Magic

Lessons

Also by Justine Larbalestier

Magic or Madness

Magic
Lessons

by
Justine Larbalestier

razor
bill

Magic Lessons

RAZORBILL

Published by the Penguin Group
Penguin Young Readers Group
345 Hudson Street, New York, New York 10014, U.S.A.
Penguin Group (USA) Inc., 375 Hudson Street, New York, New York 10014, U.S.A.
Penguin Group (Canada), 90 Eglinton Avenue, Suite 700, Toronto, Ontario, Canada M4P 2Y3 (a division of Pearson Penguin Canada Inc.)
Penguin Books Ltd, 80 Strand, London WC2R 0RL, England
Penguin Ireland, 25 St Stephen's Green, Dublin 2, Ireland (a division of Penguin Books Ltd)
Penguin Group (Australia), 250 Camberwell Road, Camberwell, Victoria 3124,
Australia (a division of Pearson Australia Group Pty Ltd)
Penguin Books India Pvt Ltd, 11 Community Centre, Panchsheel Park,
New Delhi – 110 017, India
Penguin Group (NZ), Cnr Airborne and Rosedale Roads, Albany, Auckland 1310,
New Zealand (a division of Pearson New Zealand Ltd)
Penguin Books (South Africa) (Pty) Ltd, 24 Sturdee Avenue, Rosebank,
Johannesburg 2196, South Africa

Penguin Books Ltd, Registered Offices: 80 Strand, London WC2R 0RL, England

10 9 8 7 6 5 4 3 2 1

Interior design by Christopher Grassi

Library of Congress Cataloging-in-Publication Data

Larbalestier, Justine.
   Magic lessons / by Justine Larbalestier.
      p. cm.
   Summary: When fifteen-year-old Reason is pulled through the magical door connecting New York City with the Sydney, Australia, home of her grandmother, she encounters an impossibly ancient man who seems to have some purpose in mind for her.
   ISBN 1-59514-054-9
   [1. Magic—Fiction. 2. Space and time—Fiction. 3. New York (N.Y.)—Fiction.
   4. Sydney (N.S.W.)—Fiction. 5. Australia—Fiction.]   I. Title.
   PZ7.L32073Mafu 2005
   [Fic]—dc22

2005023870

Printed in the United States of America

For Niki Bern, best sister in the multiverse

Note to Readers

Like the first book in this trilogy, *Magic Lessons* contains both Australian *and* American spelling, vocabulary, and grammar. Chapters from the viewpoint of the Australians, Reason and Tom, are written in Australian English, and those from Jay-Tee's point of view are written American style. You will find *synaesthesia* in the Australian chapters, but *synesthesia* in the American. If any of the words are new to you, turn to the glossary, where you will learn that being *jack of* something means you're *over it*, and that a *dog's breakfast* is a *mess*.

1
Reason Cansino

Once, when i was really little, we passed a road sign peppered with bullet holes. It was pretty much the same as any of the other road signs we passed out bush, but this one I read aloud in my squeaky toddler voice: "Darwin, 350. Two times 175. Five times seventy. Seven times fifty. Ten times thirty-five."

My mother, Sarafina, clapped. "Unbelievable!"

"How old is the kid?" asked the truck driver who was giving us a lift to the Jilkminggan road. He glanced down at me suspiciously.

"Almost three." Sarafina was seventeen.

"Not really?"

"Really."

When we arrived, three of the old women—Lily, Mavis, and Daisy—sat down with us on the dirt floor of the meeting place. They gave us tucker—yams, wild plums, and chocolate bickies to eat, and black-brewed, sticky-sweet tea to drink. A posse of kids hung around, darting in and out for plums and bickies, but mostly stood just out of reach, watching and giggling.

A few gum trees dotted the settlement, their leaves a dull green, standing out amongst the dirt, dry scrub, and ant hills taller than a man. Healthier, greener trees, bushes, and vines grew farther away, on the other side of the buildings, where the ground sloped into the banks of the Roper River. The buildings were low, made of untreated wood and rusting corrugated iron. The only one with four walls, a proper door, and windows was the silver demountable where school was held—the hottest, most uncomfortable building in the settlement.

"You're that travelling woman, eh?" Daisy asked. "With all them different names?"

Sarafina nodded.

"What you want to be called now?"

"Sally. And my daughter's Rain," Sarafina said, even though my name is Reason.

"We hear about you," Daisy said. "You been all over, eh? All the way down south, too?"

"Yes," Sarafina said. "We've been all over Australia."

"Seen lots of white man places, too?"

"Some." Sarafina always stayed away from cities so that her mother wouldn't find us. "I like Aboriginal places better."

The three women grunted as if this were to be expected.

"That little one, that Rain," Daisy said, looking at me. "She's countryman, eh?"

Sarafina nodded.

"Her father countryman, innit?"

"Yes."

"Where him from?" Mavis asked. She was the oldest of the three women. Her hair was all white and her skin was so black it shone. She took a piece of chewing tobacco from behind her ear and put it in her mouth.

"I don't know."

The three women murmured at this. "Don't know?"

Sarafina shook her head.

"Who his people?"

"Don't know."

"Them from desert country? Arnhem country?"

Sarafina shrugged. "He didn't tell me."

Daisy nudged Lily. "That little one, Rain? Him amari? Him munanga, I reckon."

"True," Lily said, "but him daddy still got country." She turned back to Sarafina. "Where you meet him?"

"Out west." Sarafina gestured past the water tank resting on a huge mound of dirt, to the horizon where the sun would set.

"How long you him together?"

"One night."

They nodded at this. "Drunken fella?"

Sarafina laughed. "No."

"Him from bush or white man place?"

"Bush."

"Ah," Lily said, pleased to be given something solid. "Stockman?"

"I don't know."

"Him barefoot or got boots?"

"Boots."

They nodded again. "Stockman."

Sarafina made flashcards. She cut up an old cardboard box that had once held cartons of Winnies, and she wrote on them with a fat black Texta she'd bought in Mataranka.

She wrote the names of nine recent places we'd either stayed or seen road signs for: Darwin, Jilkminggan, Katherine, Mataranka, Ngukurr, Numbulwar, Borroloola, Limmen Bight, and Umbakumba; the names of all the planets: Mercury, Venus, Earth, Mars, Jupiter, Saturn, Uranus, Neptune, and Pluto (though she said the last one wasn't *really* a planet); and the branches of mathematics: foundations, algebra, analysis, geometry, and applied.

We sat on the dirt floor under a roof of paperbark. Occasionally strands of it would drift down and land on us. The three women sat cross-legged, gutting a kangaroo and waving the flies away.

"Sally," Daisy asked, "what are you doing with your girl Rain?"

"Teaching her how to read."

They all nodded and agreed reading was important, though of the three of them, only Daisy really knew how.

Sarafina held up the cards with one hand, waving flies away, and patting one of the dogs with the other. The sky was the intense blue that only happens when the earth is the red-brown of iron. Not one cloud. Dry season. There would be no rain for months.

"Ve-nus," I read. "Dar-win. Al-ge-bra."

Sarafina held up the next card. "Nnn . . ." I said, trailing off, staring at the card with its *n* and *g* and *k* and *r*'s and *u*'s. I wasn't sure if I'd seen it before. I didn't understand how those letters went together to make sounds.

"Ngukurr," said Lily, sliding past the *g* that had confused me. Her people were from there. She knew how to read that one.

Sarafina put the cards down, realising she should, perhaps, have started with the alphabet. For the next two hours we sang, "A-B-C-D-E-F-G-H-I-J-K-L-M-N-O-P-Q-R-S-T-U-V-W-X-Y-Z." The old women laughed and lots of the kids joined us, some of them sneaking out of school in the demountable, with the drunken white teacher. I informed Sarafina that *f*, *j*, *q*, and *z* were my favourites.

Annie, Valerie, Peter, little Rabbit, and Dave said they liked *s* best, so Sarafina invented an *s* dance for them. This involved standing up, putting your hands above your head, pushing your hips to one side and your shoulders to the other, and shimmering like a snake.

We all *s*-danced, falling down and snake-bellying away across the ground, coating ourselves with red dirt. Everyone was good at it except me. I was too little and unco. Sarafina was the best, even though she was the only whitefella, faster and more shimmery than anyone else. We all laughed.

The dogs barked and jumped up, running in circles, trying to join in, but they weren't good at moving on their bellies and kept rolling over, trying to get us to rub them instead. They didn't look like snakes at all.

When we were all danced out and tired and the women had the kangaroo roasting amongst the coals, Mavis told us the story of the mermaid ancestor and how she'd made the land. She had many names, but Mavis said munga-munga was best.

I dreamed about her that night and many nights, but in my dreams when she made her giant path across the country, sparkling numbers and letters spilled out from her tail, littering the red earth, turning into valleys and rivers and hills and ocean, drifting up into the sky and becoming the planets and the stars.

The munga-munga has always been my favourite.

Once, when I was ten years old and Sarafina twenty-five, I lost my temper. Sarafina had always told me never to lose my temper, but she never told me why.

I'd only been at the school for a week. It was my first and last time in a real school, one where you had to wear shoes and be quiet when the teacher spoke and not leave the classroom unless the teacher said you could, but also one where there were lots of kids and games and books about things I'd never heard of. I was really hoping I'd be able to stay.

I was being called Katerina Thomas and my hair was cut short and dyed light brown, almost blonde. I still looked like me, though.

Josh Davidson was the class creep. He'd go around snapping girls' bra straps (those that had them), calling them bitches, and, when he could, cornering them and trying to touch their breasts (even if they didn't have any yet). He was taller than the other girls and boys, stronger, too.

He was a lot taller than me. He'd already tried to snap my non-existent bra, and I had a bruise on my arm from where he'd grabbed me when I was coming out of the bathroom. A teacher had turned the corner and told him to let me go before he could do anything else.

The next day in class, Josh sat next to me. He pushed his chair as close as he could. I felt fear and anger inside me like an intense heat. He didn't try to touch my breasts; instead, he put his hand on my thigh. I held my knees tight together. Put my hand in my pocket to hold my ammonite.

"Spread your legs, boong," Josh whispered in my ear.

I felt my anger getting bigger, uncoiling inside me. There was a scream, but I didn't open my mouth. The stone in my pocket grew warm and sweaty as I clutched it tightly. The rage was like a wave, starting small, then spiralling out of me. Growing bigger and bigger, as fast and beautiful as Fibonacci numbers: 0, 1, 1, 2, 3, 5, 8, 13, 21, 34, 55, 89, 144, 233, 377, 610, 987, 1597 . . . My eyes exploded in blinding red light.

Someone yelled out, something about a doctor.

Then, for a moment, I could see. The intense light in front of me faded away. Josh was on the floor. He wasn't moving. I felt glorious, better than I had ever felt in my entire life.

Then I fainted.

It was hours before I discovered that Josh Davidson was dead. An aneurism, they thought. The blood in his head had lumped together, had stopped the oxygen getting to his brain.

Had I made his blood do that?

I didn't ask Sarafina, but that night we left. Not just the town but the state—we went all the way across the country, as far as we could get. No more school for me.

We never talked about it, but after that, Sarafina's warnings about not losing my temper came even more often. Without explanation.

I know now. I stopped that boy's blood. I killed him.

I'm magic, like my mother, but she never told me. She didn't tell me that if I lose my temper, people might die. She never told me that if I don't use my magic, I'll go mad, like her. Or that if I do use it, I'll most likely die before I turn twenty. She never told me to choose between magic or madness.

Sarafina didn't tell me anything.

2
Back To The Asylum

Sarafina didn't look any different. She sat on one of the biggest of the ugly brown couches, still and silent, more statue than human, wearing the same white terry-towelling robe she had on last time I saw her. Only a week ago, I realised.

I wondered when time would come right again. Ever since Sarafina had tried to kill herself, it had been running either too fast or too slow. Right now it was 11 AM, but my body was convinced it was night time.

Jet lag, Tom had called it—then he'd laughed and said, "*Door* lag, really. We went by door, not jet. You get used to it. Jay-Tee and me are already on Sydney time on account of we didn't sleep away two whole days like you did."

They hadn't seemed so over it when I'd slipped out of the house, though. Jay-Tee had been sound asleep and Tom nowhere in sight. I doubted I was the only one still *door*-lagged.

The visiting room at Kalder Park was much more crowded than it had been a week ago, and hotter. The two ceiling fans didn't turn quite true and made more noise than cool air. Visitors and patients were dotted about the room, twenty-five of the first, nineteen of the latter, easy to tell apart.

Sarafina was sitting next to a much older woman with grey hair and strange, jerky movements who was trying to explain to her daughter (at least I imagined she was the woman's daughter) why Thursdays, not Mondays, were the best days for visits. It had something to do with the way *t*'s and *h*'s sounded together. Her voice was loud, carrying around the room, her cheeks red and damp. She looked exactly the way I'd always imagined a crazy person would.

Sarafina didn't look up or smile when I squeezed in beside her on the couch; her expression stayed blank and distant. I'd half expected her to tell me that I'd changed. She said nothing. She looked so much like Esmeralda. But I could see no resemblance between her and Jason Blake. It was hard to believe he was her father, my grandfather. Why hadn't she told me about him?

I reached into the hip pocket of my new pants, specially made for me by Tom, feeling for my ammonite. As my fingers touched nothing I remembered that I'd left it on the other side of the door, in New York City. I hoped Danny had picked it up.

Jay-Tee had called Danny yesterday. She'd chatted away with her brother for what seemed like hours, but I hadn't gotten to talk to him. It hadn't occurred to Jay-Tee that I'd want to. And Danny hadn't asked for me. I could call him later, when Sydney and New York time lined up properly, but I was too embarrassed.

Still, it was only Monday. I'd last seen Danny on Thursday.

No, *not* Thursday. That had been in New York City; it'd been Friday here in Sydney. It was three days since I'd last seen or spoken to him. I'd been asleep for almost two of those days, recovering from battling Jason Blake with magic. Maybe Danny had asked after me and Jay-Tee had forgotten to pass it on.

Did magic affect time? I'd first arrived in Sydney on Sunday afternoon and here it was, Monday, only eight days later, and yet so much had happened—I'd learned that magic was real, stepped through a door to another country, discovered other people with magic, made friends, met Danny, discovered what it is to be truly, truly cold. *Far* too much had happened in such a short amount of time—eight days!

My world wasn't spinning on the same axis anymore. The rules of physics had been broken. Magic was real.

The grey-haired woman's daughter leaned forward to nod at me briefly before turning her attention back to her loud, unstill mother.

I stared at Sarafina's profile, counting the freckles—thirty-eight of them—on the side of her nose. I followed the line of her gaze: out the window, down to the bay, where fifteen white-sailed boats floated on the sparkling water. Did she see any of it? Her eyes were glazed over, vacant.

Two weeks ago Sarafina's eyes had been alive, full of plans. We had been on the road together, had decided to go to Nevertire because the name made us giggle. She hadn't been sad, hadn't gotten all obsessive, insisting she count every speck of dirt or wash her hands fifty-five times in a row.

None of the usual signs that she was about to lose it. But then, she'd never lost herself completely. She'd never tried to kill herself before.

It shocked me all over again how unlike Sarafina she seemed. She'd never been a still person. Sarafina was always in motion, her face showing exactly what she was thinking. I looked at her now and saw no thought at all. It was as if she had stopped thinking, had run down and become still. All motion gone. Sarafina gone.

I tried to think of what to say. If I said, *I know about magic*, would that jerk her back to life? Not that I could say it with those two women close by. They'd think I was one of the patients. Besides, it was hardly the best way to break the news. What if Sarafina lost it again?

A trickle of sweat ran down my back. "Hot, isn't it?" I said, just to be saying something. "At least there's some breeze off the bay."

"They never open the windows," the jerky woman said, turning to look at me. Her voice was so loud I flinched. I was glad Sarafina sat between us; white, bubbly spittle formed at the corners of the strange woman's mouth, and specks flew as she spoke. "The breeze isn't allowed in. They want us to boil."

Every window was open wide.

She tried to lean closer to me. "Did they do that to your eye?" I put my hand to my still-bruised face and shook my head. "Did they put their needles right into your eyeball?"

"Mum, hush. Leave the girl alone." The daughter leaned

forward, pulling her mother towards her, and grimaced at me—though I was sure it was meant to be a smile. She looked very tired. "Sorry, love."

Sarafina wasn't hot. My mother always stayed cool when everyone else was warm. In that way, she was still the Sarafina I had always known.

I blurred my vision until I could see inside her, down to where nothing was still, to the pumping of her heart, the blood rushing through her veins, the acid roiling in her stomach, the movement of her intestines. I could see her cells, every single one of them. Hear the roller-coaster movements in every part of her, like the ocean in a storm.

Governing it all was Sarafina's pattern with its graphic confirmation that yes, Jason Blake was my grandfather. I could see both grandparents, Esmeralda and Jason Blake, in her, traces of their DNA. Like theirs, her pattern was woven through with magic. *There* in every part of her—in her cells, in the molecules that made up every cell. The magic smelled earthy, like rich black soil, but unlike my grandparents' magic, unlike Jay-Tee's, there was no taste of rust. In its place under my tongue was a sharp sourness, like an unripe lemon. The smell made my eyes water.

Sarafina finally blinked. The movement pulled my senses back to the surface, where she was still and quiet.

The crazy woman's daughter hugged her mother, stood up, and said goodbye. Her mother started to cry.

"I'll be back, I promise." She glanced at me, embarrassed,

and then away again, avoiding her mother's eyes. "I have to go. I'll bring your granddaughter next time, I promise." She left quickly without glancing back. Her mother started to rock back and forth, her cries gradually getting louder. A nurse came to quiet her and led her from the room.

When they were gone, I moved to the other side of Sarafina and screwed up my courage to speak to her. There was so much I wanted to ask. What were the feathers Esmeralda had put under my pillow? What were they supposed to do? How did magic work? How long did I have to live? I wanted to tell her about the letters Esmeralda had slipped under my door—the letters I hadn't opened, that Esmeralda had stolen back before I could read them. I opened my mouth to say, *I've been to New York City.*

But Sarafina spoke first. "You're hers now, aren't you?" She wasn't looking at me. Her tone was flat and even, but her eyes had somehow cleared.

"No. No, I'm not." I wasn't sure, though. I was staying under Esmeralda's roof. I had helped her win the stoush against Jason Blake. She was going to teach me about magic. She had put those black and purple feathers under my pillow. Did all that make me hers?

"Then why are you wearing those pants?"

I looked down at the green pants Tom had made for me, his magic sewn into every seam. I flushed.

"You're going to die," Sarafina said. "Soon."

"Then tell me what you know," I said, trying to sound

brave, though I felt ill. "Tell me what I can do. I don't trust Esmeralda. But at least she'll tell me how magic works. If I'm going to fix this, I need you to help me."

"There's no fix. You die or you end up here. This is better."

I didn't believe that for a second. There had to be a way, a path that didn't lead to madness or early death. I was going to find it. I opened my mouth to tell her.

Instead, a question bubbled out. "Why did you lie to me?"

Sarafina closed her eyes, then opened them. Turned to look at me—*really* look at me—for the first time since she'd tried to kill herself. "I never lied."

"But magic *is* real. I've seen—"

"I was trying to make it unreal by denying it. I wasn't lying."

"But what about all those things you told me? You said there was no electricity in her house. There is. That she sacrificed babies—"

"I never lied."

"What are the black and purple feathers for? What do they do? How much danger am I in?"

But Sarafina was gone, her eyes filmed over again with the drugs they'd given her. The unripe lemon taste filled my mouth, and something sharp and jolting filled my nostrils. I gagged, my eyes watering, as I realised what it was: I could taste and smell my mother's madness.

3
Someone at the Door

"At least she left a note." Jay-Tee grabbed two more slices of toast and doused them with so much strawberry jam, there was more jam than bread. Heaps more. Tom wondered why she didn't just eat it out of the jar with a spoon.

Jay-Tee was wearing a green T-shirt Tom'd never seen before. He wondered if it was Reason's. Jay-Tee'd come through the door from New York City with only the winter clothes she was wearing. Not very useful in Sydney in January. The rest was borrowed from Mere: a pair of tennis shorts and thongs . . . though what had Jay-Tee called them? Flup-flaps? Some stupid name like that.

If Jay-Tee wasn't mean, Tom would've considered making her some clothes. She'd look good in red—though really, Jay-Tee's brown skin would look good against any colour. She could even wear white or yellow. Pale people looked terrible in those colours. (Tom'd learned ages ago *never* to wear them. Or red.) But he would never make Jay-Tee anything in green. Green was a Reason colour.

Tom picked up the note and reread it. Why'd Reason want to go to Kalder Park without him? His mum was there, too, and she was as mad as Reason's. It'd be much easier if they went together. Less foul, anyway. Ever since his sister, Cath, had moved to America, Tom hated visiting his mother.

Tom missed his sister heaps, even though she was not well pleased with him. She didn't buy his crook explanation for having suddenly arrived in New York City and then even more suddenly racking off, leaving his backpack behind. Both he and Dad'd spent hours on the phone with her since, but she didn't believe a word they said, which was fair enough given that it *was* all a crock.

Tom ached to tell Cathy about magic. He didn't understand why Mere insisted she not know. Every time he asked Mere about it she'd say, *That's just part of being magic: sometimes you have to lie.* But Cath could keep a secret, and *not* telling her was wrecking what was left of his family.

"A note's better than nothing," Jay-Tee said.

"I guess," he replied. "You don't think she's run away again?"

"Nah," Jay-Tee said, mouth full of jam. "No way would she run anywhere without me."

I've known her longer than you, Tom thought but didn't say, even though he really, really wanted to. Then he realised that if he calculated the amount of time he'd spent with Reason rather than how long it'd been since they'd first met, Jay-Tee was the one who'd known Ree longer.

"She didn't take anything. Reason would take something—"

"If she'd done a runner," Tom finished for her. "Yeah, you're right. She'll be back."

"*Done a runner?*" Jay-Tee pulled her you-talk-funny face. "That's retarded. You talk even more spastic than Reason does."

Tom fake-yawned. "When in Rome, Jay-Tee." He poured some more Coke into his glass. They'd have to get rid of the bottle before Mere got home; she didn't approve of soft drinks.

"It's not Rome, Tom, it's Sydney."

"When in Sydney, then."

"No way am I ever going to talk as spastic as you guys. Except for *spewing*. I'll use that one." Jay-Tee cleared her throat loudly. "*Maaate,*" she said in the worst attempt at an Australian accent Tom'd ever heard. "Mate, Mere'll spew if you buy that Coke."

He did *not* sound like that.

"*Spew* doesn't just mean *getting angry*, you know. It also means *throw up*. You know, as in: Jay-Tee ate so much jam it made her spew. Heaps." He took another sip of his Coke, wondering if it tasted so ace because it wasn't allowed.

"As if. I never puke. Anyway, moron, *spew* means *throw up* in America, too."

"Come on, you *never* chunder? Even when you drink champagne? You said you and Reason drank that stuff *all the time* when you were in New York City."

"But I never spewed."

"Whatever." Tom wished Reason would get back. Jay-Tee wouldn't be so cranky if Ree were here. Even more, he wished it was time to start their magic lessons. Mere'd said they could

start as soon as Ree woke from her epic sleep. Which she had
yesterday, and then Mere'd said they were all still too tired and
she'd begin the lessons today, after work.

He hadn't had a proper lesson with Mere since Ree had
shown up. Unless you counted the trick Mere'd done in New
York City. She'd placed her hand on him, and then he'd started
to feel awful, a burning sensation up his arm. He wasn't in a
hurry to do that again. Still, it'd helped them find Reason.

"Do you think we'll really start today? Lessons, I mean."

Tom nodded, startled. Could Jay-Tee read his mind? "That's
what Mere said."

Jay-Tee snorted. "That's what she said about yesterday,
too."

"We would've if you hadn't kept falling asleep."

"Me?" Jay-Tee said, glaring at him. "You were the one who
kept yawning the whole time." She waved his protest away.
"What's it like?"

"What's what like?"

Jay-Tee rolled her eyes. "Magic lessons, doofus. What are
Esmeralda's lessons like?"

"Well . . ." Tom paused, overwhelmed with the urge to
string Jay-Tee along with a line of total porkies. He took
another sip of the forbidden Coke, swishing it back and forth
across his tongue so he could taste every last drop. He could
tell her that—

A tremendous thud came from the back door, as if a giant
were wielding a battering ram against it. They both jumped

up. Tom knocked over the Coke bottle. Its contents spilled all over the table with a hiss. "Bugger."

"No kidding," Jay-Tee whispered.

The sound came again, louder this time. The back door shook. Mere's brown leather, rabbit-fur-lined, ankle-length coat swung back and forth on its hook.

Tom and Jay-Tee looked at each other. They edged towards the door. Tom had to fight his body to do it; his body wanted to be at the other end of the city—back in the Shire, even.

Tom glanced at the open windows. He could see Filomena, the huge fig tree, and behind her the garage door. A flock of rainbow lorikeets flew by, fast and low under the tree, twittering and fluttering.

"It's not from outside," Jay-Tee whispered. "It's on the *other* side."

In New York City. "Do you think it's Jason Blake?" Tom asked, even though it was obvious. Who else could it be? Blake'd thought he had Reason and Jay-Tee for good, that he'd be able to take all their magic for himself. Tom didn't imagine he'd be happy about them escaping to Sydney.

Jay-Tee nodded, looking afraid.

Tom reached his hand towards the door; Jay-Tee slapped it away.

"*He's* on the other side. What if he can get you?"

Tom shuddered, even though he didn't think that was possible. They stepped back. Tom heard a dripping noise, startled, and then realised it was the Coke he'd spilled making its way from table to floor, soaking into the tiles. Mere would be thrilled. He grabbed a cloth to clean it up, tensed for the next loud bang.

"Did you see that?" Jay-Tee's eyes were so large she could've been a manga heroine.

"What?"

"The door moved!"

"It what?" Then Tom saw it, too: the texture of the door was shifting, becoming more liquid than solid, the grains flowing into one another like rivers of mercury. Esmeralda's coat started to disappear into it, as if sinking into quicksand. The coat had been her mother's. Tom reached forward to rescue it, and Jay-Tee slapped his hand away again.

"Don't!"

"Ow!" Tom glared at her. When he looked back at the door, it'd stopped moving.

"The coat's gone," Jay-Tee whispered.

He looked down at his hand, imagined himself disappearing into the door. His thoughts were shattered by another loud boom, followed by a scraping noise, like giant metal talons clawing at the wood. And then the racket stopped as abruptly as it started.

Jay-Tee screamed. A rubbery-looking, garishly banana-yellow creature was stuck to her shin. "Get it off me!"

Tom grabbed the thing, soft and malleable beneath his fingertips.

It released Jay-Tee at once, latching on to him instead,

sinking into his fingers, biting through his skin like a thousand little needles. He screamed.

The thing kept tearing at his fingers. He tried to wrench it off. It didn't budge, and then all at once, it dropped from his hand, zipping fast across the floor as if running on invisible little rollers. Tom's fingers were numb.

Jay-Tee rubbed at her calf and started to hobble after the thing. "Where'd it go?"

"What was it?" Tom stared at the pinpricks of blood on his fingers.

"I don't—"

A crash came from the front of the house, from the front door. Tom screamed. He and Jay-Tee spun around, gripping each other's hands.

Reason stepped into the kitchen.

"Jesus, Mary, and Joseph," Jay-Tee said, dropping Tom's hand and crossing herself. "Esmeralda has *got* to oil that door."

Tom flexed the fingers Jay-Tee had been squeezing. *Great,* Tom thought. *Right hand numb and bleeding, left hand practically broken.*

"Hey," Reason said, smiling and walking towards them. She was wearing the pants Tom had made her and she looked fantastic. The green of the cargos brought out the green flecks in her eyes, and her dark skin glowed. But then her face screwed up as if she were inhaling eau de dead, putrescent cat. "What's that smell? What's wrong?"

Tom and Jay-Tee glanced at each other, then at Reason. "It

bit me," Jay-Tee said. "We were attacked," Tom said at the same time.

"This thing bit us." Tom held out his right hand. "See?"

Reason peered at the tiny spots of blood, her nose still wrinkled at whatever she was smelling. "What bit you?"

"This thing. It came in through the door and ate Esmeralda's coat," Tom said. "We think Jason Blake sent it."

"And attacked your drinks?" Reason asked, looking at the mess dripping from the kitchen table. Tom realised he still had the cloth in his hand. He dumped it on the table. "Where did the thing go? How big was it?"

"Small," Tom said. "Size of a mouse, d'you reckon?"

Jay-Tee nodded. "Don't know where it went. The whole thing was freaky." She glanced at the back door.

The skin on Tom's scalp contracted. Whatever had made those noises was *very* big. Tom wondered if, despite everything Esmeralda had taught him, trolls and bunyips really did exist. Maybe Jason Blake had conjured one up.

Reason wiped at her nose as if to brush the smell away. Tom inhaled deeply, smelling the sugary-sweet spilled Coke and the musk of flying fox and rotten figs from the backyard.

Reason moved closer to the door.

"Don't touch it," Tom and Jay-Tee said in unison.

"The door *moved* before," Jay-Tee said. "In a freaky, melt-your-fingers kind of way."

Reason nodded, covering her nostrils. "The smell is really bad here."

"What smell?"

"Like . . . burnt rubber crossed with spew."

"Ewww," Tom said.

She walked away from the back door, sniffing as she went, like a tracking dog. It should have been silly, but it wasn't. Tom and Jay-Tee followed her out into the hall.

"Can you still smell it?"

Ree nodded. "I smelled it as soon as I opened the door. It's disgusting." She paused at the bottom of the stairs. The three of them stared along the line of the wide, curving banister. There seemed to be more stairs than usual.

"Yep, the scent is definitely sharper over here." Reason started up the stairs, slowly. Jay-Tee put her foot on the step behind Ree. Tom joined her; he was just as brave as Jay-Tee. He trailed his half-numb fingers along the banister, feeling the highly polished texture of the wood, until he thought of how the grains of the back door had morphed into liquid. He put his hand in his pocket. "You're still smelling it?" he asked.

"I'll tell you when I'm not, okay?"

Jay-Tee rolled her eyes at him but, amazingly, didn't make any smartarse comment.

Reason paused at the top of the stairs. Tom's stomach tightened—the house was different, the substance of it, as if the bricks had been transformed into plasticine. It felt like they were being watched. He looked up, but the mouldings hadn't sprouted eyes. He couldn't smell anything other than polished wood and eucalyptus.

Reason took a step forward and then another, leading Tom and Jay-Tee slowly toward Mere's bedroom. Tom had never been inside before; he felt his skin prickle as Reason opened the door. Mere's *bedroom*.

The room looked as though something had exploded. Clothes and books and empty coffee cups strewn everywhere. The pictures on the walls hung at wildly divergent angles. "Bugger," Tom said. "That thing has totalled it."

Jay-Tee nodded, looking as stunned as Tom. "Like it was looking for something?"

"Bugger," Tom repeated. It had gone through everything in the room. The bed was covered in discarded magazines, books, coffee cups. The pictures on the walls were on the verge of crashing down. *What* had it been looking for?

Reason laughed. "Nah. Esmeralda's room *always* looks like this. She's the queen of messiness."

"But the rest of the house—" Jay-Tee began.

"She has a housekeeper. Rita," Tom said. Clearly, Rita'd never set foot in here.

Reason picked her way through the debris to the balcony.

Jay-Tee tiptoed behind her. She seemed to think that tiptoeing decreased her odds of treading on any of Mere's stuff. Tom followed Jay-Tee. How could Mere treat her clothes like this? He knew he wouldn't make so much as a shell top for Mere *ever* again. If you cared about your stuff, you didn't drop it on the floor.

They stepped out onto the balcony. Tom breathed in the

warmer air. The sun shone down on them through Filomena, bathing them in a bright green light. The cicadas called to one another, a high-pitched wall of sound that ebbed and swelled. A large black-and-white butterfly flittered by, then dipped low and across into Tom's backyard next door. He waved flies away. The feeling of something being there, just out of sight, something that *shouldn't* be there, grew stronger.

"Do you think it's gone?" Jay-Tee asked.

Reason and Tom shook their heads at the same time. Everything was still *wrong*. Tom touched the bricks, and for a moment they felt like paper. He pulled his hand away.

"What?" asked Reason and Jay-Tee at the same time.

"It feels weird. Not like bricks." Tom looked down at his feet, wondering if the wooden boards of the balcony might suddenly change into jelly, and they'd all go sliding through.

Jay-Tee shivered, though it was hot and the three of them were covered in a light sheen of sweat. "It's still here, isn't it?"

They looked around. He couldn't see anything weird in his backyard—the passionfruit vine on the far fence and his dad's vegetable garden were intact, tomato plants tied to stakes, half-grown lettuces. Filomena's enormous spreading canopy blocked most of the view in the other directions. Tom hoped that thing hadn't climbed into the fig tree. He couldn't imagine Filomena would like being bitten by it any better than he had.

"Up there," Reason said, looking at the roof. She kicked off her ugly brown sandals, climbed onto the iron railing, sending a skink scurrying out of her way. She reached for the top of a brick.

Then, with a scream, she leapt backward and landed on the balcony with a thud. The glow-in-the-dark yellow thing was on her forearm, sinking into her. Reason tried to rip it off with her right hand. Tom grabbed at it, but the slick stuff slipped through his fingers.

It disappeared without a sound into Reason's arm.

"Get it out of me. Tom! Jay-Tee! You have to get it out of me!" Reason clawed at her own arm, smearing the little dots of blood the thing left behind.

"What do we do?" Jay-Tee was shades paler.

"Try magic," Tom said, kneeling beside Reason. He'd already used magic that week, but he didn't know what else to do. The skin across her face was tight, covered in sweat. Reason was shaking.

Jay-Tee knelt beside him. "Don't do that, Reason," she said, pulling Reason's right hand away. "You're hurting yourself."

Tom closed his eyes, determined not to let Jason Blake harm Reason ever again.

7
Door Magic

Jay-Tee pushed her leather bracelet further up her arm, thinking about her magic, focusing it. She put her hand on Reason's blood-smeared arm, next to Tom's.

Jay-Tee let her eyes blur. The thing was wearing down Reason's connection to Jay-Tee and Tom, fading the web of lines that linked her to magic and to the people around her. The usual brilliant green strands that made up the web were hazy, except for a handful of new brown threads. Those were thin but clear, the same brown as the thing had been—the same red-brown as the door to New York.

Jay-Tee pushed her magic against the brown threads, looking for weak spots, trying to break them. She felt Tom do the same. Reason, too, was drawing on her magic, fighting.

Sweat ran down Jay-Tee's back. Reason's skin grew hotter under her hand. The thing had made her feverish; her body trying to fight the invader every way it could. Jay-Tee could see the wood-brown lines knitting together and reaching from Reason's body back into the house, down the stairs—to the door, she was sure, back to New York, back to *him*. Why wouldn't he leave her alone?

She reached for the fine brown line, held it in her hands, feeling for where it was weakest.

"I see it," Tom said. "Just there. Its shape isn't true." He sent his magic rushing at the weak point, drawing Reason's and Jay-Tee's with him.

The line snapped.

Reason screamed.

The Play-Doh thing exploded from her arm through the balcony and across Esmeralda's room. Jay-Tee scrambled up, running down the stairs after it. She reached the kitchen in time to watch it disappear under the door, back to New York, back to *him*.

The noise and the shaking began again, like rusty metal fingernails dragged along echoing metal pipes. The wood rippled, looking exactly like the thing—same color, same texture, same everything.

Jay-Tee looked around desperately. She had to keep it from coming back. She snatched up a box of matches and emptied it into her hands, pushing a little of her magic into them, then she skidded across the spilled Coke to the door, spreading the matches out along the threshold, careful not to touch the wood.

She hoped the protection would hold.

"Are you okay?"

Reason walked normally, not as if her body had been invaded by some creature. Her nose was screwed up and she was wearing her something-nasty-just-crawled-up-my-nostrils face, but other than that she looked okay.

Jay-Tee, on the other hand, was so exhausted, she'd had to sit on the sticky, Coke-covered floor and lean back against the kitchen cupboards.

"I'm fine," Reason answered.

Jay-Tee looked at Tom, who shrugged.

"It only hurt while it was inside me."

Jay-Tee couldn't believe it. Her shin was still throbbing in the spot where the thing had bitten her. "You're really fine?"

Reason answered with a retching noise and followed it up by spewing on the kitchen floor. "I *have* to go outside."

Jay-Tee and Tom cleaned up after Reason, and then they tackled the sticky Coke mess.

"What do you think Jason Blake wants?" Tom asked, wiping down one of the cupboard doors.

Jay-Tee wished Tom would stop saying *his* name. She'd learned fast never to use his name—not *any* of them. Though it didn't make any sense to her, Jay-Tee knew that saying his name gave him more power. No matter how far away he was—if you said one of his names, if you even *thought* it—he'd know and show up to laugh at you and take more of your magic.

"What do *you* think he wants, Tom?"

"Our magic?"

"You got it."

"Do you think those matches will hold?" He gestured at the bottom of the door.

She shrugged. "I don't know. It's been quiet, though, hasn't it? When did Esmeralda say she'd be home?"

"Soon."

Jay-Tee dumped their glasses in the sink. "I'm going upstairs to change. These've got Coke all over them."

She went into Reason's room and picked out a pair of shorts and a T-shirt. They were pretty ugly—Reason was clueless about clothes—but they'd do. Esmeralda had promised to take her shopping for stuff of her own when there was time.

A week ago Jay-Tee hadn't even known her father was dead and would never beat her again. It had been weird telling her brother, Danny, why she'd run away. It had been such a big secret for so long. She hadn't even told Reason. And Danny had believed her, hadn't doubted for a second. It had been such a relief.

She'd felt guilty, like somehow it was her fault that her dad had gone crazy one day and started beating her. She still had no idea why. He never said anything, just laid into her, silent and furious. Now he was dead, so she'd never know what she'd done wrong. And no sooner had she run away from her dad than she'd wound up trapped by *him*. From the frying pan into the fire.

She'd spent a lot of her first two days in Sydney on the phone to Danny talking about it all and catching up on his life. He'd gotten into Georgetown on a basketball scholarship, like he'd always wanted, though he wasn't taking it up for another year because of Dad dying—plus, he'd been searching for her. He was playing ball whenever and wherever he could. Same old. He'd given Jay-Tee a majorly sketchy answer when she'd asked about girlfriends, which meant he was messing with more than one. Nothing changed there. Playing ball came first, girls a *long* way after.

Talking to Danny, hanging out with Reason and Tom, being in Sydney such a long, long way from *him*, Jay-Tee had started to believe things would get better.

But here *he* was, up to his usual tricks. Jay-Tee had forgotten that *lucky* was not her middle name, that no matter what happened she had, at best, only a few more years to live. Right now she felt every second of that short time piled on top of her, weighing her down. She was tired, worn thin like an old rag.

He'd done something to the house. It didn't feel right anymore. The three of them—Jay-Tee+Reason+Tom—had a distinctive feel together, but it was off kilter now. The thing had upset the balance. Jay-Tee could always feel the dynamic between living things. It was part of how she could tell when someone was lying or not. Or, rather, whether they *believed* they were telling the truth or not.

Since she'd laid out the matches, there hadn't been any more weird thumping or scraping at the door. Had the thing really disappeared back to New York? Was what she was feeling now just its nasty residue? Like shock waves long after an earthquake has stopped?

The thing had been the exact same brown as the door, complete with wood grains. Maybe it *was* part of the door. Did that mean the door was alive?

She'd seen that happen sometimes with dance floors,

especially old ones that had been danced on by thousands and thousands of people over the years. The dance floor absorbed all that crowd magic, began to dance a little itself. Once, in a shoe store in the city, Jay-Tee had taken one step on the old wooden floor and felt it reaching toward her, accommodating itself to the movement of her feet, ready, eager for her to dance. Instantly she'd known it had been a dance floor— people had waltzed, fox-trotted, Charlestoned, jitterbugged, boogied, and twisted across its surface for many, many years. She'd spun, feeling the floor push back, giving her extra spring and lift. She'd grinned. One of the guys who worked there had grinned back, danced toward her. "Isn't this song great? Just makes you dance."

He'd lifted her up, twirled her around, and danced her toward all the best shoes. The song changed, but he kept dancing. As they moved together she saw everyone else in the store swaying, dipping, shifting. Jay-Tee had felt the floor throughout her body, flowing in from her feet, through the fingertips of the guy twirling her around. She could have sworn, somehow, that the floor was smiling.

Maybe something similar had happened to the door. Maybe it was angry at all those generations of magic-wielders stretching it across two continents. Was that possible? Maybe it was furious at everyone who had ever stepped through it. And *he* was using the door's anger against them.

Jay-Tee knew with every part of her body that *he* was behind this. Sending that creepy thing through to terrorize them, trying to figure out a way through the door to steal all their magic—that would be just his speed.

The two of them joined Reason on the front steps, where Jay-Tee still felt her back tingling with fear.

"Esmeralda will know what to do," Jay-Tee said, trying to convince herself as much as Reason. "She'll get rid of the smell, make the door even stronger." *She'll keep* him *out,* Jay-Tee thought.

A trickle of sweat ran down Jay-Tee's spine. She'd love to go for a swim—immerse herself in cool water and float and forget that he existed.

Reason grimaced, though it could have been an attempt at a smile.

"Can you still smell it?" Tom asked. Jay-Tee nudged him in the ribs. Tom could be so dense; it was obvious Reason was still shaky and didn't want to think about what had happened. Reason didn't feel right to Jay-Tee: she was somehow separate, not connected to her or Tom like she'd been before.

"No," Reason answered, "but I can still taste it." She looked yellow.

The front gate opened and they looked up to see Esmeralda, dressed in a fancy gray suit with lots of shiny black buttons, holding a leather briefcase. Her high heels were black and shiny, too. Jay-Tee would boil in that getup on such a scorching day, but Esmeralda didn't look hot or flustered. Tom said she was forty-five, but Jay-Tee found that hard to believe. She didn't look old at all.

Jay-Tee grinned and felt herself relax. It was a huge relief to see Reason's grandmother.

"Hi, Mere," Tom said. He never called Esmeralda by her full name. Jay-Tee figured he did it to remind them that he knew Esmeralda best. Like anyone cared.

"Are you all right?" Esmeralda asked, closing the front gate behind her. She lowered her voice. "I thought you said the thing went back under the door?"

Tom nodded.

"Maybe we should talk about this inside?"

Reason shook her head. "Can't. The smell."

"The smell?"

"Reason could smell it—" Jay-Tee began.

Esmeralda shook her head. "I won't be a minute."

She took more like fifteen, returning dressed in jeans and a shirt. She was frowning. "Let's go next door."

Jay-Tee wondered why on earth they were going to Tom's place, but then Esmeralda turned left instead of right, pulling out a key to open the front door to a small brick cottage.

Jay-Tee had barely noticed the place before. There wasn't a lot *to* notice. It was only one room wide, and its tiny front garden had been bricked over to save the hassle of watering plants. The front window was closed and shuttered, as if whoever lived there was shutting out the world.

Before she stuck the key in the lock, Esmeralda turned to them. "Are you ready for your first magic lesson together?"

"But what about your house? The door? Shouldn't we be—" Jay-Tee began.

"We'll be able to do more here. Trust me." Esmeralda smiled. "So, are you ready for a lesson?"

Jay-Tee nodded and Tom said yes. Reason hesitated, looked straight into her grandmother's eyes. "I don't know," she said. "I'll have to see."

Esmeralda nodded, as if that were good enough, and opened the door.

5
A Lesson in Magic

Esmeralda waved us into a narrow corridor, closing the door, then locking and bolting it behind us.

I smelled only dust and the sweat on Jay-Tee, Tom, and me. I swallowed. The taste of that thing still lingered in my mouth. My arm ached where it had pushed its way inside me. I was warmer than I should be, glowing inside where it had been. Strangest of all: that thing was familiar—I almost recognised it. I wondered if that was because my grandfather, Jason Blake, had sent it.

The house was the perfect place for witchcraft: small, cramped, dark, and dank. There were only two doors off the gloomy corridor, which ended in what looked like a kitchen.

"These are the three rules of this house," Esmeralda said, turning to us. "Never come here unless I am with you. Always walk in one direction: counterclockwise."

Widdershins, I thought. *I never lied,* Sarafina'd said to me. I should have believed her. This was Esmeralda's house of magic. This was where she sacrificed animals and did everything Sarafina had told me about.

I never lied.

"Use no electricity—not even a battery-operated torch. Use only candlelight." Esmeralda pulled two candles and matches from her bag. She handed one to Tom and the other to Jay-Tee and then lit them, going from right to left. Widdershins.

"Why?" I asked. "I've seen you do magic around electricity." I thought of her battling Jason Blake in New York City, below streetlights, above electric cables, outside houses bursting with electricity.

"You can use magic anywhere," Tom answered me, "but if there's electricity close by, it takes more out of you." It sounded like he was quoting Esmeralda.

Esmeralda nodded as she unlocked the first door and pulled it open. "I've tried to make this house an ideal place for using magic."

Jay-Tee and I moved forward to see what we could in the candlelight. I was glad she was there, seeing it all for the first time with me. All four walls were covered floor to ceiling: fifteen bookcases crammed to overflowing with 3,635 books. And that was only the books I could see—there were more on the floor, mostly hidden behind a filing cabinet, two chairs, and a desk. If there were windows, they were hidden by the bookcases.

"The library," Esmeralda said. "Every book, paper, article, letter, parking ticket, everything I have ever found that touches on magic—on real magic—I keep in here. The collection was begun by my great-grandmother. I doubt there's another as complete anywhere in the world."

She closed and locked the first door and moved on to the

second, where Tom was already waiting. My thoughts remained in that library bursting at the seams with information about magic, real magic, the kind that had made my mother insane and was going to kill me and Jay-Tee in a few short years. Maybe sooner.

If there was a solution, an answer to the horrible choice between magic and madness, surely I would find it in there, or at the very least something that would lead me to it.

"And this is where I will teach the three of you everything I know about magic."

Everything? Seemed unlikely given how little she'd told me so far. She was hiding something. Why else had she reclaimed those letters of hers? But I'd take whatever she was willing to teach me. I *had* to know more.

The second room had three smaller bookshelves and a stack of seven boxes. It was nowhere near as overcrowded as the library but, like the library, if there were any windows, they were hidden from view. On a small round table in the centre were three single candleholders and a large candelabra with thirteen branches. Esmeralda and Tom moved counterclockwise around the table and then sat down.

Tom was familiar with this house. He knew how it worked. I thought about what that meant. Had he killed animals to work magic? Tom believed in Esmeralda, trusted her. I liked Tom, but he was Esmeralda's. I had to make sure that I didn't become hers, too.

Tom placed his candle in a holder; then he lit the large

candelabra in the centre, lighting the candles from right to left. I could see everyone's face clearly now. Tom was smiling at me and Jay-Tee, waiting for us to join him as if we were about to do nothing scarier than play cards.

No electricity. I thought of everything Sarafina had said about Esmeralda—that she had sex with every man she met in order to steal their vital energies. Did that include Tom? Was that why he always blushed around her? I hadn't seen Esmeralda with any men since I'd arrived in Sydney, but that had only been eight days ago.

And then there were the animals she sacrificed: rats, guinea pigs, cats, dogs, and goats. She used their blood for her magic. Even worse, Sarafina had told me she ate human babies bought from starving mothers.

I glanced at Esmeralda. She was smiling, encouraging me and Jay-Tee to join her. Her smile was as unguarded as my mother's. I tried to imagine her killing anything and couldn't.

It was possible that Esmeralda hadn't done any of those despicable things. Sarafina mightn't have meant to lie to me, but she had lied to herself, told herself that magic wasn't real. Maybe she'd told me so many terrible stories about Esmeralda that they'd started to grow, become worse than they really were. Or maybe it was her madness confusing her. I'd seen Sarafina turned around before. One time when we were camping in the Errabiddy hills she'd tried to push her way into a solid tree. She was catching the bus to go into town, she said. But we'd been a long way from any buses or towns.

Even so, I still didn't trust Esmeralda. There were still the letters she'd taken back before I could read them, the feathers under my pillow. And worst of all, the dried-up body of Sarafina's cat, Le Roi, buried in the cellar, its head almost hacked off.

I stole a glance at Jay-Tee, who, like me, stood frozen in the doorway. What was she thinking? She'd been doing magic all her life. She looked tired and almost frail. I wondered how all of this must be affecting her: escaping Jason Blake, finding her brother again, stepping through the door to another continent. And now having my grandfather banging at the door, trying to get to her again.

"Come," Esmeralda said, sounding exactly like Sarafina. "Sit down and tell me what happened."

Jay-Tee moved first. Took a step into the room and then made her way carefully round the table (widdershins). She sat next to Esmeralda. I followed, easing myself into the last chair. Under the table Jay-Tee's hand reached out to squeeze mine. I returned the pressure. It helped to know she wasn't any more comfortable than I was.

"What happened?" Esmeralda asked again.

"This weird brown thing," Jay-Tee began, "shot out from under the back door—"

"And attacked us," Tom said, holding out his fingers, though it was hard to see the tiny marks in the half light. "It ate your coat, too. Hang on, Jay-Tee, it was yellow."

"No, it wasn't," I said. "It was definitely a brownish colour, kind of grey-brown."

"No way," Jay-Tee objected. "It was a *red*-brown. The same colour as the door."

"You all saw it differently?" Esmeralda asked.

We looked at each other. "I guess so," Jay-Tee said. "Yellow, huh?"

Tom nodded. "Bright yellow."

"Then what happened?"

"I made a protection—"

"With matches. I saw. Well done, Jay-Tee. I added a little something. I think it will hold."

As we told her everything that had happened, I watched Esmeralda. She looked like someone you'd trust straight away. Like Sarafina. Total strangers were always telling my mother their secrets. They took one look at her and decided that she'd never betray them. (They were right, but mostly because she'd never see them again.) *She can make you believe almost anything*, Sarafina had told me.

I wondered how I could get back into that library without Esmeralda knowing. All those covered-up windows. Was there a way to break in from the backyard? I hadn't glimpsed much light at the end of the hallway. I'd need her keys. I wondered where she kept them when they weren't in her briefcase.

"What did it smell like, Reason?" Esmeralda asked. Hearing her say my name startled me. She sounded *so* like Sarafina.

I shivered, but it wasn't a fear shiver—I was cold. The boiling bitumen outside had no impact on this house. But there wasn't any breeze. The only movement of the air was caused by the four of us. The cold was coming up through my feet from the concrete floor.

"I smelled vomit and burning tires," I said, answering her question at last. "Didn't you?"

Esmeralda shook her head. "No."

"What was it? The thing that attacked us?"

Esmeralda didn't answer.

"Why did Jason Blake send it?" Tom asked.

"Why does only Reason smell it?" Jay-Tee asked.

"How did the house feel to you?" Esmeralda asked them. "In the places where the smell was strongest for Reason, did either of you feel or see anything?"

Tom nodded. "The house felt wrong, like it was made of paper rather than brick."

"The energy . . ." Jay-Tee paused, looked at her hands and then at me and Tom, her gaze travelling counterclockwise around the table. "It's kind of hard to explain, but yeah, the house did feel strange. Not like Tom said, but wrong."

"It's because all our magics are different, right?" Tom asked. "I mean except yours and Reason's, 'cause you both do numbers. But my magic is about materials and shapes. And I guess Reason's is also, um, smells."

"Yes," Esmeralda said. "Reason's magic has to do with mathematics *and* synaesthesia."

"Synaesthesia?" I asked.

"Smelling sounds? Tasting sights?" Tom said.

I thought about what I saw when I looked beneath Jay-Tee's and Esmeralda's skin. I tasted rust, smelled unlit tobacco. Synaesthesia. It sounded like a disease. But then, wasn't magic a disease? "I guess."

"So what's Jay-Tee's magic?" Tom asked, turning to look at her.

"People," Jay-Tee said.

"You're strongest in a crowd, aren't you?" Esmeralda asked, addressing Jay-Tee.

She nodded.

"People aren't merely separate individuals, are they, Jay-Tee? They're also the connections between them."

Again Jay-Tee nodded. "Like a web. A web full of magic. Well, okay, except for the occasional dead spots."

"Dead spots?" I asked.

"People without the faintest trace of magic," Esmeralda answered. "They're rare, but they exist. You can only work magic on magic. Fortunately, almost everyone has at least a smidgin."

I remembered the man in that dancing place in New York, the one who'd laughed when Jay-Tee tried to magic him.

"That thing in the house changed the way the three of us feel together. Made it wrong." Jay-Tee turned to Esmeralda. "What was that thing? I know it's from *him*, but why'd it bite us? And burrow into Reason?"

"I don't know."

The three of us stared at her. She stared back at us.

"You don't know!" I burst out.

"I'm not sure."

"So what do we do, then?" Jay-Tee asked.

"I'll teach you about magic. This incursion into my house has given us something to base our lessons around."

"You're not worried about it getting back in?" I asked.

"Jay-Tee's protections should hold. And for now, your lessons will be practical, focused on discovering what it is and how it got through the door."

"You couldn't just ring Jason Blake and ask?"

Esmeralda smiled. "Even if he took a call from me, I doubt he'd say."

"What do you *think* it is?" I asked. "You must have some idea."

She responded with another question: "What's the best and safest way to work magic?"

"Through something that's already magic," Jay-Tee responded. She touched the leather bracelet around her wrist. "This was my mother's."

Tom pulled a chain from around his neck. I'd never noticed it before. "Mere gave me this. It was in her family for generations."

They both looked at me, but I shook my head. "I don't have anything." I had never even noticed Jay-Tee's bracelet or Tom's chain before.

Sarafina didn't like jewellery, said it was pointless, but she had given me the ammonite I had left with Danny (I hoped). I'd had it most of my life, kept in my pocket during the day, under my pillow (if I had one) at night. Many times when I was little I'd woken up holding it in my hand. Every time I lost it I found it again, usually within seconds. It had been in my hand when I killed Josh Davidson.

A magic object. Something else Sarafina hadn't told me.

"The door to my house crackles with magic," Esmeralda said, "and that's where the thing entered. I think the thing you saw is some kind of golem doing its master's bidding."

"What's a golem?" I asked.

"The creepy guy from *Lord of the Rings*," Tom said.

Esmeralda laughed. "A golem is a made thing. In the olden days they were usually sculpted from clay and then filled with magic. They don't last. I imagine that's why it escaped back to New York."

"We made it go," Jay-Tee objected. "It was connected to . . . to something on the other side. We broke the connection."

"Even so, it probably wouldn't have lasted much longer. It was moving fast, yes?"

Jay-Tee nodded.

"It wanted something from us," I said. "Or it was looking for something inside us."

Esmeralda nodded. "Like magic."

"But it didn't take any from me," I said, remembering when Jason Blake had touched me. "I'm sure of it. I know what *that* feels like."

Jay-Tee made a face. "Yeah, it wasn't drinking us."

"It could be," Esmeralda said, "that the golem was gathering information—"

"Doing a recce?" Tom asked. "So it could report back to Jason Blake? Yuck."

"It's possible."

"So . . ." Jay-Tee paused. "We need something better than matches to keep it from getting back in the house. My father always used small bones."

"Bones can store a lot of magic," Esmeralda said.

I wondered where you were supposed to get bones from. Maybe magic-wielders collected wishbones every time they ate chicken. Or maybe they got them in a much more horrible way. Cats had small bones. I imagined babies did, too.

"What about feathers?" I asked.

Esmeralda did not seem disturbed by my question. She nodded. "Feathers are excellent. Darker colours seem best."

"What did you put those black and purple ones under my pillow for?"

"To protect you while you slept."

I was hard-pressed not to roll my eyes. Then I realised that neither Jay-Tee nor Tom had said anything or seemed surprised by my question. Maybe feathers really were used for protection.

Esmeralda stood up, circling the table (widdershins) until she reached the pile of boxes. She rummaged through several before pulling out a wooden box and a battered cardboard one.

She placed the wooden box next to the candelabra, removing its lid so we could all see that it was filled to the brim with a jumbled collection of stones, bones, bits of wood, and polished glass. Like all the flotsam and jetsam you might collect during a day at the beach, a beach with bones strewn on it.

"Reach in with your eyes closed and see if anything in the box pulls you towards it. Take one each."

Tom pushed the box to me (widdershins, of course). "I already have one." He pulled a milky green J-shaped stone out of his pocket. "It's a jade button from China. It belonged to your great-great-great-great-grandmother Esmeralda Milagros Luz Cansino. From her favourite coat."

"It's beautiful," I said.

I put my hand over the box and closed my eyes. My fingertips tingled, sensing a soft tug. I reached forward; my fingers touched metal. I pulled the object out, stared at it lying heavy in my hand. In the candlelight the metal shone.

A flat metal brooch engraved with a five-pointed star. In the star's centre was a rose, each petal larger than the next. I ran my thumb along the points of the pentagram, over each petal. Fibonaccis tumbled through my head and the number phi—1.6180339887—crucial for the construction of a pentagram. I thought of my ammonite, safe with Danny. This was how holding it felt. How many times had I unknowingly used the ammonite to make magic?

I pushed the box to Jay-Tee. She looked down at it a moment, her eyes squeezed shut, and plunged her hand in, pulling out a long piece of polished wood. Jay-Tee looked at it and giggled.

"What's so funny?" I asked.

She held it out to me. "What does that look like to you?" she whispered. It was longer than it was wide, with a rounded end. We both giggled.

"It was brought over here by Raul Cansino in 1820," Esmeralda said. "I suspect it's much older than that."

"But what's it for?" Tom asked.

Jay-Tee burst out laughing and then put her hand over her mouth. "Sorry," she said in a strangled voice. Tears were rolling down her face, she was laughing so hard. It was contagious; my giggles turned into laughter, too.

"Do you need to choose a less phallic object?" Esmeralda asked, not answering Tom's question. "Or do you think you two can stop giggling?"

"Less phallic." Jay-Tee cracked up again. She gingerly returned the piece of wood to the box and pulled out a large pointed tooth that looked like it had come from a big cat. In no way did it resemble a penis.

The sight of it stopped my laughter. At least it wasn't human. I shivered, remembering the thirty-three teeth that had tumbled out of a hidden compartment in Esmeralda's hairbrush my first day here. Were they magical objects? Or souvenirs?

Esmeralda cleared her throat. "The first rule of magic is to use as little as you possibly can." She was looking directly at me. "This makes it hard to teach. But to avoid madness, you have to use a small amount of magic once a week."

"Must be easy for you to remember, Tom," Jay-Tee said. "You just have to do magic every time you brush your teeth."

"Yeah, right," Tom said. "You should—"

"How do you know?" I asked, cutting off Tom. "Once a week? What happens if you do it once every two weeks or once every 153 hours?"

"Once a week worked for my mother, it's worked for me, and for your grandfather and his parents. It's the time specified in the texts I've found that touch on the issue. Once a week to avoid insanity, using only the smallest of magics in order to live as long as possible." It sounded like she was quoting.

"I imagine," she continued, "it might be more or less for different people, but, frankly, I have not experimented. The stakes are too high.

"Every time you use magic, you make your life shorter. I use as little as possible. This is especially crucial for you two." She looked at me and then at Jay-Tee, who looked down. She didn't have to say *why* it was crucial for us. We both knew that we'd used up too much already. But then, so had Esmeralda. She was riddled with rust. I wondered how long she had left. Months? Weeks? Was she afraid of dying?

"But in order to use only the tiniest amounts," Esmeralda continued, "you have to understand it.

"The three of you see magic differently. Yet you have to remember that all magic is the same. It's a system of energy that magic-wielders have the ability to control. No matter what metaphor you use for understanding it—"

"What's a metaphor?" Jay-Tee asked.

"A figure of speech. Like saying someone has a heart of stone."

I didn't think much of her example. My grandfather's stone heart *definitely* wasn't a figure of speech.

"Every magic-wielder understands how their magic works in terms of some metaphor. For Reason and me, magic is made of mathematical patterns. Tom understands it as something made up of shapes, of materials, like the clothes he makes."

"You," Esmeralda said, smiling at Jay-Tee, "think of magic in terms of the connections between people—a web, you said. But no matter how we think about what we do—what metaphors we use—we all do the same thing: we manipulate energy."

"If it's just a metaphor," Jay-Tee said, "why can't I smell what Reason smelled?"

"There's no such thing as *just* a metaphor. The way you understand magic shapes how you work your magic. Your understanding of it, the metaphor you use, is what your magic *is*. Metaphors make reality."

How could that be true? Metaphors couldn't make the world; they could only help us understand the world, and sometimes they got in the way. I thought of all the examples Sarafina had taught me, everything I'd read about the history of science. People used to think about the world as if it were a map or a table: flat, something you could fall off the edges of. Their flat earth existed at the centre of the universe with the sun rotating around it, heaven floating above and hell below. The metaphor did not make reality; it stopped people from seeing reality. When Copernicus said the world was spinning on its axis and orbiting the sun, the people of his day were horrified. They couldn't see beyond the edges of their metaphor.

"But how . . ." Jay-Tee trailed off. "Where do these metaphors come from? I mean, *why* do I see magic the way I do and Tom the way he does? My father never taught me to look for a web. Are we born that way?"

"I don't know."

There was a lot she didn't know. Esmeralda caught the expression on my face. "Why does gravity work the way it does, Reason?"

She had me. "I don't know. Nobody does."

"How did life begin?"

I opened my mouth and then shut it again.

"There's a lot I don't know about magic or how it works. Most of what I'll tell you are theories. I happen to think they're good theories, but I can't be certain.

"These objects in your hands," Esmeralda continued, "have all been used to shift magical energy for at least a century. Some of them date back to when the Cansinos first came here, some, like that phallus, considerably longer."

Jay-Tee caught my eye with a grin, but neither of us laughed.

"The energy rubs off, is absorbed by these stones, pieces of wood and bone. Because they are already imbued with magic, using them lessens the amount of energy you displace from yourself."

"So that you can live longer," Jay-Tee said.

Esmeralda nodded.

"So why not use the whole box?" I asked.

"Because it doesn't work," Tom answered. "It's like thinking that if one pill helps your headache, why not take twenty. The medicine bites back. Two is usually the limit, and even then they don't always work better than one."

"Have you ever tried to work with more than one object?" Esmeralda asked Jay-Tee.

She shook her head.

"Have you ever made light?"

Jay-Tee nodded.

"Use the tooth and your bracelet to make light. Use only the smallest amount of magic. A smaller amount than you've ever used before."

"Now?"

Esmeralda nodded. Tom sat watching. The expression on his face said he'd done this before.

Suddenly Jay-Tee's face was brighter: I hadn't actually seen her *do* anything, but it was as if a spotlight were pointed at her.

"Enough," Esmeralda said, and the light went away. "How was that?"

"Easier," Jay-Tee said. "Much." She looked at the large tooth in her hand. "Can I keep this?"

"Of course. It's yours now."

"Thank you."

"Your turn, Reason."

I looked down at the brooch in my hand. "What do I do?"

"Concentrate on the shape of light," Tom said. "Draw it towards you."

Jay-Tee snickered, like she thought Tom was being a wanker. "Just think about light."

I did. The brooch in my hand grew warmer. My body did, too, as if something were burning inside me. The whole room flooded with light.

"Stop!" Esmeralda yelled.

I stopped. The three of them were staring at me.

"Bloody hell," Tom said.

"Damn," Jay-Tee said at the same time. They both rubbed their eyes.

"That was *way* too much," Jay-Tee said. "Do you *not* want to live to the end of the week?"

"Really? I don't feel drained or anything."

"Have you ever known you were using magic before, Reason?" Esmeralda asked.

I shook my head.

"What about trying to kill *him?*" Jay-Tee asked.

"I didn't *try* to kill Jason Blake—I lost my temper. The magic just swelled up. It was in control of me, not the other way around." I hadn't been thinking of magic at all. It had been the same with Josh Davidson.

When we'd rescued Esmeralda from her strange fight with

Jason Blake, that had been magic, too. But until last week—the strangest week of my life—all my magic had been accidental. I itched to know more—much, much more. I had to get into Esmeralda's library and read every single thing in it—even the parking tickets.

"You only want a little bit of light," Tom said. "Not the full power of the sun."

"But it didn't feel like anything—"

"It didn't? What about when you worked magic against your grandfather?"

Kind of Esmeralda not to say, *When you tried to kill your grandfather*. I breathed deeply. "It felt good. But afterwards I was completely rooted." I shrugged. "Didn't get tired making the light just now. Don't feel anything."

"Nothing?"

"Well, the brooch got a little bit warm."

The three of them were still staring at me as if I were some kind of mutant. I wished they'd stop it.

"Look! I've never done magic on purpose before. I've never known what I was doing before."

Jay-Tee snorted. "You don't exactly know what you're doing now. You lit the room brighter than a thousand watts."

"What use is light against that bitey golem thing, anyway?" I asked.

"Probably none," Esmeralda said. "But I wanted to have some sense of what you can do. Now I know you need to learn control. Against the golem we'll lay more protections, not light." She opened the top of the cardboard box. It was full of feathers. Black, purple, dark blue, and green feathers. They looked like the ones that had been under my pillow.

"Jay-Tee, how do you make a protection?"

"I push a tiny bit of magic into the feathers or bones or whatever, and then, as quick as I can, I put them close to what I want protected. The magic wears off eventually."

"How do you 'push' magic?" I asked.

"Exactly the same way we conjured light."

"You just think about it?"

"Yes. But think *softly*, Reason," Esmeralda said. "Think about the gentleness of a feather. Think little thoughts."

"Not thoughts of nuclear warheads," Jay-Tee said under her breath.

Esmeralda stood up. "Ready to go back over?"

We emerged out of the dark, cool house into the intense dazzle of the bright day—even the bitumen surface of the street seemed to sparkle. I watched carefully as Esmeralda locked the door: three locks, three keys, all of which turned widdershins.

None of us said anything, following Esmeralda like obedient little chicks. Tom carried the box of feathers. I held the brooch, still warm in my fingers.

6
Feathers and Chunder

Tom could tell that Reason wasn't keen on going back in the house. It wasn't hard: her face'd gone a really weird colour. He lowered his sunglasses. Almost green.

"You can smell it already?" Tom asked. "It hasn't gone away?"

Standing outside Esmeralda's house, the late afternoon sun lanced down at them like hot angry spears. Coming out of the cold lesson house was always a shock on a hot day like this. Tom had to squint *through* his sunglasses; he could feel the sweat gathering under his armpits, on his forehead and upper lip, in the middle of his back.

Mere was examining the front door, not using magic. Even though she was wearing an old pair of jeans and a plain black shirt, she looked well groomed, neat, hair pulled back in a ponytail, in place of the formal chignon she'd had it in when she got back from work. Her make-up understated, but just so. Mere was not a bright-red-lipstick kind of woman. Tom tried to reconcile her appearance with the bomb-just-gone-off look of her room. He failed.

Reason nodded, then shook her head. "Psychosomatic," she

said, looking a little less green. "Just knowing that I *might* smell it again . . ." She trailed off, shrugging.

"Must be bad," Tom said, just to say something. It was a pretty der-brain statement.

"Yeah."

Mere stood up, opened the door. He and Reason followed her through, then Jay-Tee.

"I don't smell it," Reason said. She took several more steps forward and then gagged, her face turning a deeper shade of green. "Okay, yes, *now* I smell it. The kitchen—"

"Okay, let's do it. Quickly!"

Tom ran down the hall. The thing was at the bottom of the back door, trying to squeeze past Jay-Tee's matches.

"Drop the box, Tom," Mere said.

Tom placed the box of feathers on the floor and knocked the battered lid aside, still staring at the thing by the door. It was glowing.

Mere squatted beside the box, thrust her hand in. "Come on," she said. "All three of you."

Tom grabbed the jade button in his pocket and slipped his other hand into the feathers. Jay-Tee and Reason joined him. Like him, they were transfixed by the bright yellow thing trying to push its way back into the house. He wondered how it had broken their skin. It was all smooth edges, no signs of teeth.

"Now," Mere said. Tom closed his eyes, pushing circles of magic into the feathers. His hand tingled pleasantly as the magic built. Doing magic always felt right. Well, except that once, in New York City with Mere.

"Stop." Mere snatched up the box and then tipped the feathers onto the thing. The golem slipped back under the door before the falling feathers touched it. Mere, Reason, and Jay-Tee pushed the feathers towards the sliver of a gap between the bottom of the door and the floor.

Reason let out a yelp and stumbled away from the door. Mere shoved more feathers into the gap. "Did it touch you?"

"A little," Reason said, but she looked green.

They stepped back, staring at the back door. The feathers stuck firmly, as if held by glue. There were no gaps. The protection was working. "It's gone." Mere turned to Reason. "Are you—"

Reason moved her head slightly in what could have been a nod and then dashed to the bathroom.

Tom grabbed a clean glass and held it under the tap. The water ran hot from the pipes baking in the sun. He pulled the glass aside and let the water run over his hand until it cooled.

A deafening thud came from the back door.

"It's him!" Jay-Tee screamed.

Tom spun around, water from the glass splashing out across the kitchen. The door was pulsating, liquid ripples running across its surface, making a sound like metal on wood that set his teeth out of alignment. Then the noise switched back to dull thudding as the door bowed into the kitchen. Something large and round was pushing from the other side.

Mere and Jay-Tee just stood there staring at it.

"Shouldn't we—" he began.

"What is it?" Reason yelled over the thudding, closing the bathroom door behind her. She took the glass from Tom; their hands touched briefly and Tom gasped, jerking his fingers away.

"What?" Reason asked. No one else had heard him. She wiped her mouth, gulped down the remaining water. "Why'd you do that?"

"Nothing. Static or something." It wasn't nothing. Reason had felt wrong. For an instant her skin'd been like burnished metal—too smooth, too cool, not skinlike at all.

"He's angry!" Jay-Tee yelled. Her cheeks were flushed. "He sure isn't happy with our little feathers."

Tom looked down. Despite the convulsions of the door, the feathers hadn't shifted a millimetre.

"We made that weird-ass thing go away and he's pissed," Jay-Tee continued, still shouting. "We win. See?"

She was right. The door was still rippling, but more gently, and the noise had almost stopped. Tom felt like a giant hand had been gripping his head and squeezing and now, at last, was letting go.

"What can you smell now, Reason?" Mere asked.

Reason was leaning back on one of the kitchen stools. She did not look good. "Nothing weird. The smell's gone."

"Stopped by the feathers?" Jay-Tee asked.

"Stopped by the feathers," Mere agreed. She looked tired.

He sat down next to Mere, opened his mouth to ask how they were going to find out what the thing had been.

"Are you hungry?" Mere asked. Tom closed his mouth. He was starving. Magic always made him ravenous.

"Yes," Jay-Tee said tiredly. Reason nodded.

"How about pizza?" Mere suggested.

"Sure," Jay-Tee said. "Hey, you going to order *beetroot* pizza, Reason?"

"Eww," Tom said. "No one has beetroot on a pizza. That's disgusting."

Jay-Tee laughed. Reason didn't say a word.

7
Old Magic

i ate the pizza without tasting it. I was trying to make sense of what I had learned when the thing had touched me again. In that nanosecond of contact when the barest tips of my index and middle fingers had made contact with it . . . I had learned what it was. Why it had felt so familiar.

My fingers still felt strange, pins and needles that pulled my nerve endings the wrong way. What I had learned instantly from that moment of contact was at the front of all my senses:

The thing was a Cansino.

I recognised the core of its pattern. The same core as Mere's and Sarafina's and Jason Blake's, too. We were all related.

That thing that had crawled inside me, that had left traces of itself along my veins, my muscles—it was family.

But it wasn't human. I didn't know what it was exactly, but it was not a person. How could it not be human and yet related to me? But even more shocking was its age. It was much, much older than any of us.

The thing was a Cansino, reeking of magic rather than insanity, but it was old. Truly old. How was that possible? I *had* to get back into the library, to all those records gathered by generations of Cansinos.

"Are you all right, Reason?" Mere asked, staring at me. She was holding a glass of red wine in her right hand. Jay-Tee was drinking water. (I wondered how she felt about *that*.)

I nodded, making myself meet her eyes and smile. "I'm fine." I had to make sense of this before I could tell anyone. Especially Esmeralda.

"You don't look it." She took a sip of her wine, and for a second her teeth were stained purple.

"I'm fine, honest. The pizza's great." I took another bite to demonstrate my enthusiasm. "I was thinking about that thing," I said in between chews. "That horrible smell. What does smell have to do with mathematics? Why do I *smell* magic?"

"I don't know."

Tom looked disappointed by Esmeralda's answer, but I wasn't surprised. There was a lot she didn't know. The whole point of coming here, of living under her roof, was to learn about magic. But so far she had no answers to any of the big questions.

"It's like physics, Reason, or biology, or any scientific discipline you care to name. There are lots of theories, some of them, like evolution, very useful, but there's a great deal we don't know. We have no idea how many species there are in the world. New bacteria, parasites, jellyfish are found all the time. But there are no teams of scientists anywhere in the world researching magic.

"Most magic-wielders don't even know about it. Most of their lives, they don't know what they are, and by the time they figure it out—if they do—they're dying or they've gone mad.

"There aren't many people like me, born into a family that knows. My mother taught me everything she could. I've learned from her and from our library and from my own research, but there's so much more I don't know. And I don't have much time left."

I nodded, wishing I could get into her library myself, do my own research. None of us had much time. Except Tom. If he continued to follow Mere's rules, he could live at least twenty more years. Twenty years of small, constrained magics. How would he feel when he was thirty-five and we were long dead? I had to stop that from happening. Esmeralda had accepted that was the way magic was and lived her life accordingly. Well, I wasn't going to do that. I wouldn't accept it.

"What do you do, Esmeralda?" Jay-Tee asked. "For a living, I mean." It wasn't the question I was expecting her to ask.

"I'm an actuary."

"A what?"

"I calculate risks and premiums for an insurance company."

"Math?"

Esmeralda nodded. "Of a sort. Statistics."

"Huh," Jay-Tee said, turning back to the pizza. Tom glanced at her, looking puzzled.

"Have you ever come across anything like this before?" I asked.

"Only what I've read about golems."

I wondered where she'd read it. In her library or in fairy books? I didn't think that thing was a golem. It was alive. It was related to me, to her, and to Jason Blake.

"What should we do, then?" Tom asked.

"Guard the door," Jay-Tee said. "Make sure it doesn't get through again."

"We could sleep in the kitchen," Tom said.

"Sleep?" Jay-Tee raised an eyebrow. "Not the best way of keeping an eye on something."

Esmeralda laughed and Tom's expression fell. "Don't you think it'll work, Mere?"

"I think it's a good idea. Keep an eye on the door. Note any changes. And if the protections look like they're not going to hold, add more. You three can take it in turns to sleep."

"You won't join us?" Tom asked.

She shook her head. "I trust you." She caught my eye and smiled. "Besides, if another golem comes through, I'll hear. I'll be downstairs in seconds."

"I'll ask my dad if I can stay over," Tom said. "I'm sure he won't mind."

The three of us had li-los and pillows and bottles of water. Esmeralda had already gone upstairs to bed, saying she'd sleep with her door open.

We were positioned so that we couldn't accidentally disturb any of the feathers or each other when we got up to go to the

bathroom. Tom on my right and Jay-Tee on my left. She'd
insisted on being closest to the door. I had Esmeralda's brooch
pinned to the front of my pyjamas. Tom was wearing his chain
and Jay-Tee her leather bracelet. Their new magic things—
button and tooth—were under their pillows.

Within easy reach of the door was a tray of small chicken
bones ready to be turned into protections.

I lay back on the bedding, propped up by three fat pillows.
Tom and Jay-Tee were under their sheets, but I felt too restless
and strange to be constrained by anything other than my pyjamas. As soon as they fell asleep I was going to see if I could
find Esmeralda's keys, sneak next door, and get into the
library.

Moonlight shone in through the branches, making spooky
patterns all over the kitchen and across Tom's and Jay-Tee's
faces.

"What do you think Jason Blake wants?" Tom asked. "I
mean, beyond magic? Why's he suddenly trying to get through
the door? Why now?"

"Whatcha mean, 'Why now?' He's mad because me and
Reason escaped and Esmeralda kicked his butt in their magic
battle. He's pissed, and now he wants revenge."

"Yeah," Tom said, "I know, but he's using magic, isn't he?
Lots of magic. Making the door do all that stuff. That's way
beyond making light. Why's he using up all that magic?"

It didn't make any sense. The golem was a Cansino. Why
was it letting Jason Blake use it? I opened my mouth to speak

and then closed it again. What did being related to it mean? What would they say if I told them the golem was a Cansino? More importantly, what would Esmeralda say? I didn't trust her enough to tell her yet. And if I told Tom and Jay-Tee, there was no guarantee they wouldn't tell her. It meant something important. I needed to understand it better before I could tell Esmeralda. I *had* to get into her library.

"Seriously," Tom said, "it doesn't make any sense."

The door, which had been quiet since we set up our vigil, rippled.

Even in the moonlight I could see Jay-Tee's face change colour. "Let's not talk about you-know-who," she said, pulling her sheet up higher, as if that would protect her from my grandfather. "Let's talk about something else."

"Like what?" I asked.

"When's the first time you knew you were magic?" Tom asked Jay-Tee.

"Always," Jay-Tee said, surprising me by not telling him to stop being a stickybeak. "My mom and dad were both magic. Dad taught me bits and pieces. He didn't like to talk about it. He'd say, *You should know this.* And then tell me something quickly, mostly about being careful. He didn't want me to die as young as my mom. She was only eighteen. He'd only tell me stuff when my brother wasn't around. Danny's not magic at all."

"Wow. How old was your mum when she had Danny? Isn't he, like, twenty?"

"He's eighteen. Mom was fourteen when she had Danny, and . . ."

I didn't listen to the rest. I was thinking about Danny. Wishing I could see him again. I'd never even kissed a boy. I wanted to kiss Danny before I died.

"How about you, Tom?" Jay-Tee asked.

This I wanted to hear. I was very curious to know how Tom had fallen into Esmeralda's clutches.

"I didn't know for sure until I met Mere, you know? But I knew there was something different about me—"

Jay-Tee snorted. "What? That you like making girlie dresses?"

"Shut up," Tom said, but not nastily. "It wasn't anything spectacular. The clothes I made always seemed to fit people really well. Almost too well. I don't remember when I first saw the true shape of things. Just that sometimes I'd see things differently to everyone else. Seeing the magic, you know?"

I nodded and Jay-Tee said, "Yeah."

"I feel like I've always done it. I just didn't know what it was."

"How did you meet Esmeralda?" I asked.

"On George Street in town. I'd gone in to see a movie with some of my old Shire mates. We were mucking around, being dropkicks, deliberately bumping into people on the street and then acting like it was an accident. I bumped into Mere. And it was weird. Really weird. She looked at me strange. And I felt that magic tingle, you know?"

Jay-Tee laughed. "True love!"

Tom blushed, his pale skin darkening, visible even in the moonlight. "Shut up! *Real* magic. You know exactly what I mean! She recognised it in me, and I think I did in her, too. She was the first person in my entire life I'd met who was just like me."

"Except your mother," I said softly.

"I didn't know about mum, but. She was in the loony bin."

"What happened with Esmeralda that day?"

"She pretended to be angry, said she was going to get the cops. All my friends racked off, so it was just me and her. She said, *I know what you are.* Just like that. It was freaky."

"I can imagine," I said.

"Then she took me to get lunch in this café and told me about magic. I knew it was true. Immediately. She asked me lots of questions about my mum and my dad. Explained why mum was mad. That made sense, too." He took a deep breath and looked at Jay-Tee, as if considering whether he could trust her to hear what he was going to say. "I'd started seeing things, hearing things other people didn't hear. I'd started going nuts. Mere saved me."

"Wow," Jay-Tee said.

I nodded.

"Mere said she'd teach me, make sure I didn't end up in Kalder Park. Right then and there she taught me how to make light, explained how to use magic. What the true shapes I sometimes saw were. She told me to do a little magic once a week. Then she drove me home, all the way back to the Shire. She talked to my dad for a long time."

"You were lucky," Jay-Tee said. I could almost hear her thinking about Jason Blake.

"I know," Tom said.

I smelled Tom. There was no rust there, not like Jay-Tee or Mere. He had years left. I suddenly realised that it also meant Mere hadn't drunk magic from him. Why not? Was she saving him up for an emergency?

Something landed with a clatter on the back porch. We all gasped. I jumped up and ran to the window in time to see a cat disappearing from view.

"Just a cat."

Jay-Tee drew the invisible grid she sometimes drew when she was nervous: a y-axis from her mouth to her chest and an x-axis across her shoulders.

Tom laughed. "Scared the crap out of me."

I got back into bed.

"Do you miss your friends, Reason?" Tom asked. "Must've been horrible, being taken away from home and made to come live here."

"My friends? I've never really had any friends. I told you, me and Sarafina, we moved around a lot."

"No friends at all?" Jay-Tee asked.

"Not really. Not for long, anyway. We never stayed any-where long enough."

"But we're your friends, right?" Tom asked.

"Of course."

"And you've only just met us. You must have had friends

even if it was just for a week or two before you moved on to the next place."

"Yeah," Jay-Tee said. "When I ran away, I tried not to make friends. Getting to know a bunch of people would just make it easier for my dad to find me. But it's really hard. I ended up knowing the guys at my favourite pizza place and my favourite nightclubs and at the Korean place on the corner and the laundromat. You pass people in the street, and after you start recognising each other, you nod, and then after you've nodded a bunch of times, you start talking. Doesn't take long before you know almost everyone."

"We never stayed anywhere there were lots of people," I said. "It's hard to explain. Sarafina's really good at being, um, surface friendly. And we never used our real names. It's hard to have friends when your name and the colour of your hair and your history are all made up. It was mostly just me and Sarafina."

"What about at school?" Tom asked. "You must've made friends there."

"I only ever went to school once." I thought of Josh Davidson. "It didn't work out."

"Wow, you're lucky," Jay-Tee said. "The best thing about running away was no more school."

"I love school," Tom said. "Usually by this time in the holidays I'm dying to get back."

"No way!"

"School's great. I get to design and make all the costumes for the school pl—"

"Please! Spare us. School's—" Jay-Tee sat up. "What's *that* noise?"

The branches of the fig tree rustled violently, emitting loud squeaks and chitterings. "Just a bat," Tom and I said at the same time.

"They're noisy buggers," I finished.

I laughed. "Just a bat chasing after just a cat!"

"All we need is just a rat!"

"Very funny." Jay-Tee ran to the window. "Look! I think they're fighting. One just flew away. Their wings stretch so wide! Tom, I thought you said they were flying foxes?"

"They are," I said. "Fruit bats with faces just like a fox's."

Jay-Tee sat down on her li-lo, climbed under the sheet. "They're pretty cool."

"I ate flying fox once."

"Ewww!"

"What'd it taste like?" Tom asked, screwing up his nose. "They smell foul."

"They taste how they smell. Really, really, really horrible."

The three of us lay quietly for a moment. I liked having friends. But Jay-Tee wouldn't be around much longer. She was as riddled with rust as Esmeralda. Most likely I was, too. There had to be a cure for the rust that didn't involve losing your mind.

"So what do you want to do when you grow up?" Tom asked.

Jay-Tee snorted. "I'm not *going* to grow up, Tom. Remember? I've blown through most of my magic feeding *him*."

"And conjuring money out of nothing," I said, "and—"

"I was stupid, okay? I started doing it to piss my dad off. When he talked about magic, which was, like, hardly ever, he was all, *Don't use it unless you have to, be careful.* So I did the opposite. If he'd told me not to smoke . . ."

"But when you were little you must've wanted to be something," Tom said. "I've always wanted to make clothes. Be a fashion designer. For as long as I can remember."

Jay-Tee laughed. "I wanted to be famous."

"Doing what?" I asked.

Jay-Tee shrugged. "Didn't think about what. I just wanted to be famous."

"But you have to *do* something to be famous."

Both Tom and Jay-Tee looked at me as if I'd said something completely insane.

"What about you, then, Reason?" Jay-Tee asked. "What about your plans for the future you don't have?"

"We were going to leave Australia. Travel." Sarafina had always wanted to go to Cambodia and see Angkor Wat. "We've travelled all over Australia; we were going to explore the rest of the world."

"You and your mom?" Jay-Tee asked, yawning.

"Yup."

"Well," Tom said, yawning, too, "at least you got to see New York."

"True." I thought about what lay on the other side of the door. The strange thing that was related to me, controlled by my grandfather Jason Blake. Tom was right. What *did* he want? Why was he using so much magic?

The bats broke into another squabble, squeaking and rustling in the fig tree outside. Several of them took off, their leather wings displacing the air noisily. It was strange hearing bush noises in the middle of a city.

"Jay-Tee?" I asked softly. There was no response. "Tom?"

"Whaa," Tom answered, half asleep.

"Nothing. I'll stay awake. Keep an eye on the door."

"Wake me," Tom said through a yawn, "when you're too sleepy."

"No worries."

Soon they were both breathing heavily and evenly. I waited until I was absolutely positive they were asleep; then I sat up. Neither Tom nor Jay-Tee shifted. I stood slowly, not letting the li-lo squeak. Esmeralda's keys had been in her briefcase, which was probably in her bedroom. This was not going to be easy.

The door moaned. I froze. The wood had turned liquid again. It was vibrating, rocking, almost as if it was trying to shake the feather protections away from it. Tom grunted, then turned over. They were both still asleep. I took another step.

The door shrieked, let out a loud, piercing cry that was almost human. I started.

"What's happening?" Jay-Tee asked, sitting up.

Bugger, I thought, *now I'll never get to the library*. "The door—" I began.

A loud explosion, almost a roar, shook it. Painfully loud. We both brought our hands up to cover our ears.

Tom sat up, blinking, more than half asleep.

The door shook violently, ripples passing back and forth across its surface. My grandfather wasn't happy.

The door bowed fast and sudden, stretching out so far it whacked into me. It was sticky, spreading itself all over me, sucking me back across the room. There was pain. And whiteness and heat and then cold.

And I was lying on the ground in front of the door. In New York City.

8

Dirty Old Snow

i had a mouthful of wet, cold dirt. I pushed myself up on my elbows. They hurt. My whole body hurt. I spat several times, rolled over, stood up.

New York City again. Winter. Cold. Daytime.

I brushed some of the wet dirt from me. The *snow*. Something smelled horrible. My skin prickled, not from the cold—someone was looking at me.

It wasn't Jason Blake.

At the top of the steps, leaning against the door to Sydney, was a . . . I wasn't sure what it was—old, that was certain. A man? A monster? It had eyes and a nose and a mouth, arms and legs. It was human-shaped but it could have been anything: man, woman, black, white. It was so filthy that its clothing and skin seemed to have fused together.

It was staring right at me.

Staring at me and reeking of stomach acids, of black rubber tire remains made burning hot by the sun on the side of a highway. Burnt rubber and chunder. It smelled like the thing that had come from under the door into Esmeralda's house. The thing that was related to me—but this thing, this person, smelt even worse. It made me want to run far, far away.

Sarafina always said, *Never show that you're scared.* I stood and planted my feet firmly in the snow and stared back, trying not to think about my churning stomach, my freezing skin. I put my hand over Esmeralda's brooch pinned to my PJ top, feeling its warmth, and blurred my eyes to look all the way inside. I saw that he was a man, or at least, he'd *been* a man. I saw that he was not Jason Blake in disguise. I saw his Cansinoness. He was related to me, but he was nothing like me.

Our magic was related, too, but his was much more than mine. It was as though his magic had eaten almost everything else; all that remained were traces of what had been before— his Cansinoness, his humanity, his maleness. His magic shone throughout his body, making up the very marrow of his bones. More thoroughly magic than Esmeralda or Jason Blake, than Tom, Jay-Tee, or me.

He was old, too, older than all our ages put together. Centuries old.

The intense smell of him filled me, far stronger than that of the little golem. I pressed my lips firmly together. I would not chunder. There was no hint of unripe lemon. His reek was nothing like the madness in my mother. He was old, but he wasn't insane.

He was even worse than Jason Blake. How many people did you have to drink dry of magic to live as long as he had? The thought of it made rage swell up in me like a tumour. *Never lose your temper.* My vision shot back to the surface, where the world pulsed red. My magic swirled out of Esmeralda's brooch in a Fibonacci spiral aimed at old man Cansino. I would stop him even if it killed me.

He flicked his wrist, making a shooing motion.

My magic rebounded, exploded into me, rendered me blind and deaf, stripped of all my senses.

In this absolutely silent, scentless darkness, echoes of what I'd seen and heard on the street assailed me. All at once I realised I'd been cold, standing in snow with bare feet wearing cotton pyjamas. The wind had been cutting through me; I'd felt the uneven footpath underneath my feet, old chewing gum, salt, melting snow; I'd been smelling car fumes and steak being burnt, hearing car horns and music blaring, someone yelling out to her friends to "wait up"; I'd seen the greys and browns of a New York winter. Now I felt nothing.

Then my senses smashed back into me, like a car into a wall. I heard the bile building in the back of my throat. I blinked at a helicopter far overhead, inhaled pounding bass, felt grey and brown, stumbled over the music. What had Esmeralda called this? Synaesthesia.

I vomited onto a pile of snow in the gutter.

The old man still leaned against Esmeralda's door, comfortable, relaxed. He shook his head slowly, not in anger, more as if he was sorry for me.

With a wave of his hand he'd stopped my attack against him, stripped my senses away. What else could he do? Kill me? Easily—he wouldn't need to get angry, just flex his wrist. I took a step away, almost falling over in the snow. I didn't know what to do. He was the one attacking the door; his golem thing had crawled inside me, had bitten Tom and Jay-Tee. *Don't show your fear.* "Who are you?"

The old man laughed. Or at least I figured that's what the sound was. It sounded like a cross between a cackle and a hacking cough. I could hear the phlegm.

I stood up, stepped away from the gutter, wiped my mouth. "Why—"

Old man Cansino shook his head again, smiled, and made a shooing gesture. For a fraction of a section I thought he was going to blind me again. He shooed me instead.

I was more than willing to shoo. I wanted to be far away from him. I wanted to never see him again.

I walked hastily, awkwardly, limbs not quite under my control, wiping my mouth again, tasting vomit and charcoal. I brushed more snow and grime off my face and clothes. My eyes still stung; my heart beat so hard, I was halfway up the block before the cold started to penetrate.

I could feel the old man's eyes on my back, but when I turned he wasn't there. The steps were empty. I half turned and took a step towards Esmeralda's door, and there he was again. Shaking his head.

Adrenaline shot through me, warming me up, propelling me away. I stumbled.

"Are you all right, girlie?"

I turned to find a woman with a concerned expression

looking down at me. A shade or two darker than me, pushing a pink-cheeked baby in a pram. "You'll catch your death dressed like that."

"I'm okay," I said, though I wasn't. I smiled to demonstrate. "I slipped."

"You sure you're all right, love?" The woman peered at me. Her expression said that I must look awful, but I nodded, anyway.

"Are you sure?" a second woman asked. She was older, her skin not as dark, dressed in a red fluffy coat. The two women exchanged glances. "You look terrible."

"Do you need any help?" the first woman asked.

"Yes," said the second one. "I live near here. You can't stay out on the street dressed like that."

"She sure can't," added a man passing by, pushing a shopping cart. "Catch her death."

I was suddenly aware that almost everyone on the block was staring at me. Across the street two men on scaffolding had stopped work to watch the show.

"Did someone do something to you?"

"Oh, no. Really, no one did nothing, I mean anything. I . . . I got locked out," I told the two women. "It's a long story. I'm visiting from Australia." I added the last in case they thought my accent was strange. "I just have to call my friend's brother. It's his place." I shivered. My toes were hurting with the cold.

"Here, use my cell." The second woman gave me her phone.

I dialed Danny's number—without the prefix it was the thirty-third number in the Fibonacci series. A very good omen—not that I believed in omens, though maybe I *did* now—I hadn't used to believe in magic.

I pressed the phone to my ear, hoping he'd answer. It felt weird making a phone call with so many people watching. I shifted back and forth, trying to keep my feet from going completely numb. It was freezing, and here was me in my PJ's.

"Hello?"

"Danny!"

"Who is this?"

"Reason!"

"Reason? Julieta's friend?"

"Yes! I, um . . ." I paused, very conscious that the women were listening. "I got locked out. Can you come let me in?"

"You what? What do you mean?"

"The door slammed and I left the key inside."

"What? Where are you? Is Julieta with you?"

"Near the house. No, she's not."

"What do you mean, 'the house'? Are you here? In the city?"

"Yes!" I yelled, so relieved he'd understood. "I need you to come let me in. I'm in my pyjamas, no shoes, and it's cold. I got locked out."

"Where are you exactly?"

"Ah . . ." I didn't know. It was the East Village. A street whose name was a number, but I didn't know which one. "Very close to the house."

"Same street?"

"Yes. Same block."

"On Seventh Street."

"Seventh Street," I repeated.

"Okay. There's a café on the corner, same side you're on. You won't have to cross the street to get to it; just head towards the park. I forget the name, but it has glass cabinets full of muffins. You'll be warm in there. I'll be right over."

"Okay," I said, hoping I'd find it.

"How come you're not in Sydney?"

"It's a long story. I'm cold, Danny."

"I'm on my way. I'll see you at the café."

I handed the phone back to the second woman. "He's coming for you?" she asked.

"Yes, he's meeting me at the café on the corner." My teeth were chattering so much it was hard to get the words out. "The one with the glass counters?"

The woman with the pram nodded. "Titi's," she said, pushing the carriage into motion. "It's this way; follow me."

The other woman slipped off her fluffy red coat and draped it around my shoulders. "Come on," she said, taking my hand in hers, then, feeling how cold it was, starting to chafe it.

The two women led me to a table and called to the waitress for some towels. They pushed me into a seat and I started rubbing the blocks of ice that were my feet.

A waitress came over with two cloth dish towels. "Might

help," she said, looking at me dubiously. The same look the other two women had given me: narrowed eyes, eyebrows almost, but not quite, raised. Not suspicious of me, but of whatever or whoever had left me out on the street barefoot in the middle of winter.

"Ta," I said. I took a towel, wiped away melted snow and grit, then wrapped it around my feet.

"Now," said the woman with the baby, "are you sure you're going to be okay? I have to be going is all."

"Oh, yes," I said, teeth still clattering against one another. "I'm much warmer, and Danny will be here soon."

She didn't look like she had much faith in Danny, but she nodded. "You look after yourself in the future. No messing around outside without the key."

"I won't. Thank you so much."

The two women nodded at each other, as if to communicate that I was now the woman with the phone's responsibility. She held the door open to let the woman and her pram pass; then she sat down beside me. "How about a hot chocolate?"

I nodded. "Yes, please."

The waitress yelled the order to the guy behind the counter, then turned her attention back to me and the second woman. She looked me up and down. "Pyjamas?"

"I got locked out."

"No kidding. How'd you manage that?"

"It just shut behind me."

"That was pretty dumb."

I nodded.

"Don't be harsh," said the woman with the phone. "She's from out of town. *Australia*."

"Huh. Do people in Australia always wear brooches with their pyjamas?"

"No, it's my grandmother's."

"Huh." The waitress went to the counter and returned with a hot chocolate. "On the house."

"Thank you so much," I said, meaning every word.

I tried to keep my fear and anxiety from my face. I had no idea what I was going to do next, how I was going to get back to Sydney. If I was going to solve the magic-or-madness question, I had to get back to Esmeralda's library. With the old man guarding the way and Jason Blake lurking who-knew-where, I could see no way home.

I was onto my second chocolate when Danny showed up. Looking at him sent a jolt through me, warmed me. He was so smooth: his cheeks, his lips. His close-cropped hair. He stared and shook his head. I blushed, bent my head only to see my bedraggled PJs, my dirty feet. He wasn't thinking about how good *I* looked.

"Sorry I took a while. Was tricky getting a cab. Are you okay?" he asked.

"No, she's not, young man," the fluffy-red-jacket woman said. "You need to get her somewhere warm and dry. Do you have a bathtub? A nice soak in the bath should help, but if her toes are still blue, you might have to take her to a doctor. Could be frostbite."

The waitress came over and stood nodding, looking at Danny like it was all his fault.

"Of course," Danny said.

The woman nodded, though she didn't look like she believed him. "Sorry, cariñita, I need my jacket back." I slipped it off and handed it to her. She gave me a kiss on the forehead and headed for the door. Before she stepped out, she turned back to Danny. "You take care of her."

"I will." Danny dropped some money on the table and thanked the waitress. "Here, put this on." He handed me his coat and dragged me outside, into the street and into the yellow taxicab that was waiting.

"I called Jay-Tee," Danny said as I scooted across the taxi seat. "Talked to your grandmother a little. They're relieved to hear you're okay. They want to talk to you."

"Should I ring them now?"

Danny looked puzzled.

"On your mobile?"

"My cell, you mean?"

I nodded.

He glanced at the driver in the rear-view mirror. "We're not far from my place. You can call from there."

"What time is it?"

"It's just after one."

"In the afternoon?"

Danny nodded.

I'd asked even though I knew that. It had to be. After one o'clock on Monday afternoon. In Sydney it would be after five on Tuesday morning. What time had I come through the door? How long had I been in New York City? Half an hour? Forty minutes? I wished I'd worn my watch to bed. A week ago I would have. I'd've been ready to jump up, grab my stuff, and run. Sarafina would be shocked at how slack I'd become.

"Must be pretty early in Sydney, huh?"

"Uh-huh. Sun's not up yet."

"How come you've got that hunk of jewellery pinned to your pyjamas?"

My hand went to it. I could feel it hum under my fingers. I was cold, but it was warm. Something else nearby hummed in unison. My ammonite was in Danny's pocket. Suddenly I could feel the steady beat of the blood through his veins: the pulsing of it radiated from the stone. He'd kept it—surely that had to mean something?

Danny repeated his question.

"The brooch? Oh, it's my grandmother's. I, um . . ."

"Have to wear it all the time?" He lowered his voice. "A magic thing?"

I nodded. "A magic thing."

A snatch of song played, tinny and muffled. Danny reached into his pocket and pulled out a mobile phone. The song got louder. He looked at its screen for a moment and then answered. "Hey, Vee, how's it hanging?"

Apparently it wasn't hanging very well. Vee did most of the talking while Danny said things like, "No way"; "No, I didn't mean that"; "Of course I do"; and, "Goddamn, Vee." When he hung up, Danny looked at me and shrugged. I wondered who Vee was.

After that the taxi ride was mostly quiet. Danny didn't ask me any more questions. The ammonite continued warm and humming. Danny's heart beat regularly. I wasn't sure if mine did.

The driver kept glancing back in the mirror at me in my pyjamas, which weren't entirely hidden by Danny's coat. The last time I'd been in New York City—four days ago—I hadn't known where I was. I hadn't known I was on the other side of the world, in the United States of America. I hadn't known anyone or anything.

I was still cold. The chattering of my teeth had entered my brain. I kept thinking about the old man, wondering how he'd pulled me through the door without breaking me. I ached, but I was all in one piece. Had he rearranged the molecules of the wood to fit me through? Or had he rearranged mine? Why had he pulled me through and then let me go? Why had he sent his golem thing through the door to bite us? Did he know Jason Blake?

Mostly I wondered about how he could be related to me. It was easier to think about than how I was going to get back home.

Danny's building looked brand-new. Everything was clean and shining. The front door was massive and made of glass.

"Where are we?" I asked.

"The West Village."

"West of the East Village," I said.

"Uh, yeah." Danny looked at me oddly as he pulled out his key to open the front door. It buzzed open as he put it in the lock. "Bastard," he muttered. "Naz. The doorman. He loves doing that." He held the door as I went through. There was another set of double doors, which also buzzed open.

We were in a large foyer. One wall was sheathed in a waterfall, which flowed onto a pond full of really big goldfish. Behind a big desk a bloke sat grinning at Danny. "Gotcha again."

"Smartass."

"Who's your new girl?" Naz asked. "Don't you have enough women already?"

"Whatever. This is a friend of my kid sister. Reason, meet Naz."

I moved forward and offered him my hand. "Hi, Naz."

"Raisin? Weird name." He shook my hand.

"No, Reason."

"Reason? That's still plenty weird."

"You get used to it," Danny said.

"So how come you got no shoes? What's with the PJs—"

"Long story," Danny said. "Reason's going to be staying with me for a while."

"She is, huh?" Naz raised an eyebrow.

Danny glared at him and I wondered why.

Naz coughed. "Sure, man. Let me know if you need any-thing, Reason."

"Ta," I said.

Naz looked at me blankly.

"Thank you."

He nodded, and Danny led me towards the lift. When the doors opened, he had to put his key in a slot to make it go. He pressed the top button and smiled. "I've got views."

"Great."

The lift doors opened onto an enormous high-ceilinged room with loads of windows. I remembered Danny telling Jay-Tee that their dad had left them lots of money. Looking at this flat, I could believe it. I was pretty sure they hadn't grown up rich, though. I wondered what their father had done to sud-denly get rich. How much magic had it taken? Was that what had killed him?

"You like?" Danny asked.

"Wow." There were so many windows. It was huge.

"So, what are you doing here?"

"Well . . ." I started, but my voice faded. What *had* hap-pened? "The door . . ."

"Come and sit down." He led me to the kitchen in the cor-ner of the huge room. One wall was cupboards and bench space; the other had a stove and more bench space and a big stainless-steel thing hanging down from the ceiling. Set a little out from both kitchen walls was a solid table with cupboards underneath it, surrounded by six stools. Danny held one out for me. It was taller than Esmeralda's were, with a soft, cushiony top, and rungs to rest my feet on.

"You want something to eat? I got leftover spaghetti bolognaise."

"Spag bol, great. I love it."

"Spag bol? That's hilarious." He pulled open the fridge door. There wasn't much food in it, just tomato sauce, other jars of stuff I didn't recognise, and two plastic containers—but mostly there were bottles of beer. He grabbed the plastic containers and piled two bowls with their contents, spag and red sauce, and popped them in the microwave.

"What happened exactly?" Danny's phone rang again. Or rather *sang* again, the same snatch of song it had played in the taxi. He fished it out, looked at it closely, pressed a button, then popped it back into his pocket. "It'll go to voicemail. Was it that other guy? The one who was—"

"No, it wasn't Jason Blake."

"Really? Your grandmother seemed to think it was. Hey, you didn't run away again, did you?"

I shook my head, tried not to be distracted by my ammonite, which was still relaying the movement of his blood and heart to me.

"Your grandmother hasn't done anything bad to you, has she? Like that other guy? Jay-Tee said not, but your grandmother was standing right there."

I shook my head again. Not *yet* she hadn't. Except for the

black and purple feathers. I wasn't convinced they were to protect me. To leech my magic away while I slept?

"She's not *drinking* you?"

"No. Not Jay-Tee, either."

"Then what happened?"

"There's this old man—"

"I thought you said it wasn't that Blake guy?"

"It's a different man." I shook my head, trying to clear it.
"The door was vibrating—well, not vibrating . . ."

"Which door? The one that when you open it you're in
Sydney? If you're magic, anyway."

"Yes." Danny had been standing beside me when
Esmeralda opened the door. We'd all stepped through, back
to Sydney. He'd stayed in New York, not knowing where we'd
gone.

"The door doesn't normally vibrate?"

"No." My feet were tingling. I bent down and rubbed
them.

"Are they okay? Can you feel your toes?"

"Yes. I think they're okay. Just cold."

The bell of the microwave sounded. Danny pulled out the
bowls and handed one to me. "Careful, it's hot."

It was. I put it down on the table quickly, forking some of it
into my mouth without making contact with the bowl. The
spaghetti wasn't hot at all. Lukewarm on the outside and
almost cold in the middle, and the sauce was too salty. I ate it,
anyway. I was starving.

"So the door was vibrating?" Danny asked as we bolted the food down.

"Well, that's too little a word really—it looked like it was about to explode. And then it kind of reached for me, and I got sucked through it. Right through the wood. From Sydney to New York." I paused to take a big breath. "On the other side—I mean, on *this* side—there was an old man standing there. He made me go blind. Just for a second, but it was horrible."

"You got sucked *through* a door. An unopened door?"

It sounded strange when Danny said it like that: *You got sucked through a door.* How could anyone be sucked through wood? I'd already forgotten how the rest of the world worked, the world that was free of magic. I hadn't thought much about how it would seem to someone who was normal, who wasn't doomed. A week ago I hadn't believed in magic, either. *Less* than a week.

"He *blinded* you?"

"Yes. Made me deaf, too, and I couldn't smell. No senses at all. It was *really* scary. And then he was laughing at me, telling me to go away." Well, he hadn't *said* anything, but it had been clear what he wanted.

"Couldn't you magic him back? Turn him into a toad?"

"It doesn't work like that. Anyway, he's got more magic than me."

"Can't your grandmother do something? Blast him?"

"She's still on the other side of the door."

"You should call her."

"Yeah. But can I shower first? Before my toes fall off?"

"Of course."

He led me into a bedroom. I didn't think it was his. The walls—the ones that didn't have windows—were covered in posters of people in tight clothes. Singers or actors, I guessed. "Are those Jay-Tee's?"

"Yup. This is her room. Don't tell her, though. I want it to be a surprise. It's filled with all her old stuff."

He slid one of the posters away, revealing a wardrobe stuffed full of clothes, toys, battered board games, and boxes piled on boxes. So many things.

"Wow, Jay-Tee sure has a lot of stuff."

"Yeah, I didn't know what to keep and what to toss. Figured I'd let Jay-Tee decide."

"I'm sure she'll appreciate it."

"You can have this room for as long as you need to. The bathroom's in there."

"Thanks." It was as big as my bathroom in Esmeralda's house, only it had a window—an escape route, not that I thought I'd need one.

Danny pointed out where the towels were and shut the door behind him. I opened it again. "Uh, Danny? Do you think I could borrow some of her clothes? It'd be nice not to have to put these pyjamas back on."

"Oh, sure."

Danny started rifling through the wardrobe and picked out

a red T-shirt and a pair of blue tracky-dacks with double white stripes down the sides. "These should fit. They were always big on Julieta." He handed them to me, and though our skin didn't touch, I caught the faintest warmth radiating from him, a faint whiff of something I'd never smelled before—something vital and alive.

9
Patterns in the Door

Waiting was doing Tom's head in. He was itching to burst through the door and rescue Reason, but Esmeralda was dead against it. Especially now that they knew she was safe with Jay-Tee's brother. Tom, however, had his own thoughts about how "safe" she was with Danny.

A loud, shrill ring startled Tom into dropping the pad where he and Jay-Tee'd been taking turns describing what the door did: every stop; every start; the various gentle ripples that trembled across its surface, sometimes lengthways, sometimes across, occasionally swirling like a whirlpool. Mere wanted them to see if they could spot a pattern. So far, none of their scribbled notes looked very useful.

The phone rang again. *Reason*, Tom thought. Jay-Tee must have thought it, too: they both lunged for the receiver at the same time.

Jay-Tee was quickest, but Tom was closer.

"Hello?" he said, a little breathless. "Mere's residence."

Jay-Tee repeated, "Mere's residence," sarcastically. He waved her quiet.

"Hello, Tom?"

It *was* Reason. Tom felt his cheeks get hot. "Reason! Are you okay?"

"I'm fine."

"How? Jason Blake didn't—"

"He wasn't there. It wasn't him on the other side."

"It wasn't?" Tom asked. "You're sure? Maybe he was somewhere else spying or something."

"Maybe, but I didn't see him, Tom. Is Esmeralda there?"

"She's next door. Researching, trying to find something that will help."

"So she doesn't know what's going on, then?"

Tom hated to hear Mere being criticised, but it was true—she didn't know what was happening. "Not exactly, but she'll find something. I'm pretty sure she has lots of ideas."

Jay-Tee scooted her stool closer, crowding him. "Ask her if—"

"Shhh!"

"What?" Reason asked. She sounded tinny, like she was speaking from inside a metal box on the other end of the world, which she was, sort of—the other side of the world, anyway. Or the other side of the door. It still made Tom's head spin. In less than a second, Reason had gone from summer to winter, Southern Hemisphere to Northern, moonlight to daylight, Sydney to New York City. When she was really what? Sixteen? Fifteen? Fourteen hours and thousands of kilometres away.

"Nothing, Ree. Jay-Tee's being a pain." Jay-Tee made a face and scooched her stool closer, practically putting her ear on the receiver. Tom inched away, which left him with the kitchen table jammed into his ribs. Unfortunately, the phone was an old-fashioned one with a cord and everything. "Are you really fine?"

"Yes. Bit shaken but fine. I'm in New York."

"Yeah, we know, Danny rang. So what happened, Ree? You disappeared into the door. We both saw it. You're really sure it wasn't Jason Blake?" He pressed the phone to his ear as if that would somehow bring Reason closer. Jay-Tee's cheek was practically against his; he could hear her breathing, straining to listen. The rippling of the door stopped. He nudged Jay-Tee and she wrote it down.

The farthest Tom or Jay-Tee had been from the door since Mere'd issued her instructions and gone to her library was to the bathroom, just off the kitchen. Tom was completely jack of staring at the door and taking notes, and Jay-Tee had been getting narkier and snarlier as each minute passed.

"No," Reason said, "I didn't see Blake." She paused. Tom could hear her breathing, but in a different rhythm to Jay-Tee. She told him about an old man who wasn't human. Tom didn't understand.

"Old? How can he be old?" It didn't make any sense. "*And* do magic?" Then it hit Tom. "Do you think he's been drinking from other magic-users? Stealing their magic?"

"Could be."

Could stealing magic keep you alive for centuries? Wouldn't Mere have mentioned that? Maybe the old man was completely insane? Tom looked at the door. So did Jay-Tee. It was still.

"He's definitely magic *and* old," Reason's voice said down the telephone wire. "I don't know how he got that way. He didn't try to take my magic. I don't know why, 'cause he's *really* powerful."

"We gathered that from this end." Reason had disappeared into the door so fast. Tom'd imagined her captured by Jason Blake or broken into pieces or, worse, trapped inside the door. For a second, Tom could taste wood in his mouth, feel the splinters sticking into all parts of his body like pins and needles, only vicious and bloody. Like the biting golem thing.

"How do you *know* he's old?" Jay-Tee said loudly, so loud Tom's ear hurt. He glared at her and held the receiver tighter. It slipped in his now-sweaty hand.

"I just know," Reason said, far away. "Is that you, Jay-Tee?"

"Yeah!" Jay-Tee yelled, hurting Tom's ear some more. "So how do you know?"

"Well . . ."

"Come on, Reason," said Jay-Tee. "How do you know?"

"I can see it."

"See what?" Jay-Tee said, sounding annoyed.

"Hey," Tom said. "Steady, Jay-Tee. You don't want to lose your temper."

Jay-Tee flushed. "I wasn't going to lo—"

"So, Ree?" Tom asked, more gently. "How do you mean?"

Tom could hear Reason take a deep breath. "Well," she said, "when I look at people, really look at them, I can see down into their cells. I can see the magic in them."

"Wow," Tom said. "Like when I see the true shapes of things. I can sort of see if a person's magic, too. Doesn't always work, though. I wasn't a hundred-percent sure about you."

"Then how come you couldn't see it in Danny?" Jay-Tee asked. She didn't sound like she was losing it anymore, back to her narky self. "Remember? You had to ask me whether he was magic or not."

"I didn't know how to do it then. I do now. When I look at Danny, there's no magic. But the old man has magic all the way through. It's like the magic ate most of the human bits of him."

Tom tried to take this in. Either the old man stole magic from everyone he could or . . . "He must be really, really crazy, then."

"No."

"What? You can see whether they're nutters, too?"

"Yeah, I can, Tom. He's not crazy."

"Wow." He imagined Reason seeing the madness inside her mother. He wondered what it looked like, if his own mother's insanity looked any different. He was pretty sure it wasn't something he wanted to look at.

"If Esmeralda gets any ideas about what I should do . . ."

"She will. She'll call you when she gets back. Shouldn't be long."

"Is the door still being all weird?"

Both Tom and Jay-Tee glanced at it. *That would be a yes.* "It's stopped right now, but there's been continued weirdness. Some of the feathers burst into flames."

"You're kidding!"

"Yeah, I know. They didn't burn anything else, but. Just left a pile of ashes. I added some of the chicken bones. But it hasn't been noisy or violent since then. Now it just ripples. It's quite pretty, actually." Beside him Jay-Tee mimicked the way he said "quite" under her breath.

"Huh." Reason's voice sounded even smaller for a second.

"You okay?"

"Yeah. Tired." She paused. "And fuzzy. You know, jet lag."

"*Door* lag."

Reason laughed. "That's right."

"I wanted to go after you, but Mere said—"

"It's too dangerous? It is, Tom, really dangerous. You don't want to touch the door while it's like that. That old man is scary. When I tried to magic him—"

"You what?" Fear shot through Tom. That would require a *lot* of magic. "Tell me you didn't—"

"No, no, I didn't. Honest, Tom. The old man didn't let me. He's really powerful."

The door started up again, lengthways ripples that started swirling, turning into figures of eight. Jay-Tee was noting it down.

Tom's scalp tightened. It was as if the old man knew what they'd been saying. Tom could picture him, grinning, showing a mouth full of rotten green teeth. He took a deep breath and changed the subject by asking, "So, uh, what's Danny's place like?" Straight away the door slipped back into slower, gentler patterns. Was the old man listening?

Jay-Tee grabbed the phone. Tom's hands were so sweaty it slipped right out. "You've been on for ages." She turned to the phone. "Hey, Reason. Tom was being a hog. Sorry about before. Being cranky? It's kind of nervous-making being stuck here watching the stupid door, you know?"

Reason responded, but Tom made no attempt to hear. He stood up, stretched, rubbed his ear. Outside the world was getting lighter. The sun coming up. He looked at the clock on the stove—almost six-thirty. It had been around 4 AM when Reason had been sucked through into New York City. He was knackered.

"Uh-huh," Jay-Tee said. "You're lucky being on the other side. How's Danny? What's his place like?"

Reason said something and Jay-Tee giggled.

Suddenly, Tom had a clear image of Danny sitting at the back of that restaurant in New York where they'd found Reason again. A really good-looking guy who'd been radiating eau de Reason. Tom felt wobbly. He hadn't yet had the nerve to ask Reason about Danny, ask her if anything had happened between them. He didn't want to think about that. He shook his head, trying to kill the thought, and instead thought of worse things, like Reason not living much longer.

Tom grabbed a glass of water, gulped it down, poured another. The day was heating up. He wished Mere would get back; he was going to go mad if he had to stay here watching the door much longer.

He tapped Jay-Tee on the shoulder. "Hang on, Reason," Jay-Tee said. "Just a second. What, Tom?"

"I just need to say one thing to Reason."

Jay-Tee looked like she was going to say something mean, but then she simply handed him the receiver.

"Hey, Reason."

"Hey, Tom."

"Listen, will you do me a favour?"

"What?"

"Will you try not to use any magic? I mean, not unless you really, really have to."

Reason didn't say anything.

"Will you promise?"

"I'll promise to try, Tom, but I might have to. That thing . . ."

"I know, but try really, really hard, okay?"

"Sure, Tom. I promise."

"Good. 'Bye, Reason."

"'Bye, Tom." He handed the receiver to Jay-Tee, who nodded at him.

The first thing she said to the phone was, "You're going to promise me the same thing, right, Reason?"

10

Ammonite

"You don't have much furniture," I said. Danny's hair was damp, making the curls cling even tighter to his head. He'd changed clothes, too, but my ammonite was still in his pocket.

Danny was bone-meltingly gorgeous. His brown eyes were huge and almost slanted, with the longest, blackest eyelashes. His hair was cut close to his scalp, leaving lots of tiny little curls. His skin was a gorgeous shade of brown, darker than mine or Jay-Tee's. It glowed. Looking anywhere other than at him was an effort. So I did an inventory of his furniture: a couch, two comfy chairs, a huge television, and six stools around the kitchen island, one of which I was sitting on. In the giant room, it seemed like no furniture at all. He pulled up one of the stools and sat opposite me.

"So, Reason?" he said. I bit on my tongue to stop myself from blushing or shaking or doing anything that would make him realise that I liked him. I wanted him to realise, but only if he liked me, too, and not just as Jay-Tee's friend.

"Uh-huh?" I said, barely opening my mouth.

"What did your grandmother have to say?"

"I didn't get to talk to her, just Tom and Jay-Tee. She was out doing something. They didn't know much. They said they'd get her to call me back."

He pulled the ammonite out of his pocket, placed it on the benchtop, where its browns, greys, and blacks almost disappeared into the marble counter. "This is magic, right? How come you gave me this?"

Now I *was* blushing. "I . . . You know when we were at that dancing place?"

"You mean the club, Inferno?"

"I guess. The place where you introduced yourself to me? You know, when you were looking for Jay-Tee?"

He nodded.

"Well, I didn't know if you . . . You might've been like Jason Blake. I know you're not *now*, but I didn't then. I gave it to you so I could follow you. Then if you kidnapped Jay-Tee or something, I could find her again."

"You can follow it even when you can't see it? So it *is* magic?"

I nodded. "I can always feel where it is. Well, not if it gets too far away, but."

Danny and I reached for the ammonite at the same time, our fingertips touching briefly. "Sorry," we both said.

"Take it."

I did. It was warm. The feel of Danny from it was overwhelming.

"Good to have it back?"

I nodded. It did feel good. I slid it into my pocket but kept it in my hand, between forefinger and thumb.

"How does it work?" Danny asked. "I mean, the whole time I had it with me the stone never felt cold. Very weird."

I tried to explain about magical objects, how magic rubs off on them. It was hard because it didn't entirely make sense to me. I could almost hear my mother scoffing at the explanation. I tried to think of it as like the sun's energy being absorbed by a dark stone, but longer lasting so that instead of staying warm part of the night, it stayed warm forever. I thought about Danny as his heart continued to beat between my fingers. Had part of him rubbed off onto the ammonite? Had he absorbed something of me from having it in his pocket the last few days?

The phone rang. Danny handed it to me. "Your grandmother."

"Hi, Esmeralda," I said, glad for once to hear her voice.

I needed to think about what Esmeralda had said. I walked to the sliding glass doors and opened them, stepping out onto the balcony. The wind was bitter, but no snow fell, and the sky was perfectly blue, with tiny pockets of stringy, feather-thin clouds. On the ground, piles of snow lingered. I could see a large body of water, but I couldn't smell much salt in the air so I figured it must be a lake or a river, not the sea. Close to the shore were sixty-two rotten wooden posts sticking up, looking like a flock of drowning giants only able to get one arm above the water. It must have been an old pier that had rotted away. Seagulls glided by. One hovered for a moment, as if frozen, and then drifted away. The sea must not be far. I wondered why the gulls would stay here in the cold when they could fly to summer.

The door slid open and then shut. I looked at Danny and saw no magic, no rust inside him. He was completely normal. He handed me a big woolly jumper.

"You must be freezing." His words made little puffs of condensation.

I was. I put the jumper on. "Great view. New York City is so big."

"That's New Jersey over there."

"Is that a different city?"

Danny looked at me oddly. "Yes."

"Huh." It didn't look very different. Grey and brown buildings. Hardly any trees. Beside the water, on the New York City side, people rode bicycles and jogged and took their tiny dogs for walks at the end of long leashes that from this distance looked more like kite strings. On the highway beside them, trucks and cars zoomed by. I could hear the rumble of the traffic, punctuated by the sudden squeal of horns and brakes and then by the bit of song that meant Danny's phone was ringing.

He pulled it out, examined the screen, pressed a button, put it back in his pocket.

"How come you didn't answer it?"

"Huh? Oh, it was a friend of mine. Don't feel like talking to them right now."

"How could you tell who it was?" I asked.

Danny raised an eyebrow—clearly, he thought it was a dumb question. "I can see the name of the person calling."

"Then how come you didn't know it was me when I called you? Didn't my name show up?" I slipped my hands up into the sleeves of the jumper. It was freezing.

"Er, no." Danny stared at me as if he was trying to figure me out. "That wasn't your phone, was it?"

"No, of course not. I've never owned a phone."

Danny laughed. "I can tell."

"What time is it?" I asked, wondering how Tom and Jay-Tee were doing.

"Quarter to two."

"Huh."

"Do you know how long you'll be staying here?"

I shook my head. "I guess it depends on what happens with that old man. I can't go back to Sydney until he's gone or lets me past or something."

"You could always take a plane, you know."

I hadn't thought of that. How much would that cost? Plane rides were expensive, weren't they? I took in Danny's apartment. So big, such a huge television. He had a *lot* of money now. All of it from his dead magic father. Esmeralda had money, too. I wasn't used to a life where money *solved* problems; I was used to money—or, rather, not having any—*being* the problem.

Sarafina never had enough. She worked lots of different jobs—barmaid, under-the-counter accountant, fruit picker, maths coach—anything she could find. Sometimes I helped, too. When we didn't have money we'd make instant noodles go a long way or live off the land, find wild grub. Not something you could do in a big city.

Danny and Esmeralda were both casual about money, as if it was there to pluck from the air. Apparently, it was: I'd seen Jay-Tee make money appear in her hand where there'd been nothing.

"I'd pay for the ticket," Danny said, as if he were offering to buy me a newspaper.

I shook my head. It wouldn't make any difference. "He'd still be on the other side of the door trying to get through. We have to figure out what do with him on this side. Maybe there'll be clues or someone here who knows what to do. It's a big city—I can't be the only magic one. Esmeralda had some decent ideas." I shifted my feet. They were starting to go blue and tingle again.

"Do you like being in Sydney with your grandmother?"

I considered this. "I get to see my mum. And it's nice being with Jay-Tee and Tom. I don't trust Esmeralda, but so far it's been okay. I just have to stay alert. Anyways, it's warm there. Summer."

Danny slid the door open. "Come on in, then. No need to freeze if you don't have to."

I followed him in. "Esmeralda wants me to try and track down where the old man comes from."

"How, exactly?"

"With magic."

"Okay," Danny said, as if he understood, which, of course, he didn't. "What kind of magic?"

"I can smell him. She wants me to follow his trail."

His phone rang. He shrugged in half apology, pulled it out. "This friend I better answer," he said to me before putting the phone to his ear. "Hi, Sondra. Uh-huh. Oh, sure, me, too." He went into his room and shut the door.

I wondered what it was like for your friends and family to be able to get in touch with you whenever they wanted. What it was like to have so many friends that your phone rang several times a day. Strange to think of. Did Danny carry his phone with him wherever he went? Into the dunny even? Did everyone with mobile phones do that? Out bush some people had mobiles, but they hardly ever worked. You had to be in one of the big towns before there was any signal.

Fifteen minutes later Danny came back out with a large piece of paper in his hand. He didn't say anything about the phone call. I wondered who Sondra was. How many friends did Danny have? "Okay, you'll need clothes. Not to mention shoes."

"Oh, yeah." I felt like a der-brain for not having thought of it.

He put the paper on the floor and knelt beside it, holding it in place. "Put your foot on this." I did and he pushed the pen around my left foot, his hand brushing past my ankle. "Next foot." I switched feet. The ghost sensation of his skin on mine lingered. He traced around my right foot, his inner wrist touching the arch of my foot, my ankle. I fought to keep my blush down. "Now," he said, looking at me, completely unaffected. "What else are you going to need?"

"Um," I said, trying to focus my brain on something other than his hands against my feet. "Socks. I'll need socks."

He nodded. "Socks, shoes, winter coat, a hat, gloves. Shirts, jeans." He wrote them down beside the outline of my feet, then held his hand out palm first. "Put your hand against mine."

I did. His hands were warm and dry. Smooth. I felt my cheeks grow hot again. My hand was only a little bigger than his palm.

"Okay. Itty-bitty hands. I'll get you a scarf, too." He wrote it down. "That should be enough."

"Um, I'll need knickers, too," I said, embarrassed. Sarafina would not think much of my embarrassment. She didn't approve of people being embarrassed by everyday things like knickers or menstruation or anything, really. You should only be embarrassed by your own bad behaviour, like lying. Yet she had lied to me about magic. I was going to die young because of her lies.

"What?" Danny asked, looking confused.

"Undies."

"Undies?"

"You know? I'll need a bra and—"

"Panties. Oh, yeah. I gotcha. Sorry."

I told him my sizes. He had no idea if they would translate or not.

"What's your favourite colour?"

Red, I thought, *the browny-red of the ground up north.* Then I realised that I was in New York City, so it wasn't north at all. Dizzying.

I thought about Jay-Tee. Red-brown was the colour of the rust throughout her, the colour of the smell and taste that meant she didn't have long to live. Neither of us did.

"Blue," I said. "Deep blue."

11
Fading

"It's not moving," Mere said. Jay-Tee hadn't heard her coming into the kitchen, but she managed not to jump. Unsurprisingly, Tom almost leapt halfway across the room. At least he managed not to knock anything over. Mere put the box she was carrying down on the counter.

"No," Tom said, trying to sound calm. "It stopped about . . ." He looked at the stove clock. "Ten minutes ago."

"Thirteen," Jay-Tee said, glancing down at the pad. She'd been sitting on the kitchen floor, staring at the door ever since Reason'd hung up, noting down changes, almost—but not quite—letting herself fall into a trance. Both Esmeralda and Reason seemed to think it was important. They both knew numbers. Tom was annoying her so much she now greeted his endless comments and questions with grunts or with silence. His words were wearing her down, making her even tireder than she already was.

"Here," Mere said, reaching out for the pad. Jay-Tee handed it to her. She leafed through a few pages. "Good work. Thank you."

"Reason rang," Tom said. "She wanted to talk to you."

Mere nodded.

"Did you find anything next door?" Jay-Tee asked, eyeing the box. She wondered what was in it. More feathers? Bones?

Mere nodded. "One or two things. I have some ideas."

"Like, for example?" Jay-Tee asked.

"You two must be a bit sick of sitting here guarding the door."

"Too right!" Tom said.

Jay-Tee said, "Yeah!" even louder. No way was he as sick of her as she was of him.

"Why don't you both take a break?" Mere looked at her watch. "Come back in an hour and I'll tell you—"

Jay-Tee didn't wait to hear the rest. Suddenly she was jumping out of her skin with the need to be moving, to run, to be out of there and looking at anything in the world but that damn door. She exploded out of the kitchen, bolted out the front door, jumped the front gate, went sprinting down the narrow, uneven sidewalk, past trees, some with such low-lying branches that— short though she was—she had to duck to avoid being clobbered. Houses flickered by, squat and low, pressed together closer than teeth, leaning in on the street as if they wanted to consume it. She felt her mother's leather against her wrist, the vibration of the animal tooth in her pocket.

She didn't pause at the end of the block, just lifted up her knees and ran harder. The only cars were parked and still, metal guardians of a road so narrow that in New York it would have barely qualified as an alley. For the length of the next

block a flock of red-green-blue chirruping birds kept pace
before disappearing into a shaggy tree covered with shaggy red
flowers. The air was utterly still, but it didn't matter—Jay-Tee
ran so fast, she created her own wind.

She sailed over a pile of dog poop, sprinted across the next
narrow road, and ran down the next block, where the trees
were so out of control that their roots turned the sidewalk into
a broken-down earthquake survivor. To keep from tripping she
stepped lighter, lifted her knees higher, but she didn't slow her
pace, so it wasn't until she hit the end of the street and
zoomed left to avoid the heavily trafficked road that she real-
ized how good the shade had been, how strong the sun now
was, how overheated she was.

Her black hair radiated more heat than tar on a city roof in
the middle of August. She streamed water, salt stung her eyes.
Up ahead she saw tall trees shading a low brick wall in front of
an ugly block of orange brick apartments. She slowed and sank
down onto the bricks, scorching despite the shade. Jay-Tee
didn't care. She slipped her hands under her thighs and leaned
forward, breathing deeply.

She felt dizzy, empty. If she was shaken maybe she would
rattle; maybe she would break. But after being stuck in the
house all morning staring at the stupid door, everything looked
so good. She grinned, sat up, still breathing hard. In the distance where the road disappeared, shimmering heat danced
over the line of cars and trucks waiting for the lights to
change. She glanced up at the blue, blue, blue sky, but it was

too sharply, vibrantly light for her to look at it long. She shielded her eyes with her hand. "Wow."

Jay-Tee had never seen light so intense before. Despite the traffic fumes, everything had such sharp, clear lines, as if the cars, the trees, the old chewing gum stuck to the sidewalk had been freshly cut from glass with a laser. Another flock of the red-blue-green chirrupers zoomed by. Each one of them dazzling: greener greens, bluer blues, redder reds than she'd ever seen.

"Wow," Jay-Tee said again. Somehow she'd managed to forget she was in a whole other city, a whole other country. She'd never been farther away from New York than Jersey City. Never been some place where every single person spoke completely different than her, where the cars drove on opposite sides of the road, where the light was so bright it cut her eyes.

Jesus, Mary, and Joseph—I'm in Australia! She crossed herself, thanked God that she'd gotten to see a little more of the world before she died. She hoped she'd get to go into the outback like Reason had promised, finally see some kangaroos. How cool would that be?

Jay-Tee glanced at her watch. "Wow." It was only eight-thirty. Morning still. She'd thought it was like noon or something. How could it be this hot so early in the morning? The thought made her dizzier. Time had totally slowed down. She wondered if it was a jet-lag thing. Or a staring-at-the-stupid-door thing.

"Jay-Tee!"

She turned. It was Tom, wearing a dorky hat and clutching his sides. He sat down beside her.

"Bugger, you can run fast."

"Yup. You make dresses, and I can run faster than a jet plane."

"You think it's magic?" Tom asked once he got his breath back.

"Oh, sure. I went even faster with the extra talisman Esmeralda gave me." She reached into her pocket to feel the tooth. It was almost as hot as the bitumen road. "I kind of know where I am all the time."

Tom gave her a look. "Um, yeah, Jay-Tee, me, too. Right now we're in Newtown—"

"No, no, not like that. I meant in space. I know where I am compared to everything else around me." Tom still looked confused. "I never bump into things, Tom. Not ever. I'm like the total opposite of clumsy. 'Cause I just know—I mean, my body just knows—where everything is, especially people. Someone jumps out suddenly, I can get out of the way. 'Less they're faster than me, of course." She thought of her father, and then of *him* and felt momentarily chilled. "Anyway, *that's* what helps me go so fast. I think I'd still be a fast runner without magic, but not that fast."

"Cool."

"Ain't it?"

Tom nodded. "Your brother knows about magic and everything, doesn't he?"

"Yeah."

"Huh," Tom said.

"Why?"

"Nothing."

Jay-Tee shrugged. "Your country sure is bright."

"You taking the piss?"

Jay-Tee giggled. "You talk funny. Is there somewhere we can get some water? I'm so thirsty I'm about ready to faint."

"Sure. Corner shop just around the corner."

That struck Jay-Tee as funny, too, and she giggled again.

"What?"

"Corner shop around the corner."

Tom sighed and stood up. "You know, I'm getting a bit jack of you always—"

Jay-Tee started to stand, felt dizzy, and sat back down again.

"You okay?"

She nodded, though there were dots in front of her eyes and her fingertips tingled. Light-headed, that's how she felt, like her head was hollow, except it wasn't only her head; her whole body was lighter than it should be.

"You sure? You don't look good." Tom squatted in front of her and stared into her eyes; for a moment he was so far away it was like seeing through a telescope. Then he was so close she could count every freckle on his skin; some of them were gold. There were so many of them, they made her dizzy all over again. She wobbled. Tom put a hand on her knee to steady her and just like that Jay-Tee knew what was wrong.

She was dying. Right-here-and-now dying. Magic-used-up dying. She knew it because she could feel Tom's magic pulsing in his hand on her skin; she could feel her cells screaming at her that she needed it, that she had to take it. She was too weak to tear it from him.

This was it. So much sooner than she had ever expected. Jay-Tee's head tumbled with all the things she should have done, or rather *shouldn't* have done. If only she hadn't helped with the protection spell or run crazy fast. She'd thought having two talismans would make her magic last longer. If only . . . She should have listened to her father. *Be careful. Don't use magic unless you have to. Don't conjure money out of air. Don't dance too hard, run too fast.* Don't, don't, don't. But she'd done everything she wasn't supposed to.

I'm too young for this. In front of her eyes the world was narrowing. The hazy distances, the cars, the road, the strange trees and birds—all disappearing.

Jay-Tee had never really believed she would die. Not now. Not her. But here she was, and her energy, her life, whatever it was that made her who she was—was vanishing, run down into almost nothing. Jay-Tee didn't want to die.

"I need your magic, Tom."

His eyes, opened wide, were all whites. "What?"

"I'm dying. I can feel it. I need you to give me some of your magic. I won't take it from you. I wouldn't do that to you." Jay-Tee was lying. She *couldn't* do that to him. "I don't think I have much longer." She was fading, getting smaller and smaller. She wondered if her skin was shriveling like a mummy's or like a vampire in the sun. She shouldn't have run like that. It was the running that had pushed her over. She shouldn't have—

"How much will you need?"

"I don't know." *All of it.* "But you control how much you give me, Tom. When you can't spare any more, you stop."

He looked afraid; the patchy crimson flush of his cheeks had all but vanished as if they weren't sitting outside in hundred-degree heat. It was true, then: Esmeralda really hadn't ever drunk from him.

"What do I do?" he asked, his voice even softer than hers.

"You let me touch you and you say yes." She could barely see him. "You let me take your magic. It won't feel good. It'll be horrible—you'll want to hurl. You'll hate it. I hated it. Will you do it for me, Tom? You have so much." Her voice was breaking, her eyes leaking. "I don't want to die. Not this soon."

Tom moved his head. She couldn't see whether he was nodding or not. She reached forward, felt for his hand, and put hers on top. "Pull away, say no as soon as you need to." It was getting harder and harder to get the words out. "I'm weak, Tom, I'm not sure I'll be able to stop this myself. Okay?"

"Okay," Tom whispered, so faint she could barely hear. As if he were the one dying, not her.

"Will you give me some of your magic?"

"Yes."

His magic streamed into her, clean, strong, alive.

12
Smelling Magic

Before Danny went out to buy me clothes, he showed
me how his television worked. His phone rang again, but he
didn't answer it. I'd never been around anyone who got so
many phone calls. But I hadn't been around many people who
had mobile phones before. Maybe it was normal.

I sat on the big couch, waiting for him to come back, pressing the remote control to change the images on the huge
screen. Going faster and faster, watching a kaleidoscope of
images zipping by, startling and strange. I glimpsed a person
flying, not in a plane but like a bird. Magic flying. Except it
wasn't real, just how the rest of the world imagined magic
would be: careless and easy. Fun.

I thought about my grandmother's plan, about trying to
find out where the old man had come from by following the
trail of his scent. He reeked much more strongly than his
little golem, so Esmeralda figured it should be a lot easier to
follow him.

I wasn't quite so sure, but at least there was a plan now. I
stopped on a channel that played loud music while a girl in
tight black pants and a top that hung off her shoulders and

barely covered her breasts jumped onto the hood of a battered car and waved her arms around. Her lips were moving as if she were singing, though the voice sounded more like a man's than a woman's.

There were so many words said so fast that they all jumbled into one another. I wasn't sure if the song was in English or not. I think I heard *baby* and *love*, but those were the only words I understood. All around her were piles of rubble and crumbling buildings. Everything was grey and cold-looking except the girl with her brown skin, orange hair, and unnaturally blue eyes, and the sky, which was the same plastic blue.

I thought about how the old man had smelled; my stomach tightened. If I were going to track him, I'd have to remember it perfectly. He smelled like the golem thing in the house, but more intense.

The girl on the television jumped from the hood of the car to the top of the tallest crumbling building—an impossible distance. From the top of the building, you could see green hills.

More intense, because not only did the smell make me chunder, but somehow it managed to curl around me, insinuate its way into my body. Was that because he was related to me? Because he was a Cansino? But so was the golem thing, just not as much as he was. The golem was merely a copy, I decided. He was the original.

Danny came through the door loaded up with shopping bags, talking into his mobile phone. "Call you later," he said as the lift closed behind him. "Yeah, me, too." He pressed a button on the phone and slipped it back into his pocket. "Christmas time!" he called out.

"Yay! Pressies!" I jumped off the couch and ran over to him, regretting my hasty movements instantly. I was dazed. I'd been lost in television land, and here I suddenly was in the real world, only it was hazy, not as distinct as television land. I blinked slowly, trying to clear the haze.

"You okay, Reason?"

"Yep. Just fine."

He handed me seven different bags, all of them overflowing. I'd never been given so many presents before (I wasn't counting the books and pyjamas in my room at Esmeralda's—those weren't presents, those were bribes). For my birthday and for Christmas Sarafina only ever gave me one, but it was always perfect: an ammonite, a compass, an atlas.

When I was eleven she'd given me Darwin's *The Origin of Species*. It had taken me a while to get used to how it was written, so old-fashioned and roundabout, but natural selection, evolution—amazing. There were thousands of fossils in the outback, every step we'd take, practically, and we'd feel history going crunch under our feet.

Sarafina had found my ammonite in the Kimberleys, hundreds of kilometres from the sea. And yet once—millions of years ago—the stone had been a shell, home to a creature that might have resembled a cuttlefish. It had once lived in a straight shell—but slowly it evolved, becoming a spiral-shelled creature.

I wondered how magic had evolved. What had been its straight shell? Where had it come from? What was being selected for? Were humans the only ones with the trait? Surely it must be an evolutionary dead end? How far could you go with genes that drove you to madness or death?

"You like?" Danny asked.

"Wow," I said, peering into the bags and seeing blues and blacks. T-shirts, jeans, lots of woolen things, three shoe-shaped boxes. I could barely hold it all. "There's so much. You didn't have to buy this much!"

Danny shrugged. "I got the money, you know? Why not? I figured it was better to give you some choices. I bought you this, too." He pulled a small box out of his jacket pocket.

I opened it. A watch. Digital, with a black face and bright blue digits. The strap was blue, too.

"So you don't have to keep asking me what time it is."

I hugged him. "Ta heaps, Danny!"

"Go get changed." Danny grinned and saluted me. "Make sure you have lots of layers."

"No worries. Jay-Tee taught me how you dress for the cold."

Danny raised an eyebrow and looked pointedly at my dirty pyjamas. I giggled.

He'd bought me four pairs of jeans, six normal T-shirts and four long-sleeved ones, three jumpers, eight pairs of socks, underpants and bras (which sort of made me blush—Danny had touched my underwear! Sarafina would not have been impressed), a huge coat, two pairs of gloves, two scarves, and a knitted blue-and-black hat. So much! And all of it fantastic. How had he chosen so well? There was nothing little-girlie or stupid.

I chose a pair of black jeans that were a size too big, transferred my ammonite from my hand into the right pocket. I pulled on a blue T-shirt with the word *Forever* written in red, also too big. Was that a message from Danny? And if it was—what was for forever? Or had he liked the way it was lettered—kind of scribbled, almost falling over? I liked it.

The next layer was a black long-sleeved T-shirt that had a hood. Then a blue woollen jumper. I pulled the hood from the long-sleeved T-shirt so that it hung outside the jumper. Then I pinned Esmeralda's brooch on the front.

I put on black socks and opened the three boxes of shoes. One was a pair of boots lined with sheepskin. The other two were fancy sneakers. A red-white-and-blue pair covered in stars, and then the best pair of sneakers I'd ever seen. I pulled them on. They were the first things to fit right. *Just as well*, I thought. *Shoes that don't fit are way more of a problem than too-big jeans and T-shirts.*

The shoes were the deep blue of the sky in the desert when there's a full moon. Almost, but not quite black. Silver streaks ran down the sides as if the sneakers were ready to take off. They made me feel like I could run faster than anyone else in the world. Faster than Jay-Tee even. Or that I could if I wasn't going to die so soon.

I pushed the thought away, grabbed the big blue coat.

"It all fits?" Danny asked. "Hmmm, well, sort of. You're littler than I remembered. How about the shoes? At least they should fit. One of the girls in the store, her foot matched the outline of yours exactly, so I made her try on all the shoes. Lucky, hey?"

"Very." I could imagine all the girls in the shop going out of their way to help Danny. If I worked there, I would, too.

"Clothes seem okay," he said, looking at me. "Even too big and all."

"They're perfect. Thank you." I gave him a big hug and he returned it. I could feel his strong hands on my back. A warmth spread all the way to my soles. "Let's go," I said. "I'm starting to get hot."

Danny nodded. "Winter's all about being too cold when you're outside and too hot inside. You can't win. Have you got your gloves? Scarf? Hat?"

"Oops!" I dashed back to Jay-Tee's room and scrabbled about for them. So much stuff to wear! Then I thought about that bitter cold and wrapped the scarf firmly around my neck.

We took a taxicab because Danny said it was too cold to walk all that way and we'd be walking around enough once we got there. It took ages to get a cab. They kept sailing by, even though Danny stuck his arm out and waved like crazy.

On the way we decided that we'd begin three blocks from the door and walk until I picked up the old man's scent, without getting close enough for him to spot us.

We'd walked blocks, and Danny's phone had rung five times (but not once from Sydney) before I smelled the old man for the first time. I stopped and inhaled. There in the midst of traffic fumes and cigarette smoke, I caught the tiniest hint of burnt rubber and acid—essence of old man Cansino, but not enough to turn my stomach.

It was coming from the same restaurant Jay-Tee had taken me for breakfast a week ago, when I'd first stumbled through the door between Sydney and New York City; when I'd no clue where I was and Jay-Tee'd been working for Jason Blake. It felt strange being back here. I wasn't exactly who I had been that day. Neither was Jay-Tee. The world had shifted on its axis several more times since then.

"The smell's coming from in there."

"You're sure?" Danny asked.

"Yes." It was faint but definitely there. I pulled the coat Danny had bought me tighter, glad of it in the cold, and of the hat and gloves. I glanced at my gorgeous new shoes. The jeans were fine, too, though they kept slipping down too far on my hips, and I couldn't help comparing them with the wondrous pants Tom had made me. None of the clothes, not even the shoes, fit me the way those pants did. I wished I had them here. I bet Tom's magic would make them work as well in this cold weather as they had in the Sydney heat.

"Can you go and check on the old man? See what he's up to? Esmeralda seems to think that he won't have much interest in anyone who isn't full of magic." That's what my grandmother said, but I wondered if the old man could sense that Danny had been *near* a magic-wielder.

"Check for what, exactly?"

"What he's doing. Is he still just standing there, leaning against the door? Or does he seem to be doing something?"

"Okay, then." Danny didn't sound convinced it was the best plan in the world. "I'll meet you back in here. Once you've finished sniffing around, grab a table and order something. Don't go too far."

I nodded and pulled open the door. "Be careful."

He raised his eyebrows. "I thought he wouldn't be interested in me."

"Esmeralda says not."

"No need to be careful, then?"

"I don't think he's stupid, though. If you stand there gawking, he's going to think something's up. He's dangerous." I thought of what I had done to Josh Davidson. "He can hurt you."

"True enough. You be careful, too."

"Of course."

As he walked off to do his recce, I heard the fragment of song that meant his phone was ringing again. His *life* was ringing. That phone was where Danny's many friends lived. If he hadn't been rescuing me, helping me, he'd be doing other things, spending time with other people. Whereas me, well, I had exactly four friends in all the world: my mother, Tom, Jay-Tee, and Danny. And I'd only just met three of them. Would Danny still be friends with me when he didn't *have* to look after me?

Inside the restaurant I was assailed by the smell of freshly baked cakes and breads, hanging heavy in the air, slow-cooking meats, the lumpy brown soup a man was sipping from a cardboard cup as he pushed past me out onto the street, detergent, sweat, steam. I lost the faint trace of the old man.

I walked further into the restaurant, past the counter and the kitchen, closer to the other entrance. The scent of Mr Cansino curled past my nose, making bile rise in my throat. There and then gone. I stopped, breathing deeply, trying to catch the elusive foul smell again. Gone.

"You want table?" a waitress asked in an accent I didn't recognise. "Seat yourself," she continued before I could respond. She pointed at a sign with those words written on it and then walked away.

The smell wafted past me again, just outside the two dunnies. I went into the nearest one.

Inside I smelled antiseptic, soap, toilet water, and the lingering smell of the last person's visit. Since I was there I went to the loo myself, adding the smell of my pee to the mix. If the scent of the old man was in here, it was completely lost in everything else. I flushed and washed my hands with the strange foamy soap that came out of the wall yet didn't lather. It left my hands feeling oddly dry and itchy.

Outside the toilet my stomach contracted. I smelled him again. I took a step towards the other toilet door, and the acid and burnt rubber started to slide away again. I stepped back. The smell was still there. I took a step away, closer to the exit with its smells from the street outside, and of the food conveyed from kitchen to table. It started to fade again. I moved back towards the loos.

Right here between the two toilet doors, next to the metal stand loaded with postcards. This was where I could smell him most strongly, where I most strongly wanted to chuck. I tilted my head up, wondering if the smell was coming from a vent. It was no stronger or weaker. I knelt down. I had to press my hand to my mouth and concentrate to keep from bringing the spag bol back up. There was a crack about ten centimetres long on the linoleum checked floor. It wasn't wide, no more than two or three millimetres, but it looked deep.

"Can I help you, miss?" a waiter asked. He was holding a jug of water and looking at me as if I were mad. "You drop something?" He had the same accent as the waitress. Not American like Danny. Something else.

"Um," I said between my teeth. "I'm fine." I stood up and walked over to an empty table. The smell vanished. The first waitress came by, slapping a glass of water and a menu down. I guzzled the water, hoping to rinse the taste of him away. When the waitress returned I ordered hot chocolate, not at all sure I'd be able to stomach it.

On the floor near the bathroom the smell had been so strong. Was it somehow in the floor? Coming from underneath? I had no idea how I was going to get down there. And if I did, how was I going to keep from chundering every two seconds?

The waitress sloshed the hot chocolate down on the table in front of me. Maybe it would settle my stomach. I took a sip and almost spat it out. Too hot. I blew on it. Then sipped again. It tasted awful, like vomit and burnt rubber. The smell of him was coating my mouth.

Danny came in, talking on his phone. He said goodbye, slid into the chair opposite me. "You okay? You look green."

I screwed up my face. "I'm fine. His smell is kind of foul."

"That sucks, having to track by a smell that makes you want to hurl."

"Can we not talk about it?"

"Sure. Sorry. There wasn't anyone there."

"There wasn't? No one?" If the old man wasn't there, I could go back to Sydney, call Esmeralda and walk back through the door. But I wanted to stay here, with Danny. At least for a little bit.

Danny shook his head. "Nope. No one."

"Can you call Australia on your mobile?"

"My phone?"

I nodded. "Can you call Jay-Tee? Right now?"

"Sure." Danny dug out his phone and pressed a few of the keys and handed it to me.

Esmeralda answered; she sounded tired. She must be. I doubted any of them had gone back to sleep after I'd been sucked through the door. Come to think of it, I hadn't slept since yesterday (Sydney's yesterday). I pushed back layers to look at my watch. It was 4:33 PM here, so 8:33 AM there. I wondered if my grandmother had decided to take the day off work.

"It's me, Reason."

"Hello, Reason. Have you found something?"

"Sort of. Danny walked along Seventh Street, and he says the old man isn't there anymore."

"Really? That's interesting, because the door on this side is perfectly still."

"Huh. You think the door only goes crazy when he's nearby?"

"It's a possibility. Are you close? Can you go around and check that he's not there? Cautiously? If he *is* there, I don't want you to set him off again."

"We're not far," I said, though I really didn't want to risk seeing the old man again—it was bad enough following his vomitous trail.

"Go back, see if he's there, but stay on the phone."

"Okay." I put my hand over the receiver. "She wants us to check the door." I took my hand away. "If he isn't there," I asked my grandmother, "what then? I mean, if I go back to Sydney, aren't we back to where we started?"

"I don't know. But we'll get you back here somehow, Reason. I promise."

13
Magic Lies

Tom went home. All the cells of his body had turned into concrete. Walking was harder than running had been. He ached. His body wanted him to lie down and sleep in the street. He ignored it, kept guiding one foot after the other, over and over, until he was outside his tiny house and his key was in the lock and the door was open, then closed, and he was pulling himself up the stairs, one foot after the other, over and over.

The handle of the door of his bedroom wouldn't fit right in his hand, kept slipping. It wasn't a tricky door. He'd never struggled to get it open before. Only when he used both hands would it open and then shut behind him. He pushed the blue gaberdine aside and fell onto his bed.

He was knackered. Like Reason had been when they came back through the door, back from New York City. Like he had been after Mere had drunk from him.

He touched the wool gaberdine, pulling across the grain— it was sturdy but soft. He felt soft but not even faintly sturdy. He was drained. He tried to remember his plans for the fabric. There was so much gaberdine, and it was such a dark blue.

Midnight blue, the sales assistant had called it, but midnight in Sydney was never blue.

A coat. It was going to be a coat for Cathy. The least daggy coat in the universe. A long coat, three-quarter length or more. He was going to line it with synthetic fur or maybe quilting or polar fleece, though something that thick might wreck the line. Cotton wool? Spider webs? Something warm. It was going to be cool and warm. Best winter coat ever. For his sister in New York City, where it snowed and people took your magic without asking you.

Tom was *so* tired. He'd only ever been this tired once before, and then he'd slept a whole day. More, according to his sister's flatmate. That had been at Cathy's place, sleeping on her ugly yellow couch, just after Mere had drunk from him.

Mere had drunk from him.

Tom pried his eyes open, made himself sit up, draped the fabric across his knees, nice drapes. *Full-length coat*, thought Tom. *That'd be better*. Maybe the synthetic fur should only be at the cuffs and collars? He picked up the phone and dialed his sister's number. The fifteen digits went beep, beep, beep, but slowly. It was more like beeeeeep, long pause, beeeeeep, long pause, beeeeep.

Then there was silence. Lots of silence. Tom wondered if maybe New York City and Sydney weren't talking to each other anymore. He was thinking about never talking to Mere again. The phone made an abrupt scratchy noise. Almost a burp. Tom giggled. The phone connected, Australia to the U.S.A. Tom wondered if monkeys had anything to do with it. It had sounded like a monkey burp. The phone was ringing, but not properly—just one looong ring at a time.

A male voice answered. "Hello?" it said, talking funny.

"Is Cathy there?"

"No," said the voice. There was a click, and the phone returned to dial tone. The dropkick had hung up. Tom groped through his memory, trying to place the voice—Cathy's mean flatmate, the one who'd said Tom'd slept for twenty-six hours, the one with the expensive bathroom products. He wished Cathy would find somewhere else to live. He tried her mobile and got voicemail. He left a message asking Cathy to call. He missed her.

He thought about calling Reason in New York City, telling her . . .

It was all too hard. He lay back on the bed. Closed his eyes and saw thousands of tiny triangles falling through blackness like rain, or snow, more like. What would he tell Reason? That Mere had drunk from him? That she was every bit as dodgy as Reason thought?

He opened his eyes. The ceiling had a giant plaster thing around where the light hung down. He couldn't remember what those things were called. He wasn't sure he'd ever known. It had flowers and leaves and grapes on it. A few cob-webs between the light fixture and one of the bunches of white plaster grapes. It hurt his eyes to look at it.

That's just part of being magic: sometimes you have to lie.

Mere had lied to Tom and told him it was something else, a searching spell? Something. He couldn't remember. But she'd drunk from him. Placed her hand on his arm, asked him if he'd share his magic with her. He'd said yes, because he didn't know what the real question was. Tom decided to never say yes to anything ever again. Safer that way.

They hadn't shared. Tom'd gotten nothing from Mere. He'd felt weak and strange afterwards, heavy, like he felt now. He'd slept for *a whole day!* Now he wanted to do the same. Close his eyes and not see the cobwebs and white plaster grapes and flowers.

Tom'd thought Mere'd been tired, too. But she hadn't been. She'd been energised on *his* magic. She'd lied to him. She'd drunk from him the same way Jay-Tee had, but Jay-Tee'd asked; she'd told him exactly what she was doing. And anyway, she'd only asked him 'cause she had to, because she was dying.

Jay-Tee had looked wrong. Her skin suddenly seemed almost transparent. Like she had only seconds left. Jay-Tee was only fifteen. It wasn't fair.

Then it occurred to him. Mere was *forty-five.* What if she'd taken his magic because she felt herself dying, too? Like Jay-Tee had? About to keel over and die that very second.

It wasn't a what-if, Tom was suddenly sure. The haze of his exhaustion seemed to lift in the face of his realisation: that was why Mere'd taken magic from him. She'd felt herself dying, and she'd been afraid. It made perfect sense. Mere'd never taken magic from him before. Never. Tom knew that for a fact, because now he knew exactly what being drunk from felt like. He'd felt that hideous sensation twice in his life. First Mere, then Jay-Tee.

He'd been with Mere for over a year, seeing her every day, and only once had she'd taken magic from him. She must've been desperate.

She *was* dying.

Recently Mere'd been so cautious with her magic. More cautious than he'd ever seen her. She'd hardly used any while she instructed the three of them. She'd just made the candles go out. That was nothing.

He wished she hadn't lied, though. If she'd've asked, he'd've said yes.

Tom's eyes closed again. He dreamed of nothing.

14
Old Man Cansino

"Okay, we're about to go around the corner," I told Esmeralda. "Are you sure the door's not moving?"

"Positive."

"Huh." I leaned against the café window, touched my cheek to the cool glass for a split second before shifting quick smart to put cloth between me and it. The temperature had dropped. Only 5:19 PM and the sun was already disappearing. Still Monday. It felt like Tuesday was never going to arrive. In Sydney it was 8:19 AM and they were already there, living in Tuesday while I stayed in Monday forever. My eyes stung from cold, fatigue, door lag.

Ever since Sarafina had gone crazy and I'd been sent to Sydney, the days had swelled into years. Seconds dragged, and then minutes sped up and disappeared. Time was happening somewhere far from me. A week ago I'd turned fifteen. Now I wasn't sure what age I was. A hundred? Five?

In the window were nineteen different muffins and cakes. I couldn't smell them, though—all I could smell was him. His vomit-and-charcoal coated my tongue, made my stomach feel like it was full of bile all the way to the back of my throat. The hairs on my arms stood on end. It was bitter cold, my nose, cheeks, and eyes stung with it, but the rest of me was swathed in warm layers. I wasn't tired anymore.

"Is he there?" Esmeralda asked, her voice sounding as if it was hauling its way through spinifex to get to me.

"Ah—" I began.

"I could go first," Danny said close to my ear.

I put my hand over the receiver.

"I can make sure he's not there," Danny continued. "Or you can walk behind me. I'm big enough to block him from seeing you. You don't look good."

"He doesn't need to see me to know I'm here." I took in a deep breath. It was icy and made me cough. Danny patted me on the back and I shook my head, swallowing. "I'm okay. I'll go first."

Easier said than done. *I* might want to get it over with, but my body was deadset against ever seeing the old man again. My ears didn't want to be shut off from sound, and my eyes were uninterested in repeating their brief experience of blindness.

"It's okay to be scared."

"I'm not scared," I lied.

"What's going on?" Esmeralda asked from the other side of the world.

"Nothing," I said. "We're about to go around the corner."

I took a step forward, neatly avoiding a pile of frozen poo, barely managing not to skid on the salt and ice. The street was familiar to me—even though it was like so many other East Village streets, I *knew* this one. This was where I'd first stepped from summer to winter. This was where I'd first seen snow, fire escapes nailed to the outside of buildings, New York City.

I couldn't see the old man. But further along the block, a tall man I thought I recognised disappeared around the corner.

"Do you see him?" Esmeralda asked again.

Should I tell her that I had possibly seen my grandfather, Jason Blake? That the old man was a Cansino, like us? "No," I said. I glanced at Danny, who shook his head. He couldn't see any old man, either. "I can smell him, though, stronger than ever." I thought about going to a chemist, getting something to stop the chunderous feeling. Esmeralda hadn't been able to smell him.

I looked around as much as I could with my movements restricted by scarf and hoods and hat. "But it's getting dark, so it's kind of hard to tell." Which applied to my possible Jason Blake sighting, too.

"The door still isn't moving," Esmeralda said, her voice coming through more clearly this time. She sounded like Sarafina. More like Sarafina than Sarafina had when I'd seen her last.

"It's good to have proof that there *is* a connection—you know, between the strangeness with the door and—"

"The old man," Esmeralda finished for me. "Yes, it is."

Danny and I walked closer. In all my winter clothing I was starting to sweat, yet my nose was running because of the cold. Up above, the sky was turning a strange orangey-brown colour. If the old man's vile smell had a colour, that would be it.

Pollution brown. I couldn't see the moon or any stars, and even if I could they'd be the wrong ones. The Southern Cross, Carina, Centaurus couldn't be seen from so far north. I had no idea which was east and which was west.

"Let me know when you're on the steps."

"Okay," I said into Danny's mobile.

"I'm going to try opening the door," my grandmother said, her voice breaking up a little.

"Won't that muck up those feather protections?"

"No," she said, without offering any explanation. *Some teacher*, I thought.

"And what if he's just hiding? I can smell him really strongly." I turned to look behind me.

"I'll be ready."

I wondered how she could be so sure.

"We're at the door now. Oh . . ."

Something grey-brown was oozing out of the top step in front of the door. Something that smelled so intensely, my mouth flooded with bile. It began to bubble, get bigger and bigger.

I took a step back. "Bloody hell."

"The door's started again," I heard Esmeralda say.

The stuff was surging upwards, shaping itself into something human, into old man Cansino. I turned to run. He froze me in my tracks, then, without using his hands, pulled me back towards him. I opened my mouth to scream and he closed it for me. If I vomited now, I would choke on it. I wished he had stopped my nose so I couldn't smell him.

"Oh, there he is," Danny said, as if the old man had been there all along, as if he hadn't just bubbled out of the ground. "That's gotta be him, right?"

"What's happening?" Esmeralda asked. "Are you okay, Reason?"

I tried to say no, but my mouth wouldn't open.

"Is he there?" asked Esmeralda. "The door's gone mad. Reason? What's happening at your end? Should I come through?"

The old man moved his hand slightly; I felt his grip on me lessen. A little.

"No," I said to my grandmother, relieved I could talk. "He's here. Don't come through!" My right hand with the phone dropped. I strained to pull it back up again; sweat started to trickle down my back.

The old man was leaning against the door in the same position as when I'd last seen him. As if he'd never moved. I turned again, more slowly this time, hoping he wouldn't notice. I wanted desperately to run, to get away from the smell, from him. The old man stopped me. His fingers flickered up, slighter than a butterfly's breath, but I knew that was why I wasn't moving. Esmeralda was asking questions. I could feel the buzz of them from the phone in my hand that I could not raise up to my ear.

"Bugger," I said. I thought about my magic, tried to think about sending it at him, stopping him. My magic was as far away as Esmeralda's squeaking voice on the phone. I had never felt so helpless in my life. There was nothing I could do to stop him.

The old man smiled. Or at least, the expression on his face

shifted in a way that could have been a smile. There was something completely wrong about his face. It was *too* mobile. Expressions flitted across like the ripples in the door. His flesh moved the same way his strange clay golems moved. His flesh *was* the golems, I realised. He had shifted up from the cracks in the ground, oozing that same grey-brown substance. They weren't golems; they were pieces of him. That was why they had the exact same horrible odour—not because he'd made them, but because they *were* him.

"He looks like a mummy," Danny said. "He's so dry and old." He stood in front of me, blocking my view of the old man, but I could still smell him, still feel him. I still had to concentrate to keep from chundering until there was nothing left to chunder. "Don't worry, Reason. He may be magic and everything, but he's not much taller than you. I'm way bigger and stronger than he is. I'll take care of him."

The old man did something. Without wanting to, I stepped around Danny, fighting each movement of my legs. My left foot moved to the first stair.

"What are you doing, Reason?" Danny asked. "Don't go near him!"

I opened my mouth; the old man closed it, pulled me up another step.

"Reason!" Danny jumped beside me. "What the hell are you doing?"

Old man Cansino made me take one more step. Two more steps and I'd be standing beside him. My body screamed at me, every muscle twitching, desperate to run. I was so close now I could see the grey-brown texture of his flesh, the way it moved as if his muscles were made of plasticine. He didn't look dry at all—more like an overripe piece of fruit: if touched, he would explode with rot. My stomach began to turn; he stopped it cold. I didn't vomit; I remained stuck in the moment before vomiting, my eyes watering, my nose breathing cold acid, my mouth tasting nothing but him.

Danny jumped in front of me. "Leave her alone," he commanded.

"Careful, Danny!" I yelled, before the old man waved my mouth shut again. Esmeralda's bleating in my hand got more frenetic.

Danny turned and grinned. "You said he wasn't interested in me."

The old man punched Danny in the stomach, then the face, and then kicked him in the knee, sending him stumbling back down the steps, barely missing me. I flinched, or at least my brain told my body to flinch, and it sluggishly obeyed, working against the old man's hold. My stomach stayed locked. Danny landed steady on his feet, almost like he'd meant to come down the steps that fast.

"Are you—" I began. The old man closed my mouth and pulled me up the last two steps so that I stood beside him. He smiled. Even on his strange face there was no mistaking that expression.

Danny plunged back up the stairs, aiming a punch at the

old man's head that would have landed if Cansino hadn't dissolved into grey-brown clay, disappeared into the steps, then reappeared out of the path of Danny's fist. All before Danny had time to blink. As soon as Danny *had* blinked several times, perhaps wondering if his eyes were packing it in, and realigned himself to the old man's new position, Cansino was already dissolving again. Danny had no chance. The old man wasn't even looking at him; he was looking at me. The smile did not leave his face. I amused him.

"Reason," Danny said, sounding breathless, "back away, get out of here."

I tried to move. I couldn't.

"I—"

The old man shook his head. My mouth closed again.

Old man Cansino continued to duck Danny's blows, dissolving out of his way, melting in and out of the steps. Danny was getting slower; sweat dotted his upper lip. Him and me both— I kept trying to move, but all it did was make me damp with sweat.

The old man punched Danny's cheekbone, making a loud, smacking sound, like flesh against flesh rather than clay. Danny stumbled, managed to jump out of the way of Cansino's foot before misstepping and landing on the step below. The old man shimmered forward and kicked him hard in the knees. Danny fell backwards, swearing his head off.

Old man Cansino turned to me, still smiling. The edges of the smile flickered as his plasticine face wavered. He cupped his empty hands together, then they weren't empty anymore; he threw something at me. Instinctively, I caught it. It was grey-brown. A piece of him. I felt it all again, that we were related. I felt our Cansinoness, his age, his magic. The smell of him overwhelmed me, invaded my cells. There was no other smell in the world, just him. The chunder remained trapped in my stomach.

The small piece of him, like the golem, began to dissolve into my hands, pushing its way into me. It hurt. More than it had last time. Like thousands of pins and needles. It—he—was doing something to me. He still stared at me, with his wavering smile. The pins and needles felt like they were piercing my bones, penetrating my marrow.

He nodded and waved his hand, pushed me backwards down the steps. Released his grip on my muscles. I stumbled to the gutter and chundered and chundered until I was chundering nothing but air.

Danny helped me up, pushed snow on top of the mess I'd made.

I glanced up at the old man, still there against the door. He made his shooing gesture. Without any magic coercing me, I obeyed, grabbed Danny's hand, and got away as fast as I could. The thing he had thrown at me was sharp and cutting inside me. It felt like I was being operated on. Changed. What had he done?

I could feel him still watching. I broke into a run, half afraid that running would make whatever he had thrown at me cut even deeper. I didn't stop until I turned the corner and was out of the old man's sight, but not out of his smell.

"Are you okay?" Danny asked. He'd easily kept pace with me. We were back in front of the café with the cakes and muffins; there were only seventeen now.

I nodded, though my mouth tasted awful, my stomach hurt, and there was something alien slicing into my bones. I glanced nervously at my hands, but I was wearing gloves and couldn't see the thousands of little pinholes I was sure would be there. The sensation of cutting was fading, but I could still feel whatever it was inside me. "I'd give my right arm to brush my teeth."

"I bet. We'll get you a toothbrush."

"You?" I asked. His right cheek was very red, and a trickle of blood ran from the corner of his mouth. I wiped at it with my glove.

"It's nothing. Just a split lip."

"You're lucky he didn't do worse. He could have used magic against you." *He could have killed you, like I killed Josh Davidson.*

"Oh," Danny said smugly, "he *was* using magic."

"No, he wasn't. Not *against* you he wasn't. He didn't turn you blind or control your movements as if you were a doll." I shuddered. Would he be able to control me even better with the stuff he had put inside me? It didn't hurt anymore, but I could still feel it there, throughout my body. What was it?

Danny snorted. "No dude that old beats me in a fight without magic." He drew in a deep breath. "Is your grandmother still on the line?"

I looked down at the phone in my hand. "Uh, yeah."

Danny took it from me and started talking to her.

I took a deep breath of the frigid air, managing not to cough this time. I looked up and saw a smoky grey-brown trail cutting through the air. From him, I was sure.

I peeked around the corner. There he was, guarding the door, staring right back at me. Dozens of grey-brown trails flowed out from him. I hauled myself out of his sight before he could put another spell on me.

Why hadn't I seen them before? What were they? Trails of where he had been, trails of where he had sent parts of himself? The one that came around the corner was the thickest. I decided to follow it.

15
Dying

"You missed some excitement," Esmeralda said as Jay-Tee walked into the kitchen. Esmeralda didn't look up, kept her eyes fixed on the door. She nursed the old-fashioned, very heavy, very corded phone on her knees. Jay-Tee couldn't decide whether she was waiting for Reason to call again or was planning to use it to bludgeon to death whoever (or whatever) came through the door.

The door was moving, but in total slow motion. As if someone was hitting the pause button over and over to shift it frame by frame. Too weird. The door made Jay-Tee's skin crawl. It was like a wild animal, toying with them, waiting for them to relax before it leapt out and tore them into pieces as small as the feathers that lined the bottom of the door. Jay-Tee had a sudden, very clear image of feathers soaked in blood and guts. Very ewww.

"Where's Tom?" Esmeralda asked, still not looking at Jay-Tee.

"He went home to sleep."

"But it's so early."

"He couldn't keep his eyes open any longer. We didn't get much sleep last night." Jay-Tee wondered if Esmeralda wasn't

looking at her because she knew what Jay-Tee had done. She
had never done to Tom what Jay-Tee had. He'd said so himself. Before Tom and Reason had come to New York, they'd
never even heard of drinking. *She must hate me*, Jay-Tee
thought. *I hate me.*

Esmeralda nodded and made a note on the pad.

"So what was the excitement?"

"Reason rang. We were able to establish that when the
door isn't moving, the old man isn't there on the other side.
He's definitely controlling it."

"Huh," Jay-Tee said instead of saying, *Duh.* She'd thought
that was pretty obvious. Though you'd think that anyone with
enough magic to make the door so weird for so long would've
died when Moses was a baby.

"He's very powerful," Esmeralda continued, as if she were
talking about something unimportant—the weather, or what
she'd bought at the local store. "He was able to stop Reason
from moving or speaking while he held Danny off. Easily."

"Is Danny okay?"

"Yes. He's fine." Still she didn't look at Jay-Tee.

"You sure?"

"Yes. I spoke to him."

"And *he* hasn't shown up?"

"You mean Reason's grandfather?"

Jay-Tee nodded and sat down on a stool, instantly feeling
the soreness in her butt. She'd sat on one of these kitchen
stools staring at the stupid door for way too long.

"No. Not yet."

Jay-Tee slipped off Reason's sandals and folded her feet up under her. She looked at her watch and tried to calculate what time it was in New York. What had Reason said to do? Add six and swap AM for PM? Or was it add eight? It was after ten here so that made it—Jay-Tee counted it off on her fingers—6 PM there. Or eight. Either way, it'd be dark already, and cold. Not brighter than a movie star's teeth, and not deliciously hot.

"I don't know what to do," Esmeralda said.

"Huh?"

"I don't know what to do." She hugged the phone closer; her eyes were wet. Jay-Tee watched her blink rapidly. "I don't have much magic left."

Jay-Tee turned away, staring out the window at the enormous prehistoric-looking tree. Fronds hung down from it, as if it was meant to be in a dark, dripping jungle somewhere, not in someone's backyard in the middle of a city. If Esmeralda asked, Tom would probably give his beloved Mere some magic, too. But how long could he keep doing that? What would be left for Tom? Eventually they would have to die. Nothing to be done about it. Not unless they wanted to drink Tom dry.

"We're dying," she said.

This time Esmeralda turned to look at her. She nodded. "I feel like I'm wearing thin, floating away from the world."

"Fading."

"Yes." Esmeralda sounded sad and defeated.

"Me, too."

"I know. I saw it in you."

Jay-Tee wondered what it was she could see. The absence of magic? The damage magic had done to her? Why couldn't Jay-Tee see it? Did Reason see it, too? "I . . ." Jay-Tee stopped. She wasn't sure she could tell Esmeralda what she had done. "I think I understand *him* now. Drinking my magic like that."

Esmeralda bowed her head. "Yes."

"But it only delays the inevitable."

Esmeralda looked at her, smiled briefly. "I would give anything for a few more weeks, a few days. . . ."

"Anything?"

She nodded. "If I could, I'd take it. . . ."

"But we don't have enough left to take it with, do we? We can only ask and hope."

Esmeralda sat up, staring at Jay-Tee. "You did, didn't you?" Her eyes went soft, unfocussed for a moment. "You did." It wasn't a question.

"I explained it to him. . . ."

"As Alexander did with you."

"Alexander?"

"Reason's grandfather. Jason Blake."

Jay-Tee felt sick. She wasn't like him. "Is that his real name?" She'd thought she'd heard all his different names, but she'd never heard that one. She wished Esmeralda hadn't said it out loud.

"I don't know. It's what he called himself when I first met him."

How could Esmeralda say Jay-Tee was like that man? She

wasn't. "Tom gave me his magic because we're friends. It wasn't like with *him* at all."

Esmeralda laughed. "I'm not accusing. I'm hardly in a position to be casting stones."

"Have you done it? Drunk from someone?"

"Yes."

"Who?"

For a long while Esmeralda said nothing. The door had shifted to lengthwise ripples. It would be pretty if it wasn't so weird and if Jay-Tee didn't half expect it to bulge forward and suck them through any minute now. She wondered if that would be a bad thing.

"Mostly from my daughter."

"Reason's mom?"

"Yes."

"Oh."

"Indeed. I didn't ask her; I took it."

"You . . ."

"Yes. She wouldn't use her magic. She refused to learn. She refused to believe it was real. So . . ."

"So you just took it from her. Wow, no wonder she hates your ass."

Esmeralda laughed, but she looked like she was going to start crying. "Sarafina has reasons beyond counting for hating me. I wasn't a very good mother."

Jay-Tee cracked up. "You weren't a very good mother! That's hilarious. Man, you must've been Cruella De Vil!"

"I didn't mean . . . It wasn't supposed to be like that." A tear rolled down Mere's cheek. "I didn't want her to go crazy. I thought if I just took it . . ."

"And it didn't hurt that it also meant you were going to live longer."

"No, it didn't. Oh! I never meant any of it to turn out like this. If I could change it all, I would. If I could go back in time . . ."

Jay-Tee snorted. "If I could go back, I'd snag the basketball genes, not the skanky evil magic genes. In a heartbeat."

"Oh, yes," Mere said with so much longing Jay-Tee could almost taste it. "Get rid of the curse. Nothing is worth this. Nothing."

The door wasn't moving. Jay-Tee wasn't sure how long it had been still. They'd stopped taking notes. "Hey, didn't you say that when the door isn't moving he's not on the other side?"

Esmeralda wiped her eyes. "Yes."

Jay-Tee stood up, walked toward it. "Come on, then. Let's check it out. We're going to die, anyway, right?"

16
Magic Trails

"Where are we going?" Danny asked.

"That way." I gestured to the thickest trail.

"Your grandmother said you should keep trying to find out where he came from."

"I *am* trying to find out where he came from."

"Won't it make you sick again? Shouldn't we rest for a bit?"

"I'm fine." I kept following the trail.

"Why are we going north? Are you smelling him?"

I shook my head. "I don't have to; I can see him now."

Danny stopped dead, turned around, his hands curled into fists. "Where is he?"

"Sorry, not *him* him. I can see where the old man's been. His, um, residue? The stuff I was smelling before, I can see it now. It's like a misty trail."

"His *residue?*" The part of Danny's face that was visible between his scarf and his hat screwed up like he'd eaten something truly disgusting. "What do you mean *residue?*"

"When he moves he leaks stuff—like dead skin cells."

"Eww. Magic dead skin?"

"I guess."

"We're following a trail of magic dead skin cells. You know that's weird, right?" Danny was grinning at me. He reached out and touched my nose. Though it was nearly numb with cold and he was wearing gloves, I felt his touch tingle throughout my body. "No wonder it made you barf."

"Yeah, it's pretty foul." And then I realised that it *wasn't*, not anymore. I could smell the old man, but it wasn't making me want to chunder. He didn't smell bad to me anymore. Why? I could feel it, the stuff he had put inside me, crawling around me—it ached, made me feel uncomfortable in my own body. Like it wasn't my own anymore. He'd changed me so that he smelled good now, not foul. How else had he changed me?

"Lead on," Danny said.

After seven blocks the trail disappeared into the footpath. I pulled up and a woman ran into me. "Sorry," I said, trying to step out of her way and running into a man carrying a small child in his arms. "Sorry," I said again. The man didn't say anything to me, just scowled briefly and kept walking.

"What?" asked Danny. "Why have we stopped?" He pulled me out of the pedestrian traffic to the front of a run-down shop selling shoes. The shop next door was just as run-down and seemed to specialise in tat: old baby dolls in faded dresses, plates with different people's faces on them—including Elvis Presley and a blonde woman in a white dress—and large plastic crosses that lit up in red and blue. Even pressed up against the shop window, people passed by so close their winter coats brushed against us. I was never going to get used to such massive mobs of people. What were they doing out at night in the cold?

I stared at where the old man's trail disappeared. Through the passing crowds I saw no grate, no vent, no cracks in the concrete. He must've sunk down into the ground here. I wondered why. I wondered, too, if he could reappear here. The thought made my stomach contract. If he could disappear into the ground anywhere he chose, then he could reappear anywhere, couldn't he? With that piece of him sunk into my bones, could he find me whenever he wanted to? I glanced behind me. People everywhere I looked, but none of them a centuries-old relative of mine.

"It disappeared," I told Danny.

"Your magic trail disappeared?"

"Yes."

"Shouldn't your grandmother know about this?" He started to get out his mobile phone.

"Not yet, not until I have something to tell her."

I looked around, searching for old man Cansino's trail. We were standing on the footpath of a big street; the footpath was wide, but the street was even wider, with four lanes of traffic— six if you counted the cars parked bumper bar to bumper bar, with barely a centimetre between them. I had no idea how you could get a car out that was parked in that tight. Maybe they had special forklift trucks for that, or maybe they pulled them out with helicopters.

Even at night with pretty coloured lights, the shops on the other side of the street were as run-down looking as the shoe and the tat shop, all of them jammed up against each other. I hadn't yet seen a single building that stood on its own. Most of the shops looked more or less the same, just like all the houses. It was hard to note landmarks when there was no visible landscape. No hills or mountains or rock formations and what few trees there were had no leaves, making them look almost as identical as the buildings. If Danny decided to rack off, I would have no way of finding my way back to his place. "Where are we exactly?"

"Fourteenth Street. Between First Avenue and Avenue A."

"Okay, I have to find the trail again. I'm going to start searching that way." I looked up at the strange night sky that lacked stars and blackness. "What direction is that?"

"East."

"If I can't find the trail again, you can get me back to this spot, right?"

"No problem."

"Do you see it yet?" Danny asked. We'd walked half a block east. I stopped to peer up and down Avenue A, seeing no hint of Mr Cansino's trail, half-wondering why all the streets here had such boring names. Numbers are wonderful and letters are fine, but streets should have *actual* names.

I shook my head. "Nah. Don't smell anything, either."

"What does it look like?" Danny asked. He was looking in the same direction as me, his eyes narrowed as if he was trying to see with my eyes.

"It's like thick mist, but kind of concentrated. I can't see through it. It's the colour of a mouse's fur—halfway between grey and brown."

"So not like floating dead skin cells?"

"Nah."

"Where next?"

"How about we keep heading east?"

"Sure."

It didn't feel like east. Without any stars or the moon, I had to take Danny's word for it. We kept walking until we hit the river. I didn't catch the old man's scent once.

"So, your place must be near here," I said.

"This is the East River, not the Hudson." He pointed back the way we'd come. "My apartment's way over there, on the other side of Manhattan."

"Huh. So is this an island?"

Danny looked at me with the exact same expression Jay-Tee always used when she thought I'd said something der-brained. "Yeah, Manhattan is an island."

"But I thought this was New York City?"

"Wow, Reason—you really don't know anything, do you?"

"Not about New York City I don't. I bet I know heaps of stuff you don't know. Like how to make a fire out of—"

Danny laughed. "I bet you do, too." He pointed to the other side of the river. "Over there? That's Brooklyn. Further up that way—that's Queens. We're standing on the island of Manhattan. They're all boroughs of New York City."

"Boroughs?"

"Parts? Districts? Districts. That's probably a better word for it. They're all districts of New York City. There are five of them: Manhattan, Brooklyn, Queens, the Bronx, and Staten Island. Julieta and me grew up in the Bronx, which is way up north." He pointed along the black river. I wondered what it would look like during the day.

"But the East Village isn't a borough?"

"Nope. It's a neighbourhood. Boroughs are much bigger: they're made up of lots of little neighbourhoods, like the East Village."

"Okay," I said, feeling overwhelmed. The East Village seemed so big just on its own. "So this river here is the East River that the East Village is west of?"

Danny grinned and nodded.

"And the river near your place is the West River?"

"Nope, the Hudson, but it *is* west of here."

"I like this river better. More trees. Must look nice in summer."

"Yeah, it does."

I hadn't seen any trees from his flat, just a lot of concrete. Here, we were in parkland. If you could call it that when nothing was green. The trees were tall, with lots of branches but not a single leaf.

The old man had not been here. We headed back west on Tenth Street. There were fewer people than on Fourteenth Street. It was much narrower. I still felt hemmed in. I didn't like not being able to see the horizon in any direction. Too many buildings.

When we hit Avenue A I thought I saw something, but when

we got there it turned out to be a grey ribbon tied to a pole. I was cold and hungry and tired, and I didn't know what the old man had done to me. I took another step down Avenue A. The next street sign I saw was for Ninth Street. "Hah!" I said.

"You found it!"

"Nope. I just figured out how this city works. Wow, I'm slow."

"And, er, how does New York work, then, Reason?"

"The street numbers go down as you go further south. Tenth Street is south of Eleventh Street."

"Uh-huh." Danny didn't sound very impressed by my revelation.

"But the avenues run from the east to the west, so First Avenue's closer to the east side then the west."

"Well done."

"So if you lived on the corner of 190th Street and Fourteenth Avenue, you'd be very far north and west."

"Yup. Except that there is no Fourteenth Avenue—you'd be in the Hudson River or, worse, New Jersey, and there are streets above 190th. Manhattan goes all the way to 218th Street."

"Huh. What's your address, then?"

"I'm on West Street, which is basically the West Side Highway. That's the farthest one west."

"What number street is closest to you?"

"Ah, actually, it's kind of different in the west village. The streets are called things like Horatio and Jane. They're not numbered."

"That's annoying," I said. Now that I knew what the numbers

were for, I approved of them as street names. "So why is this Avenue A?"

"It used to be a park."

I looked across at the east side of the street where there was a park, if you could call it that with snow instead of grass and leafless, dried-up trees. "Like that?"

"All of this land used to be park, not just that bit. There didn't used to be any avenues here. So when they added more avenues, the numbers had been used up running west; they used the alphabet instead. The next avenue east is Avenue B."

"Then C, D, E, and F?"

Danny laughed. "Just C and D and then the highway and then the river."

We reached Seventh Street. I peered west along the street, and there it was, a fat rope of mist emerging from a grate in the middle of the footpath. "Eureka."

"You see it?"

"Uh-huh. Right there." I walked up to the grate; mist coiled out of it, the same grey-brown as the thing he had sent spinning into my hands. The smell intensified as I got closer. But it wasn't the same smell. Or rather it *was*, the stuff inside me had softened it—the burntness had become something freshly toasted, the bile was now like lemons. It didn't make me feel sick. It smelt good. And yet it was the same smell. It hadn't changed: I had. The old man had put something in me so that he now smelled like lemons and cinnamon toast. I shuddered. Somehow it was worse than when he had smelled like chunder and burnt rubber.

I could still feel that lurking strangeness, the pieces of the old man floating in my marrow. I peered down into the grate. The trail disappeared into darkness. I tried not to think about the old man bubbling up out of there, grabbing me. Or him bubbling out of me.

"Which way is it heading?"

"That way, west," I said, following the trail along the street, being very careful not to touch it. I didn't want to find out what happened if I did. At the corner of First Avenue I had a clear view of the trail winding a long way down the avenue. "It's moved out into the middle of the road. It goes south for blocks."

The trail led us along Second Street, yet another street with rows of cars parked on either side, some lightly dusted with snow, others almost buried. On the south side of the street the houses were the same I'd been seeing everywhere, jammed together, four or five or six stories high, brown and grey, presenting flat, indistinguishable faces to the street. In the middle of the block stood a large church, its doors shut and steps covered with snow.

The north side of the street had only a few houses before the trail led us to a high—almost three metres—spiked metal fence. Behind it—right in the middle of the street—was a cemetery, blanketed with clean white snow, sparsely dotted with ancient-looking gravestones and monuments. A low stone wall covered with a brown, withered, treeless vine ran along the back of the cemetery, towered over by the rear ends of more tall, skinny houses.

The trail we had followed was not the only one leading to the cemetery. Three came over the low stone wall in back. Five more came from the west. They all went into the cemetery, into the ground, over and over again. The web of his trails running in and out of the white-covered earth hovered like an eerie mist above the gravestones and monuments.

"Bloody hell."

"What?" Danny pushed up to the icy fence, trying to see. "What is it?"

"He's all over this place. He's been in the ground here."

"What do you mean? He's a ghost?"

"No. His trail, it leads in and out of the ground, all over the cemetery. Like he's been . . ."

Danny stared at me. "He's a grave robber?"

17
Touched by the Devil

The door didn't open. They were both swaddled in warm clothes, ready for winter on the other side, and yet the door wouldn't budge. Esmeralda turned the handle back and forth, leaned into it as she turned, but it made no difference. Jay-Tee started to sweat just watching. Well, actually she was sweating because she had several layers of winter clothes on and she was standing in a Sydney kitchen in the middle of summer.

"Why don't you use the key?"

"I told you, I don't *need* the key. The door just opens for me."

"But maybe he's changed it?"

"That's not possible."

"Well, according to you, a man who's older than Moses and has that much magic shouldn't be possible, either."

Mere glared at Jay-Tee, and if magic could have turned her glare into lasers, then Jay-Tee would've fried. Then she laughed. "Okay, you're correct: the meaning of *possible* appears to be in flux right now."

"Huh?"

"I'll go get the key. Stay back from the door. It's not moving, but you never know."

Jay-Tee rolled her eyes. She wasn't stupid. She took off all her winter gear and opened the fridge, wanting some Coke or any kind of soda, but not finding any. There was an open bottle of wine, though. She pulled it out and poured herself a large glass. She took a sip—it was pretty nasty, but she'd tasted worse.

She pulled herself back onto the uncomfortable stool and peered at the door for the gazillionth time. It still wasn't moving. She'd kind of thought Esmeralda rattling away at the handle would've attracted the old man's attention. She took another sip of the wine, not *quite* as nasty on the second sip. What if the scary old man on the other side was just waiting for them to come through the door so he could pounce and steal their magic? Reason had told Mere that he'd made no move to drink from her even though he could have anytime. But maybe he didn't want *Reason's* magic?

"What are you doing, young lady?" Esmeralda asked, taking the glass from Jay-Tee.

"Hey!"

"You're fifteen years old, Jay-Tee! I don't care if you're going to die any second now—I'm not having you drinking, and particularly *not* in the morning!"

"*He* let me drink."

"I'm sure he did. You're free to go back to Alexander's exemplary care if that's what you want."

Jay-Tee had no idea what *exemplary* meant, but she knew sarcasm when she heard it. What difference did it make if she had a glass of nasty wine?

Esmeralda put the key in the lock, but before she could turn it, the door shook wildly, turned from solid to almost liquid. The molten wood surged around her gloved hand. "No!" she yelled, pulling at her wrist with her other hand, but the door swallowed it as well. She was being dragged forward into the door. Her body arced backwards, the winter hat tumbling from her head. "Jay-Tee, help!"

Jay-Tee jumped up, poised to do something, but wasn't sure what. If she used her magic to help, she'd die.

The door swallowed Mere up to her elbows. She arched back, pulling away, desperately trying to keep her face and legs from disappearing, too.

Jay-Tee tried to get hold of Mere's legs or her coat and pull, but the stuff came surging at her hands. She jumped back, looking around the room wildly, saw the glass of wine, grabbed it, and doused the top of the door. The wine ran down over the strange bumps and rivers of the molten door, over Mere's submerged arms, and down to the floor, where it floated some of the feather protections away. Instantly the door pulled Mere even farther in. Only her head and feet were visible now.

"Damn."

Then Esmeralda started to glow. Threads sprouted in her back, reached back into the kitchen. They looked like the connections between people that Jay-Tee saw when she was dancing, the threads that bound everyone's energy together, that turned them into a crowd.

Jay-Tee took the risk. She grabbed at the threads, pulled

them together in her hand, and stepped back, pulling as hard as she could. Fighting to use only her muscles and not her magic, she pulled and pulled, until she felt the skin across her palm breaking open. She ignored it and pulled harder.

Jay-Tee's back was to the door, so she couldn't see what was happening, but she could hear Mere breathing hard; she could feel the magic growing.

All the air vanished out of the room in a wave. Jay-Tee staggered—the threads in her hands went limp, disappeared. She lost her hearing as if she had dived to the bottom of a deep, deep pool. She turned. Esmeralda was lying on the floor in front of the door, blinking rapidly, red-faced, her mouth opening and closing like a fish. She was drenched. Her winter clothing was in tatters, her gloves entirely gone. In her right hand she still clutched the large, ornate key that opened the door.

Jay-Tee rubbed her own ears. Held her nose and breathed in as if she was trying to clear her ears of water. Her ears popped, and she was awash with sound. The door was making the horrible, grinding, metal-on-metal noise. Mere was panting louder than a German shepherd. The fridge was clunking. Outside birds were squawking and chirruping at one another. Somewhere else a dog was barking.

Jay-Tee crossed herself, said a Hail Mary, then knelt down beside Mere.

"Are you okay?"

Mere nodded, then shook her head. "It hurts." She used her elbows to sit up. Her expression was far away, dazed.

"You sure?"

Mere closed her eyes, opened them. She looked scared. "There's something. . . . Could you get me a glass of water?" She was looking down at her hands, still clutching the key. They were covered in tiny dots of blood.

Jay-Tee fetched water, handed it to her, watched her drink.

"You don't look okay. You look like you saw the devil."

Mere looked up at Jay-Tee; she half smiled. "He may have just touched me."

Instinctively, Jay-Tee moved back. "Not really?"

"I should be dead. I don't understand." Her gaze returned to her arms, searching for something. "I used my magic to get away. I should be dead. He put something in me and I'm not dead."

"The devil did?"

"The old man. He's so very old, Jay-Tee. I didn't think that was possible. I feel good, warm inside, stronger." She put her hand on Jay-Tee's left arm. "Here," she said. "A present."

Jay-Tee didn't feel Mere's hand; she felt hundreds of tiny paper cuts, sharp and fine. Something thin as a ribbon and sharp as a blade cut its way into her, slid its way down into her bones.

Esmeralda had turned on her. It was what her father had done and *him* as well. She didn't know why she hadn't expected it. This was what adults did: betrayed you. Esmeralda was taking all her magic, killing her, and there was nothing Jay-Tee could do to stop her.

Jay-Tee felt a white-hot flash of rage, but then it faded. She didn't even have enough strength left to be angry. Tears leaked out of her eyes. All her regrets flooded her, multiplied, and then the pain grew so great there were no regrets, no thoughts, no nothing at all.

18
Green Tea

"I don't think he's a grave robber. Look at the snow. It's not disturbed."

"Couldn't he spirit whatever he wants out of there?" Danny asked. "Use magic?"

"I guess. I don't know."

I was knackered again. My eyelids were rebelling against staying open. My brain was finished with thinking. Through half-closed eyes I looked at old man Cansino's grey-brown trails swirling into one another, sinking into the ground, and rising back out again. They danced together, twisting and twirling. It was pretty.

"Reason?"

"Mmm?"

"What's wrong?"

"Sleepy."

"Let's go home."

My stomach contracted, but not with nausea. I could smell the old man everywhere around me, but now he was lime juice and fresh toast. I tried to recall what it had been like before. I couldn't.

"Hungry." I yawned. We'd been walking around for hours, it felt like. Longer. It had been day; now it was night. The sky was the same grey-brown as the old man. Everything was. I wondered if I was, too.

"There's a sushi place near here. Have you had sushi before?"

I shook my head. "Never heard of it."

"Are you game?"

I nodded, too tired to say yes.

Getting to the restaurant was hard. My legs decided they'd done enough walking. I had to use my tired brain to tell them what to do, but they weren't much chop at listening. In my mind I called them mongrels, but they didn't care. Finally Danny put one arm around my shoulders and another under my knees and swung me up into the air like I was a princess. It felt wonderful.

"Wheee! Better than last time." I had been chasing Jay-Tee, running away from Esmeralda. I'd only just met Danny, but I hadn't been running fast enough for him, so he'd hurled me over his shoulder.

He laughed. "You didn't like the sack-of-potatoes carry?"

"Nup."

In his arms I started to wake up, to feel the increasingly cold air on my face. For the first time in hours I could smell something other than old man Cansino. I could smell Danny. His stale sweat, his shampoo, something musky and sweet that slid off his skin, making me shiver. His arms around me were strong and still. I suddenly longed for him to run his hands along my back. To hold me rather than carry me.

"Are we there yet?" I asked.

"What am I? Your father? A taxi driver?"

"You're Jay-Tee's brother who has the good basketball genes."

"That's me."

"Hey, do you do that for a living? Play basketball?" I wasn't sure if that was possible, but Jay-Tee seemed to think that her brother playing basketball was a fabulous thing.

"I wish. One day, maybe. I got into Georgetown on a basketball scholarship, but they let me take this year off, what with Dad dying and me wanting to look for Julieta and everything. I do what I can to stay basketball fit. I train every day—well, most days—play a lot of pick-up games, and I'm with a West 4th street team. Then in September I'll go to school and train big-time. They've got a great starting point guard, so it's gonna be tough to get minutes."

"Huh," I said, not having understood much of what Danny said. I wondered what Georgetown was and why he was talking about school when he was eighteen and must be finished with school already. "Sorry to stop you training."

"No big deal. I let the guys know I wouldn't make the game tonight. I did a session at the gym this morning. It's no biggie. Today *this* is more important. I can go a day without basketball."

"I wish I could go a day without magic."

"That's what Julieta says. Here we are."

He let me down gently and I wobbled on my treacherous legs.

"Steady."

Danny opened the door for me, and I walked into a blanket of warmth.

Sushi turned out to be rice wrapped in dark green paper stuff with fish and vegetables in the middle. It tasted great. But it didn't put much of a dent in our hunger. I had to eat twenty-six pieces before my stomach stopped grumbling.

The waitresses wore fancy Japanese clothes and smiled and bowed a lot. They brought us hot tea in tiny cups, which tasted bitter but was somehow refreshing. Green tea, Danny said. One sip and all the door lag and fatigue melted away.

"How come you know nothing about New York? And you've never tried sushi?"

"Didn't Jay-Tee tell you?"

"No."

"I travelled around a lot with Sarafina, my mother. In Australia, but not in the cities—in the bush. There's not a lot of sushi there." I wondered why it was called sushi.

"But you went to school, right?"

I shook my head. "Not really. Sarafina preferred to teach me herself. But she taught me mostly maths and science. I'm really good at numbers."

"What about television? You *must* have seen this city on TV."

I shook my head again. "Nut. The most I've ever watched television in my life was at your house today."

"No!" Danny looked shocked. "Not really?"

"Really. I'd see television in pubs sometimes. But it was always the races or footie or some other sport, and I never got to watch for very long. I've read lots of books."

"But not any about New York City."

I shook my head. "Mostly books about maths and science. I know the name of practically every small town in Australia. There are *lots* of them. I can navigate by the stars. I can identify hundreds of different plants and animals, I can calculate the Fibonacci series—"

"I bet you can. I mean it, that's all amazing. It's just so different. I've never met anyone who hasn't grown up with a TV before. I mean, this is the most famous city in the world. It's so weird that you don't know anything about it. That you'd never even *heard* of it before you stepped through that door. To me that's almost weirder than magic being real. And trust me, that's plenty weird enough."

"I'd heard of New York City!"

"But not of Manhattan? Or Brooklyn? Do you even know what *NYPD* stands for?"

"New York, um, something." I shook my head, feeling really stupid.

"New York Police Department. It's amazing to me that you don't know that."

"I do now."

Danny rolled his eyes. "Can you name any other cities in the U.S.? In the world?"

"Sure. Paris. Tokyo. Phnom Penh. Jakarta."

"Do you know anything about them?"

"Paris is in France. Right now it's . . ." I looked at my watch. "Eight thirty-seven PM here, so it's . . . 2:37 AM there. Phnom Penh's in Cambodia and it's four hours behind Sydney so it's 8:37 AM there. Jakarta's in Indonesia, where it's the same time as Phnom Penh."

"You forgot Tokyo."

"It's in Japan, and right now it's 10:37 AM."

"Okay, you got me. How do you do that? Know what time it is in all those cities?"

"It's easy. There are only twenty-four hours in a day, so the math's not hard. The tricky bit is remembering where the time zones are. I don't know *all* of them. Some are kind of arbitrary, and daylight savings makes things more interesting. I'm better at countries that are closer to Australia."

"I can see that. I never heard of Phnom Penh before."

"I don't really know much about them as actual places. I wouldn't know what bits of those cities are called, their—what did you call them? Boroughs?"

Danny nodded.

"If there's a door that leads through to any of them, I'd be as lost as I was here."

"Do you think there are?"

"What?"

"Other doors that connect cities."

"I don't know. Maybe. I mean, I guess so. Why would there be only one?" Until that moment it hadn't occurred to me that there would be more than one. How stupid was that? I wondered if the old man had come to New York from some other faraway city through a door like the one at the back of my grandmother's house. Maybe if we kept following his trails, we'd find other doors?

Again I wondered how old man Cansino had lived for so long. Was he stealing magic? He'd made no attempt to steal mine.

"What's it like being magic? It must be amazing."

One of the waitresses came over, taking teeny-tiny steps because the skirt of her Japanese dress was so tight. She put down a card that listed desserts and then cleared our plates.

"Green tea ice cream. Like the tea we had? That must taste foul."

"Actually, it's good. You want to try some?"

I nodded. "New things are good."

Danny signalled to the waitress and ordered. He did it easily, lifting his hand, raising an eyebrow—I'd never signalled to a waitress in my life.

"So, magic. What's it like?" He leaned forward, staring at me as if he could see the magic inside me.

"I'm not really sure yet. I only just found out I was magic."

"Really? How could you not know?"

Good question. How had I not known? "It's kind of hard to

explain. Until I stepped through the door, I didn't know. And to
be honest, even going from Sydney to New York City like that,
well, I didn't figure it out straightaway. I was kind of slow."

"Huh. Jay-Tee says she's always known. What about that kid
Tom?"

"He's only known for a year. Esmeralda says it's possible to
be magic your whole life and never know."

"No way. How could you not know?"

"What's Jay-Tee told you?" I was starting to think not much.

"Not a lot, really. That she's magic and our parents were,
too."

"Magic isn't as amazing as you'd think. It's not like any of
us can fly or anything." I wondered if that was true. I wondered if I could fly if I tried. Except that it would use up so
much magic I'd be dead on the spot. "It's mostly small things,
like being able to tell when people are telling the truth or not.
And the door working for us, but not for you. It's pretty easy
not to know, really. Esmeralda says almost everyone has a certain amount of magic. You know that feeling you get that
someone's looking at you? Even when you have your back to
them?"

"Nope." Danny's eyes were wide. He seemed confused by
the question.

"What do you mean, 'Nope'?" I thought of Esmeralda's
other example. "How about when you go to pick up the phone
just before it rings, and it's as if you knew it was going to
ring?"

"That happens?"

"Esmeralda says it does. You've never felt deja vu? Or dreamed something that came true?"

"No, never."

"Wow, you must be a magic dead zone. Huh." No wonder the old man hadn't used magic against Danny. He *couldn't*.

"I guess. So you're saying that most people have some kind of magic, but some of it's really small. Like deja vu or whatever? So most people have lame, not-very-useful magic." He was smiling. I liked his smile.

I laughed. "Trust me, they're better off with only that much."

"Why?"

That put me on the spot. Jay-Tee mustn't have told him about the less good side of magic.

"It's not as much fun as you'd think."

"Why not?"

"Well, um, it kind of tires you out."

"So does playing basketball. Doesn't make me love the game any less."

"I guess not. Jay-Tee hasn't told you anything about . . ." I trailed off, not knowing how to say it or whether I even should. How would Jay-Tee feel if I told him the truth? Not that she'd been great at telling *me* the truth. Still, wasn't it up to Jay-Tee to decide whether she wanted to tell him or not?

"About the downside of magic? No, she hasn't, but I get the feeling there is one."

Downside! I almost laughed out loud. That was one way of putting it. *I'm fifteen and I might not make it to sixteen.* Some downside. "Maybe she should tell you."

"I'm asking you." He was looking straight at me with his huge brown eyes. His face was so close I could hear him breathing. If I leaned in a little, I could kiss him. I wanted to tell him everything he wanted to know. I knew exactly how it felt to be kept in the dark, to have other people decide what you should and shouldn't know. My mother, my grandmother writing me letters and then stealing them back before I could read them. Jay-Tee and Jason Blake. And now old man Cansino. He hadn't asked my permission to hurl a piece of himself at me, to alter my sense of smell and who-knew-what-else.

"How old was your mother when she died?" I asked him.

"Eighteen."

"And your father?"

"Thirty-seven. They were very young when they had me and Jay-Tee."

I nodded and took a deep breath. "Most magic people don't live very long."

"What do you mean?"

"I mean that, according to my grandmother, your father was an old, old man by magic standards. Not many of us make it into our twenties. That's your *downside*."

The waitress placed two bowls of green ice cream on the table. Danny stared at me, and I lowered my gaze to stare at the ice cream.

19
Dead

Esmeralda let go of Jay-Tee. That hurt, too.

"What did you do to me?" Jay-Tee asked. She could feel whatever it was pushing deep into her body. It didn't feel right. It unbalanced her, wrecked her rhythm. The web shattered all around her. She felt hot. Not from the outside, from the inside. There were spikes inside her, twisting around, burning her. They didn't belong inside her. She could see a thin thread running between her and Esmeralda, but the thread wasn't right either: it was jagged and frayed.

"I'm sorry," Esmeralda said. "I don't think it works for you."

"What? What isn't? What didn't? I don't understand." Jay-Tee started to shake. The kitchen moved. She swayed on her knees, then leaned back. The floor slid from under her, pulled her down. Her cheekbone hit the tiled floor. It hurt, but not as much as the things impaling her from the inside. Besides, the floor was cool. Green and black tiles arranged like a checkerboard. "I hurt. What did you do to me?"

Esmeralda put something cold and wet on her forehead, but seconds later it was hot again. Her body would not be still. The spikes jiggled at her.

"I'm sorry, love. I didn't realise. Will you let me try to get it out?"

Jay-Tee started to shake harder. "It hurts!"

Esmeralda put her hand on Jay-Tee's arm. It didn't feel right. Nothing felt right. Jay-Tee shook harder.

"Don't," she said. "Don't." But Esmeralda's hand stayed locked on her, sucking at her, pulling something out.

Jay-Tee shook so hard her head banged back into the tiles. There was a smacking sound. Jay-Tee wondered if she was bleeding. Probably. She couldn't see any threads between her and Esmeralda. The something inside was trying to crawl out, something hard and sharp and angled. It would rip her to pieces. Esmeralda was calling the thing toward her. She fought as hard as she could to get away from it, away from Esmeralda. She tried to scratch Esmeralda's face, but Esmeralda held her hands down. She was stronger than a man, stronger than Jason Blake.

The world narrowed to Esmeralda's head bent over her, the woman's eyes closed, concentrating. *She's stealing all my magic,* Jay-Tee thought. *She's killing me.*

She convulsed again, head and legs and arms smacking hard onto the tiles. The pain burst inside her like a rotten tomato. The narrow slit that was the world shaded into nothing.

Jay-Tee was unconscious, she was gone, she floated. She wondered if she was dead.

20
So Little Time

"You're telling me that Julieta's going to die young?"

I nodded. Neither one of us had touched our ice cream. It was starting to melt into green puddles.

"And you, too?"

"Yes."

"How young?"

"I don't know." I especially didn't know now. What old man Cansino had done to me must have eaten away even more of my magic. Had I lost minutes, days, months? I wished I could look inside myself, see my own rust. "It depends on how much of your magic you've used. I don't know the precise formula. I don't think anyone does."

A string of tinny notes bleated from inside Danny's coat. His phone again, I realised after a confused half second. He made no move to answer it. "So why use your magic at all?"

I sighed. "That's the other downside. If you don't use your magic, you go insane. My mother, and Tom's, too—they're in a loony bin in Sydney."

"Wow. *That* is messed up."

"Yeah."

"It's like a disease."

I burst into tears.

I didn't mean to. I didn't know I was going to. It exploded out of me. Tears poured out of my eyes, snot from my nose, and choking sobs from my chest. I cried so loud, Danny looked around nervously. One of the waitresses brought tissues and patted me on the back.

"Family troubles," Danny said, which almost made me laugh.

The waitress nodded. "Ah, yes." She cleared away the melted green ice cream. "I bring you more. Colder."

Danny pulled out one of the tissues, pushed my hair out of the way, and held it to my nose. I took it from him and blew. More tears and snot came flowing out of me. Danny pushed the box closer. Half blind through my tears, I groped for another tissue, blew my nose again, even though it felt like I'd have to blow it a thousand times before all the snot would be gone.

"I'm sorry," I said, finally getting some words out. Then I started sobbing even harder. "I don't want this."

Danny reached under the table to hold my hand. "Who would? It sucks."

I was crying so hard my chest and throat ached. I thought of Sarafina, empty and numb at Kalder Park. Of Jay-Tee dying one day soon. Of Tom. Of what the old man had done. I cried and cried and cried.

Danny moved beside me, put his arms around me. His

phone rang again. *He must have thousands of friends,* I thought. *And I have only four.* He ignored the insistent snatch of song, pulled my head to rest on his shoulder, stroked my hair.

"I'll look after you," he told me. "We'll fix it. If it's a disease, then we'll just have to find the cure. For Julieta and for you."

Danny took me back to his flat, insisting that there was nothing more we could do that night, that I was tired, but I wasn't. Midnight in New York City; four in the afternoon in Sydney. I lay in Jay-Tee's bed wearing one of her old T-shirts, staring at the ceiling. The outside streetlights made shadows stretch out across it like claws. For a heart-stopping moment I thought the hand was reaching down at me. The old man's hand.

I could hear cars and trucks still thundering along the highway. Occasionally car horns and sirens. Was this city ever quiet? I had been overwhelmed by Sydney, but it was orders of magnitude calmer than this place. All those noises outside made me feel even more alone. Sarafina was far away, and even if she'd been right there with me, she wasn't able to help me anymore.

I missed her. I missed how she'd been *before*. Whenever I'd been scared in the past, she always reassured me, talked me out of it. "There are worse things," she'd always say. But now I was caught in the midst of those worse things.

I tried to think of something else. How would Jay-Tee feel

when Danny told her that he knew about magic, *all* about magic. That I had told him what lay ahead for his sister. Would she be angry?

My mind veered back to the old man, to the grey-brown stuff lodged inside me. I got up, went into the bathroom, peed, washed my hands, stared at my face in the mirror.

I didn't look any different. My skin didn't have a tinge of grey added to its brownness. Nothing scary bubbled out of my pores. I don't know what I expected to see, but it wasn't there. I could feel it inside me, though. I wasn't the same. I wished fervently I could blur my eyes, see inside myself, see what he'd done, and, more importantly, undo it.

I didn't go back to bed. I couldn't. I opened the door quietly and peeked outside. All the lights were out, but there was so much light streaming in from outside that I could see well enough. Cities, I decided, were never dark.

I tiptoed into the kitchen and opened the fridge door. There was nothing in there to eat, just endless cans of beer. I shut it again. I wished Danny was up. I needed to talk to someone.

There wasn't any light coming from underneath Danny's door. That probably meant he was asleep. I crept over and put my ear against the door and listened. I couldn't hear anything.

I opened his door slowly, my heart beating fast, and slid inside. I wasn't quite sure what I was doing. I just knew I couldn't be alone with old man Casino's golem thing chewing away inside me, changing me.

His room was dark. I couldn't see anything. I took another

step forward and stood there listening, waiting to hear something other than the loud thumping of my heart.

My eyes still hadn't adjusted to the blackness. Maybe he
had heavy curtains. I heard a siren outside. Then another.
They rushed by, fading into the distance, and there was silence
again.

Then I heard Danny breathing. The light, even breath of
sleep. *I should go.*

"Danny?" I asked instead. "You awake?"

Nothing. I thought about going back to bed, lying there and
feeling the old man's creature crawling about inside me.

I took another step into the room. "Danny?" I repeated a
little louder. "Danny?"

His sheets shifted. I took a step towards the sound.

"Danny!" I called, louder still.

"What? Huh?"

I heard him sitting up, his skin sliding against the sheets. I
moved towards his voice. "It's me, Reason."

"What is it? Is something wrong? Is that old man here?" All
of a sudden he sounded a lot less sleepy.

"No, no, nothing's wrong. I, ah, I couldn't sleep."

"You what?"

I took another step forward and bumped into his bed. I sat
down, put my hands on my lap. They were shaking.

"It's still early in Sydney, so I'm wide awake."

"Huh."

"So I was hoping you were awake—"

Danny snorted. "I wasn't."

"Sorry."

"I'm awake now."

"Sorry."

I shifted further up the bed, closer to his voice. "I, I wondered if . . ."

"What?"

"Do you have any video games? I've heard of them, but I've never played any and I wondered what it was like."

"You what?" Danny burst out laughing. "Sure. Sure thing. What the hell—I got the TV all set up."

We played a game full of dark alleys and underground passages and cellars. It was a world of grey and brown and black and white, so that the explosions of red blood were shocking. We were attacked by zombies who we had to kill by cutting off their heads (Danny was horrified that I hadn't known how to kill zombies properly) and vampires who we killed by banging thick wooden sticks through their hearts. He was even more disgusted by my vampire ignorance, groaning aloud when I asked what the garlic was for. We had to shoot werewolves with silver bullets (which was annoying, because our guns had plenty of normal bullets, but we had to go find the special silver ones) and mad people with guns, who died in all the ways that normal people do. Not from lack of magic.

I wasn't very good, but it was fun, and I could die as many

times as I wanted and always come back. I got lost in the strange world on his huge TV screen, which vaguely resembled New York City but was darker and gloomier, with no gleaming white snow or dazzling neon lights. I became so absorbed in trying to stay alive and out of Danny's way so we could blow up our enemies (those that could be killed that way) that I forgot there was anything else in the world outside the television screen. I could understand why people spent so many hours shooting and running in imaginary worlds.

Danny sat next to me, controls balanced on his knees, eyes intent on the screen. He wasn't wearing a shirt, just pyjama bottoms. In those seconds in between my deaths and resurrections, it was hard not to look at his smooth, brown skin. The lights of the game flashed across him. I wanted to kiss him.

"Come on, Ree! Pay attention. You got killed again. Sheesh!" He turned to me, grinning. "You gotta be faster than that."

I swallowed and leaned forward. He looked at me oddly. "There's something on your chin," I told him, brushing the imaginary something away. His chin was a little scratchy, like sandpaper.

He rubbed his chin where I had touched him. "Need a shave. Want another game?"

"Sure," I said, but I didn't, I wanted to kiss him. "No, I want to . . ." I swallowed again. "I want to . . ." I leaned forward fast. My mouth bounced into his, teeth clashed against teeth, and yet it made me shiver. "Oh, sorry." I looked down, feeling like an idiot.

"Reason?"

"Yep." I didn't look up.

"You're my sister's friend. You're fifteen."

"You're only eighteen. That's only three years older."

"But you're way young for fifteen even. When I picked you up today, you had jewellery pinned to your pyj—"

"That brooch is magic! Like the ammon—"

"Reason. You're really pretty and everything, but Julieta—"

"I'm pretty?"

"Sure, you're pretty, Reason, but you're a kid. You didn't even know that Manhattan is an island."

"I do *now*."

"Reason, that's not the point. You're just a baby!"

"No, I'm not. I'm an old woman. For a magic-wielder I'm old. I could die tomorrow. I don't want to die without ever having kissed anyone."

"You've never been kissed?"

I shook my head. "Not ever. I'm fifteen and I could be dead tomorrow and you smell good and I want to kiss you."

Danny laughed. "You smell pretty nice, too, but I can't. You're Julieta's friend. It'd be too weird."

I leaned closer to him. He was rejecting me, but I leaned closer. My body was doing it, not me—my brain had lost all control. I felt my nervous animal responses: pulse rate, sweat, my eyelids fluttering, an uneven twitch in one of the muscles of my left cheek. Just like any other animal, Sarafina had told me when she explained the facts of life. I didn't feel like any other animal. I felt like me.

"I can't kiss—"

I put my lips against his, gently this time. Neither of us moved a muscle. His lips were warm, soft, dry. I was terrified he'd move away, terrified that he wouldn't. What was I doing? The old man's pins and needles shifted inside me, pushing me closer to Danny.

His mouth opened; so did mine. I felt his tongue on mine. It felt good, not gross at all. I hoped I wouldn't forget to breathe. His hands slid over my cheeks, so big they covered my entire face. He pulled me closer to him. All my senses were focused on the connection between our two mouths. There wasn't anything else. I didn't know if my eyes were opened or shut. I swivelled around onto my knees to reach him more easily, put my hands on his shoulders. They were hard with muscle, smooth and warm. My fingers glided across, onto his back. His hands slid from my face onto my back, the two of them almost covering it entirely. There was so much of him, so much more of him than me.

Still, we kissed. Sharp pins and needles danced throughout my body, pushed me closer to him.

Danny pulled away. "Are you sure?" he said. His voice sounded odd, throaty. It made me want to kiss him more, touch him more. There was a sweet smell filling the air in between us.

"You smell like limes," I said. "You smell good." It wasn't

just him: everything smelled of limes, of lightly toasted bread, of cinnamon.

He slipped an arm under my knees, gathered me to him, went up onto his knees, grunted a little, and then stood. "Are you sure?" he asked again.

Sure of what? I wondered. I was sure I wanted to kiss him a lot, touch him, and I wanted him to touch me. "Yes."

He carried me into the bedroom, stumbling in the darkness before he laid me on the bed, leaned over me, kissing me again and again and again. Finding each other by touch, by taste. "We shouldn't," he said, his mouth so close to me I was stealing his breath. "I shouldn't. Tell me no."

I kissed his mouth. The smell had come with us. The room was full of sweet limes, of something fresh and newly baked. The smell was so familiar, so good. I felt Danny's hand moving up my waist as he pulled my T-shirt over my head. I heard him pulling at his pyjamas. "Are you sure?" he asked again, his voice beside my ear.

Every cell of my body wanted to touch every cell of his body. *Had* to. "I want to bury myself in you," I said.

"Oh, God," Danny said. "I have to bury myself in you." But he pulled away, took a deep, noisy breath, said something fast in a language I didn't know.

I couldn't see him in the dark, so I let my eyes blur, to see what was there beneath his skin, what he looked like right down in his cells. He was so clean he glowed. There was no magic there, none at all.

I moved across the bed to the sound of his breathing. Reached out my hands, touched his chest, ran my fingers along his body till I found his chin, his lips. I kissed him again. He groaned and returned my kisses. We leaned back onto the bed. Sheets against my back, his hot skin against my front. We rolled, sheets and skin wrapped around each other.

"I'll try not to hurt you," he said.

I couldn't imagine how he could.

21
Family Secrets

"Tom! Tom! Wake up. It's morning."

Someone with giant hands and sharp teeth covered in feathers was shaking him.

"Tom!"

"Nyahunh?" Tom said, trying to open his gluey eyes. "Don'hur'm'."

"Tom, Tom, it's just me. Wake up! Are you sick?" Tom felt a hand on his forehead. "You don't feel hot."

"Nahmk," Tom said. In his head it had been, *No, I'm okay.*

"Are you sick, Tom?"

"I'm okay," he said, more clearly (he hoped). Through the gunk in his eyes everything was blurry.

"You've been asleep a whole day."

Tom's eyes opened. He wiped sleep away, sat up a little. There were no monstrous hands, no feral teeth, and no feathers. "Hey, Da."

"Hey, yourself." His dad leaned forward and sniffed his breath. "You weren't drinking, were you?"

"Dad!" Tom sat up and glared at his father.

"Well, what am I supposed to think? I get back from getting

the groceries yesterday at eleven in the morning and you're out cold, and I keep checking on you throughout the day and you're still off in the land of Nod. And it's the next morning and you still haven't woken up!"

"I have now." Tom yawned. "Sort of."

"You weren't drinking? You didn't take any other kind of—"

"Dad!!"

"You're telling me you were just very tired. Twenty-four-hours-of-sleep tired?"

"It was a magic thing."

His father's mouth closed, his lips went thin, and he got that tight expression he always wore when Tom said the word *magic*.

"Well, come on, Da, what d'you reckon? I mean I only just slept this long once before—*exactly* like this—in New York. You're the one who lied to Cath about it and told her I have . . . whatever illness it was. . . ."

"Thomas Sebastian Yarbro!" His father was looking at him with an expression Tom had never seen before, halfway between gobsmacked and killing rage. Right now Tom didn't care, though he had a feeling he would later.

"How dense can you be, Da?" Tom had never spoken to his father like this before. He wasn't sure what had gotten into him, except that he was really, really, really ropeable, and his dad'd accused him of being a drug addict, when what'd really happened was that he was . . . was that he, Tom Yarbro, was the drug. "Didn't it occur to you to connect the two? Big sleep in New York, magic thing; big sleep a few days later in Sydney, possibly also a magic thing?"

The expression on his dad's face faded. "There's a stack of phone messages. Mostly Niki, Ron, and Scooter. You can't just dump your old friends when you get new ones. You need to call them back. Oh, and Jessica Chan rang."

"You what?"

"Something about another dress. Apparently it's an emergency."

"Da, you can't not talk about—"

"Tom, I can't." His father stopped, took a deep breath, looked right at Tom, into his eyes, but as if he didn't quite recognise him. "I just can't. I don't understand any of"—he waved his arm in the general direction of Mere's house—"*that*. I just don't. All I know is that you were . . . you were becoming like your mother, and now you're not. You're happy—well, mostly—and Mere had a lot to do with it, and I'm grateful. But that stuff scares me. I guess I'd rather you *had* been drinking, because that I'd understand."

Tom stared back at his father—his turn to be gobsmacked.

"I accept that it's real, but it doesn't mean that I *like* that it's real. How am I supposed to deal with knowing that I'll most likely outlive you? Or that the only way you can live much past forty is if you go mad like your mother?"

"Cheer up, maybe you'll have an accident and die first."

His dad sighed. "Very droll. Parents shouldn't outlive their kids."

"Actually, Lien says—"

"Your old history teacher?"

"Yeah. She says in the olden days parents mostly outlived their kids."

"Indeed. Infant mortality's still disgracefully high amongst Australia's indigenous population." Tom's father taught sociology at Sydney Uni and had lots of books with tedious titles like *Archaeology of the Meaning of the City* or *The Idea of the Theory of Knowledge,* which were written by people with names like Habermas, who Tom privately thought of as Mighty Mouse, and Foucault, who Tom thought of as . . . well, something pretty rude.

"I don't have anyone to talk about it with, Da."

"What about Mere? Or her granddaughter? Or that American girl?"

"I just met them, Da, and Esmeralda's . . ." Tom wanted to tell his dad what she'd done to him, but he didn't know how. "They're not family. I want to talk to *you,* to Cathy."

"Cathy doesn't know anything about—"

"I want to tell her."

"Do you think that's fair?" his father asked. It was not what Tom was expecting; usually his father stuck to repeating all Esmeralda's arguments for secrecy.

"How d'you mean, 'fair'?"

His father stood up, walked to Tom's balcony, treading on the fabrics underfoot. Tom winced. His dad looked out at Esmeralda's huge fig tree, Filomena. In the bright sunlight the leaves glowed. It was a cloudless day, but it didn't feel as hot as the last few days. Tom wondered what time it was. He sat up, realised that he was still wearing his clothes from yesterday. No wonder Da'd thought he'd been drinking.

Tom's father turned to him. "I think your sister's better off not knowing. I wish *I* didn't know."

"I hate having secrets from her. It's not fair to me or her."

"How's your sister going to feel when she discovers that you don't have long—"

"If I had a disease that was killing me, would you keep it a secret from her?"

His father didn't answer for a long time. "Okay, yes, I would tell her. But a disease is different. It's within the bounds of what one can expect from life. *This*, this isn't."

"Cath's suspicious, Dad. For the past year she's felt left out. Is that fair? Every time I talk to her she begs me to tell her what's going on, and I really, really, really want to. 'Cause it's all scary and weird and I need to talk to someone." Tom felt his eyes getting damp. He blinked. His dad looked away nervously.

"All right."

"You mean I can tell her?"

"Yes, tell her."

First his father made them both a huge fry-up breakfast. Sausages, eggs, onions, potatoes, tomatoes, cheese—even the bread was fried. All of it dripped grease and yumminess. Tom squeezed a tonne of oranges to make them as much juice as they needed to wash it all down. One of his few memories of his mother before she went crazy was that she only ever squeezed enough oranges to fill four small glasses. Tom was always left wanting more.

"It's fantastic, Da," he said, enjoying the not-quite-burnt onions. "Perfect."

"Isn't it?" said his dad. "Your mother would never let me make a real breakfast. She was against butter—too much cholesterol—and if you let anything get even vaguely brown, she'd get all upset about carcinogens."

Tom had never heard his father say anything negative about his mother before. He wondered if he'd somehow put the thought in his head, remembering about the tiny glasses of orange juice.

"Was that before she went mad?"

"Sometimes, Tom, I think she was born crazy. I met your mother when we were fourteen, and she was *always* obsessed with something or other: eating right, her motorbike—"

"Mum had a motorbike!"

"Oh, yeah. She used to be wild, your mum." His dad smiled softly, in a way that made Tom uncomfortable. He *really* hoped his dad wouldn't tell him what he was remembering. "Very wild. Her craziness was mostly good. Fun. Until she *really* lost it."

His father didn't need to say anything else. Tom remembered vividly the day his mother had attacked him and Cathy. He would never forget it.

"So, how are you enjoying having two new girlfriends?"

Tom blushed hot and prickling from head to toe. "They're not my girlfriends!"

His dad cracked up and Tom knew he'd been had.

"Bastard."

His dad kept grinning. "They're nice-looking girls."

Tom was torn between hotly retorting that Reason was way better than "nice-looking" and trying to ignore him. "I hadn't really noticed."

His dad laughed again.

"Dad!"

"Though it must be good for you to have kids your own age who have the, ah . . ."

"Who are magic-wielders, too?"

"Uh, yeah."

"It's all right." Tom thought about Jay-Tee dying, drinking magic from him; Reason off in New York City with tall, dark, handsome, and *very* poxy Danny. "Yeah, it's great. After breakfast I'll go over and see how they're doing."

"You're not going to call your sister?"

"I think I need to talk to Esmeralda first."

"Fair enough. Tell Mere hi from me."

Tom half nodded. He had a lot he wanted to say to Esmeralda; none of it involved passing on greetings.

Tom decided to see Jay-Tee first. He climbed from his dad's balcony to the front balcony of Esmeralda's. First he pressed his face against the glass of Reason's door, hoping she'd come home. But her room was empty, her bed unslept in.

He turned the door handle. Not locked. He opened the door slowly, peering through the door. No one there. He checked the bathroom and then tiptoed out into the hallway, pausing to listen for any movement. He didn't want to see Esmeralda until he was ready. He heard only birds outside, a car driving by— nothing from within the house. No noise from the kitchen, no noise from the door.

Tom crept along the hallway to Jay-Tee's room, stopped outside the door listening. Nothing. He knocked as quietly as he could. If Jay-Tee was there, he wanted her to hear, but not anyone (Esmeralda) downstairs.

"Jay-Tee?" No response.

He opened the door slowly, peeking his head around. Jay-Tee was in bed. He crept closer. There was a giant bruise on her cheekbone.

"Jay-Tee? Are you okay?"

He sat down on the bed beside her. "Jay-Tee?" She didn't stir or do any of the things a sleeping person should be doing. Tom could feel his heart beating faster.

He stared at her eyes. Her eyelids didn't even flicker. He held his hand up to her mouth. His hand shook; seconds went by. He felt nothing. He held his hand closer, bare millimetres away from her lips. This couldn't be real. Why wasn't she moving? Why wasn't she breathing?

"Please, Jay-Tee, breathe. Please."

Then he felt it, the slightest featherweight of warm air. Her breath on his hand. She was alive. Unconscious but alive. What had happened to her? He could think of an explanation. He hoped he was wrong.

What had Esmeralda done to her?

Tom sped out of the room, took the stairs three at a time, jumping the last six so that he landed in the downstairs hallway with a thud, and ran into the kitchen. Esmeralda jumped up, dropping paper and pen to the floor. She looked like she'd never done anything wrong in her entire life. Her scrubbed, fresh-looking face, her young-girl ponytail. Even in a faded T-shirt and jeans, she looked good. Her looks were a lie.

"Tom! Are you all right? You startled me."

Good, thought Tom.

"What's wrong?" she asked.

As if you didn't know! Tom found that he was shaking too much to get his mouth open. The room was shifting as if he were viewing it through a kaleidoscope. He couldn't see anything but true shapes: triangles, squares, hexagons, rhombuses, and trapezoids.

"What did you do to Jay-Tee?" he shouted at the mass of geometric shapes that had been Esmeralda. "Did you drink her dry? I know you lied to me, I know you drank from me. Have you done it to her now? Is Jay-Tee going to die today? I'll kill you if she dies. I'll kill you." Tom's voice was tight, as if his vocal cords were ready to snap.

"Tom, I—"

"Lied to me, lied to Jay-Tee, lied to Reason. Her mum was right to run away from you. You're evil. You're worse than Jason Blake. How could you do that to me? If you needed magic, I'd've given you some of mine. Like I did for Jay-Tee. Why'd you just *take* it from me?"

"I didn't—"

"You know what? I don't even know why I'm talking to you. What are you going to do? Tell me more lies? It's pointless. I'm going to go upstairs and give Jay-Tee some more magic—"

"Tom!" Esmeralda took a step forward, reached out a hand to touch him with her trapezoidal fingers. Tom pulled the shapes towards him, twisting them into acute triangles, sharp and broken.

Esmeralda cascaded into a shower of jagged shapes. She screamed. "No!"

Tom fell, the kitchen falling apart as he descended. A dog's breakfast of triangles, rhombuses, and trapezoids. When he hit the floor, his eyes snapped shut. Tom watched dodecahedrons form and crumble on the backs of his eyelids. Darkness threatened to draw him down, but he forced his eyes open and the shapes trickled away from him. The room lost its true shapes, became Esmeralda's kitchen again.

"Tom," Esmeralda said, leaning over him. "You lost your temper. You know you can't ever lose—"

"I know." It had felt so good, though. Like something his body had always wanted to do, needed to do. "What's wrong with your hand?"

"You broke three of my fingers."

"I hope it hurts." Tom had never felt as calm as he did lying on the cool tiles of Esmeralda's kitchen floor. "Did you drink from Jay-Tee?"

"No."

"Then what happened to her?"

"Tom, sit up. We need to talk."

"We *are* talking. I'm asking you questions. Why did you drink from me without asking?"

Esmeralda sat beside him, nursing her broken fingers: the index, middle, and ring fingers of her right hand. They were all bending the wrong way and swelling up into weird potato fingers.

I did that, thought Tom, satisfied. Her hands and arms were covered with tiny dots of blood. Like the creature had left on him and Jay-Tee.

"I was afraid."

"Afraid that I'd say no if you'd asked me the real question?"

She nodded. "Afraid of dying."

"I trusted you. You betrayed me."

Esmeralda's cheeks went red. "I did. I betrayed you. I lied to you. I took your magic without asking. There aren't any excuses, but I was close to dying. I was afraid. I shouldn't have done it. I should have asked you. It was wrong."

"Very wrong."

She nodded. "But I don't need to anymore."

"Don't need to what?" Her fingers were so swollen they

were like pumpkin fingers. The middle one was bleeding slowly from the fingernail.

"Take anyone else's magic."

"Then why did you take Jay-Tee's?"

"Tom! I *gave* her magic—at least I tried to. I didn't take it away."

"Sure you did." Tom didn't believe her, but her lies weren't making him angry anymore. He didn't think he had any anger left in him. He would probably live the rest of his life (which he'd just made shorter) without ever losing his temper again. Not many people could say that.

"Look at my fingers, Tom."

Tom laughed. "I *am* looking at your fingers."

The middle finger moved, began to straighten. The blood on the fingernail dried; the swelling started to deflate, like a balloon slowly losing air. Then the index finger straightened and began to shrink, then lastly, the ring finger. They were unbroken. Slowly Esmeralda flexed each one. They moved as if they'd never been broken.

Tom sat up, stared at Esmeralda, who was looking back at him with the same brown eyes as Reason. "How?"

"I have magic, Tom. I don't need to steal Jay-Tee's."

"But in New York . . ."

"Sit down at the table with me, Tom. Let me get you a cold drink."

Tom stood up, feeling wobbly, walked to the table, pulled out a stool, sat down. How had she done that? Why was he doing what she told him to?

Esmeralda was looking at her right hand as if she didn't believe it, either. "You know the old man? The one guarding the door? He did something to me. Put his magic inside me. He didn't ask, either, just pushed it into me. I thought he was killing me, but he wasn't. Now I'm full of it, Tom. I can feel his magic in every cell. I feel different. I'm stronger than I've ever been. I'm not dying anymore. Every time I do magic now I feel stronger, not weaker."

"The old man?" Tom tried to take in what she had told him. He took in the tiny wounds all over her arms, looked at his own fingers. The dots there were dried, but they were still there. "When he sent that golem through, it was trying to give us magic?"

Esmeralda nodded. "I think so."

"He's trying to get through the door to *save* us?"

"I don't know what he wants. I tried to give some of his magic to Jay-Tee, but . . . well, it didn't work. It made her sick."

Tom looked at Esmeralda, trying to read her face, but he didn't have Jay-Tee's ability. He had no idea whether she was lying or not.

"Her body couldn't take his magic."

"His magic isn't like ours?"

"No, it's something different."

Tom tried to take this in. Mere had unbroken her fingers. He hadn't even known something that complicated was possible. There were so many questions he wanted to ask her. "Why didn't it work for Jay-Tee?"

"I don't know."

"Could you give it to me?

"We could try, but it was bad for Jay-Tee. She was convuls-ing. . . . I thought she was going to die. But I tried to give her a lot. Maybe if I only gave you a little . . ."

"Do you think she'll be okay?"

"I do. Her cells . . . When I look at them they don't seem any more damaged than they already were."

"What do you mean?"

"What I tried to give her didn't take, but I don't think it damaged her. Her body fought it, expelled it."

"So where did it go?"

"I don't know. Into the air? Maybe it burned up in her fever. I think she's okay, Tom."

"But you're not sure?"

"No."

"If she wakes up okay, will she have enough magic to last a little while longer?"

"Yes. I'm just not sure how much longer. She has the magic you gave her and whatever skerrick she had herself."

Tom nodded, satisfied with Esmeralda's answer. "I'm going to go sit by her."

"Yes," Esmeralda said, as if she were giving him her permis-sion. Tom was thankful that she made no move to follow him.

22

Waking

Jay-Tee woke to bright daylight stinging her eyes, making them water. She closed them again. She woke to a thudding pain in her head, but when she shifted position there was just more pain. Her throat was dry and raspy. She coughed.

"Here's some water."

Jay-Tee turned to the voice, to Tom. She half opened her eyes, sat up, groaned, took it from him. "Thanks," she said, draining the glass and holding it out for more. Tom poured the water quickly, splashing drops of it onto her hand.

He stacked a monster pile of pillows and cushions behind Jay-Tee. She leaned back into them, relieved that her muscles no longer had to work to hold her up. Everything ached.

"My head hurts," she told Tom. Talking made her cough. She finished the water and then held out her glass for more. Tom poured it.

"Want me to get you some aspirin?"

Jay-Tee nodded and Tom went away. She drained the glass again. It had no effect on her thirst, on her feeling of dryness. The water vanished before it reached the back of her throat, leaving her mouth as moisture-free as a ten-day-old slice of bread. But the jug of water was on the floor. The thought of getting out of bed to refill her glass was too much.

She closed her eyes, resting the empty water glass on her lap and thinking about what Esmeralda had done to her. Jay-Tee felt terrible, but she didn't have that floating-away feeling, she didn't feel like she was dying. Not immediately, anyway. What had Esmeralda said? It hurt trying to think complicated thoughts.

Tom came back with a bottle of aspirin and shook two onto her palm. She swallowed them. Their journey down her parched throat was scratchy and uncomfortable. "Could you close the curtains, Tom? Make it less bright?"

She heard him bustling with them. When the other side of her eyelids got darker, she ventured to half open them again. The searing whiteness had softened, making the room shadowed and spooky. Much better.

Tom came and sat beside her. "More water?"

She held out the glass, drained it, held it out for more until Tom had emptied the jug and gone into the bathroom to fill it again.

"Thirsty," she said.

"Well, der," Tom said, smiling at her. He had a nice smile, she decided. White teeth. Very blue eyes. She wondered if they seemed so blue because his skin was so pale.

"You're so white. You've got lots of freckles," she told him, draining her glass again.

"Yeah, and invisible eyebrows."

"I can see your eyebrows. They're goldy-white."

"Ah, yeah. Do you think you're brain-damaged, Jay-Tee?"

Jay-Tee giggled. "Maybe. My brain sure does hurt."

"Do you know what happened?"

"Esmeralda did something to me. I thought she was steal-ing my magic, but she didn't." *Because I still have magic and I'm alive.* Jay-Tee frowned. What had Esmeralda done? "She put her hands on me, but they hurt. Her fingers put something in me, something sharp and horrible. Worms with teeth."

Tom poured her more water. She drank it, her mouth finally feeling a little damp. She held the glass out for more.

"I swear you're going to pee for a month."

Jay-Tee began to shrug but it hurt. She tried an eye-roll, but that shifted the pain of her headache from the back of her skull to her eyes. She settled for silence.

"Do you know why Esmeralda hurt you?"

Jay-Tee went to shake her head before she remembered the ow-ness of any movement. Instead she said, "I thought she was trying to suck me dry. Take everything. But she didn't: I'm alive. Why am I alive, Tom?"

"Esmeralda claims she thought she was giving you magic, but she says your body didn't like it."

"Huh." She shook her head a fraction, careful not to shift the headache again. "Didn't feel like magic."

"The old man's magic," Tom said. "It's different. *Really* dif-ferent. Esmeralda's turned into a superwitch. She unbroke her fingers."

"She . . . ?"

"She, uh . . . her fingers were broken and she fixed them with magic."

"She broke her fingers?"

"They broke, but she fixed them."

"What do you mean?

"I saw her do it. Her fingers unbent, the swelling disappeared, and then they weren't broken anymore. It was—"

"Freaky?"

"Bloody oath."

Jay-Tee half smiled. "'Bloody oath.' That's funny. But how did her fingers get broken?" Jay-Tee shifted her head to look at Tom's face.

He blushed.

"What? What happened?"

Tom looked down. "I lost my temper."

"You broke them!" Jay-Tee winced, she'd spoken too loud. "You punished her?"

Tom nodded. "It felt good."

"Mere's like me, Tom. She's been bad. Badder than me, because I asked you if it was okay. I didn't want to be like *him*. She deserved broken fingers."

Tom looked confused. "Asked what?" Then he blushed again. "Oh, right," he said. "She *should* have asked."

"Mere was afraid. She should have trusted you. Trusted that you'd be good. I did."

"What would you have done if I'd said no?"

"Died," Jay-Tee said. "Yesterday, with the cutting magic inside me . . . Are you sure it was magic?"

"Esmeralda thinks so."

"Huh. Anyway, when the cutting got really bad, I thought I was dead. I floated. It was really boring. Being alive is better."

"Too right it is."

"I definitely want to make it past fifteen."

"Yeah, I want you to, too. And Reason, and me."

"Reason's sure there's an answer. Well, she was before she went through the door."

"Ree told you that?" Tom's tone was sharp. Jay-Tee wondered what was bothering him.

"No, but when Mere was explaining magic to her, the limitations and everything? She got this look."

"What look?"

"Reason gets this look when she's figuring things out, looking for answers. She's a . . . a solver of problems. I think it's the math thing. I think she thinks our problem is a math thing. I hope she's right."

"Me, too." Tom was smiling again. He looked warm and sort of glowy. Jay-Tee blinked, wondered if she was seeing right.

"So you're saying Esmeralda has this new kind of magic? Where did it come from?"

"The old man—"

"The guarding-the-door old man?"

"Yes. Esmeralda has the same little bites on her arms that we had when the golem bit us, same as what Reason had."

"Huh. It did feel like that. But the golem thing gave me a tiny nip compared to what Esmeralda forced inside me." Jay-Tee paused. "You know, Reason felt different afterwards. After the golem attacked her. Out of kilter."

Tom nodded, remembering. "I touched her and she felt wrong. Too smooth, like her arm was made of metal, not flesh."

"She made way too much light. Her magic was so big she couldn't control it!"

"You're right. Reason must have some of the old man's magic, too."

Jay-Tee closed her eyes. She could see it. That stuff coming out of the door, trying to suck Esmeralda into it. That stuff had been the same color as the old man's golem. Was that what had gone inside her? Jay-Tee's head hurt. "Where's Mere?"

"In the kitchen, watching the door."

"And Reason?"

"Still in New York City. I haven't talked to her since yesterday morning, though. After . . . after you drank from me I slept. A lot. It's not long since I woke up."

"Okay, then," Jay-Tee said, pleased to be decisive. "Let's call Reason. We have to tell her about this."

23
Inside and Outside

A song rang out. Or a portion of it. I wondered why it stopped so abruptly; then it started again, the same fragment of music. I'd heard it before somewhere, but I couldn't think where. Everything had been dark—now it was lighter.

"Hello," Danny said, sleep in both syllables. "Oh, hi, Julieta."

I heard the sound of a voice far away and small, but not any of the words. I opened my eyes, shifted a little closer to where Danny was. He didn't have a shirt on. Neither did I. I remembered why. I pulled the sheet up higher. I blushed, my cheeks so hot my eyes watered.

"Why didn't you tell me?" Danny asked. "Julieta? How long have you got?"

I was glad I couldn't hear anything Jay-Tee said. I tried not to listen to what Danny was saying, tried to think of other things, like the old man's golem inside me, like what Danny and I had done together. If Jay-Tee wasn't already cranky with me, that piece of news would make her totally ropeable. For a second I wished Sarafina had never gone mad and that we were still on the road, out bush, her and me. No magic, no madness, no imminent death, no evil grandparents, no New York City. And no friends to be cranky with me. We could go back to Jilkminggan like I'd always wanted. The women there could teach me more stories about their mermaid ancestor, the munga-munga.

"Leave Reason out of it—"

Oh, great, I thought.

"Come on, Julieta. Why didn't you—"

I eased myself back to the other side of the bed. It was a big bed. I had to stop listening to this. I should get up, shower or something.

"Julieta, you're my sister. Of course I wanted to know!" Danny looked in my direction, but I wasn't sure he saw me. "What if I never see you again? I don't want to lose you all over again!"

Jay-Tee said something that made him laugh, but it was a bitter laugh. "Friends are *not* the same as family, Julieta. We're Galeanos." He turned his back to me, lowered his voice. "You know I love you, right? I wish you'd come to me instead of running—"

Danny didn't say anything for a long time, then he was murmuring that it was okay, that he was sorry. I imagined Jay-Tee crying. I had to stop listening. I threw myself into the Fibonacci series, let myself float away on the wave of each number: 0, 1, 1, 2, 3, 5, 8, 13, 21, 34, 55, 89, 144, 233, 377, 610, 987, 1597, 2584, 4181 . . . A spiral unravelled in my head. It was grey-brown, the room filled with the smell of limes. I was floating in it, drowning in it.

"Reason!"

I blinked, spluttered. Opened my eyes on Danny's bedroom. New York City. Danny lying by my side.

"Reason!" Danny called out again as if I wasn't lying there right next to him. He had his hand over the receiver.

"Julieta wants to talk to you," he said after a moment, handing me his mobile phone.

I took it but didn't look at Danny directly. "Hi," I said into the receiver, hoping I didn't sound like . . . I wasn't quite sure what it was I didn't want to sound like. I hoped Jay-Tee wouldn't yell at me.

"Hah," Jay-Tee said. "You sound sleepy, too. Isn't it like four in the afternoon there?" She didn't remotely sound like she'd just had an intense conversation with her brother.

I looked at my watch. "No, it's 6:13 PM. We, ah, we were, um, doing a lot of research and running around yest—today and didn't sleep much last night and—"

"Sure," Jay-Tee said. "We've been sleepy, too."

"You do sound kind of funny."

"My head got banged," Jay-Tee said, as if it was nothing. "I'm fuzzy."

"Are you okay?"

"Oh, yes," she said. "Just fuzzy."

"I'm, ah, about telling your brother—"

"It's okay. I mean, I'm mad at you. You shouldn't have told him. But you did. So, you know . . . Let's just say we're even, okay? I didn't exactly tell you stuff I should've when you first came to New York. You know, with *him* and everything. So we're even, right?"

"Okay." I shifted back onto the pillows, holding the sheet to my throat. I was sore. My thigh muscles ached. Danny and I, we hadn't gone to sleep until long after the sun had come up. My face got even hotter. I decided not to think about it. I closed my eyes. On the backs of my eyelids I saw the curve of muscles across Danny's stomach and my hand touching them. I wasn't sure Jay-Tee would still think we were even when she found out.

"We've been running around, too," Jay-Tee continued. "Well, apart from the monster-huge sleeps."

Danny slipped out from the sheets. I watched his back as he retreated into the bathroom.

"Monster-huge sleeps?" I peered over the edge of the bed and found the clothing I'd been wearing. I held the phone between the side of my head and my shoulder and tried to get the T-shirt on but ended up tangled. I heard the sound of a shower going on.

"Yeah, ah, well—"

"Can you hang on a sec?"

"Sure."

I put the phone down and got my makeshift PJs on. "Okay. What's happening?"

"The old man gave Mere his magic."

"What?"

"He or one of his golems got into Mere just like it got into you. Only it stayed in. It gave her magic and then she gave it to me. But it cut me up, made me really sick—"

"Cut you?"

"Like worms with sharp teeth. She thought it would help me. I'm . . ." Jay-Tee hesitated. "My magic's worn thin. Mere thought I was dying. I *was* dying, *am* dying—so she thought it would help me. But it didn't work for me the way it did for her. I got really, really sick. Convulsions and everything. You should see my bruises."

"You were dying?" But I wasn't anywhere near finding a way to keep her alive. Jay-Tee couldn't die so soon.

"Uh-huh. I felt thin, like a piece of saran wrap."

"Like *what?*" Jay-Tee had almost died? She couldn't die. Not *yet*.

"Like a piece of glass. As if you could see right through me and I was about to float away. It was . . . it was horrible."

"It sounds horrible." How did I feel? Was I lighter than I had been? Hollow? I wished I could turn my gaze on myself, see my own rust.

"Yeah, but I'm okay now. For the moment . . ."

"But . . . how did you get bruised?" I was bruised, too, but my bruises felt almost good. I looked at the closed door to the bathroom, heard the sound of Danny showering, wondered if he was thinking about washing me off his skin. I hoped not. I blushed again.

"The magic Mere put inside me—it made me convulse. It kept pushing deeper and deeper into me, and my body tried to fight it. It didn't do that to you. We think you're more powerful now, like Mere." Jay-Tee's voice sounded far away, suddenly exhausted.

The phone was muffled, then Tom came on. "Hi, Ree. Jay-Tee has to lie down. That stuff, whatever Esmeralda did to her, it *really* hurt her," he whispered. Then he asked a question in such a soft voice that the only way I could tell it was a question was by his rising tone at the end.

"What?"

"Hang on a mo." I heard his hand going over the receiver and sounds in the background that I couldn't figure out. "Okay, I'm in your room now. When the golem got inside you? We think it gave you magic. Like what happened to Esmeralda."

"Magic? No, I don't think so. . . ." I trailed off. I could feel it inside me. Not as sharp as it had been, but prickling at me, deep inside, moving inside the marrow of my bones. "I don't think he made me powerful."

"But remember? It bit Jay-Tee and me, but it *burrowed* into you. And when we were having that lesson—your light was so intense, so out-of-control bright."

"But it came back out again. It didn't stay. It went back under the door. Remember?"

"That's because we chucked it out. Me and Jay-Tee and you."

"No." It didn't make sense. A different kind of magic? Wasn't that like saying there were different kinds of gravity?

"Esmeralda can do bigger magic now. What if you can, too?"

"It didn't stay in me." Except that it was inside me now.

"Are you sure, Reason? Esmeralda might not die now. This might change everything. So maybe you won't have to die, either. Maybe me, too. Jay-Tee almost died."

"She really almost died?"

"Yes. Her magic ran out. Esmeralda reckons the old man's doesn't run out."

"It has to have limits. Everything has limits."

The shower in the bathroom shut off. I slid out of Danny's bed, took a few steps to the door, and was shocked to discover that walking was ouchie. I glanced back at the crumpled bed. What would Sarafina say? I'd had sex for the first time at the same way-too-young age she had, and just as stupidly I hadn't used any protection. Everything she'd told me about sex diseases—AIDS and gonorrhoea and syphilis and chlamydia (which somehow also affected koalas—I didn't want to think about that)—and none of it had crossed my mind even once.

"Esmeralda doesn't think this magic has any limits."

"But it does. It didn't work for Jay-Tee."

"Ree, Esmeralda says using this magic makes her stronger."

"But how does it work? Where's the energy coming from? If it doesn't take energy from her body, where does it come from?" Danny came out of the shower, a towel tied around his waist. He looked at me, half smiled. I smiled back and my cheeks got hot. I nodded and walked out of his room, shutting the door behind me and leaning on it. What was Danny thinking? Was he regretting what had happened?

"Ree? You still there? Why wouldn't it work?"

"Sorry, Tom. I need to think about all of this." The living room looked as dark as it had when I'd left my (Jay-Tee's) room last night, looking for something to eat. Eighteen hours ago. I wondered when time would stop running circles around me, always going either too fast or too slow for me to get a grip on it.

"Esmeralda really is much more powerful. She healed her broken fingers. Right in front of me."

"She had broken fingers?"

"Yeah, long story. Her healing herself was heaps more impressive than making light, let me tell you. It took *seconds*."

"I bet."

"You don't think you're supermagic, too?"

"I don't think so." I moved away from Danny's door and into the kitchen, ignoring the soreness of every step. I yawned. "I'm hungry."

"The light you made during the magic lesson in the cottage. It was so big, Reason. And remember? You said you didn't feel at all drained."

I opened the fridge door: there was still no food in it. I wished Danny had as much food in his fridge as beer. If there was magic coursing through me like Tom thought, why didn't food appear out of thin air? *That* would be useful.

"Do you feel different?"

I did feel different. But not just from what Cansino had done to me.

There was a loud buzzing sound and Danny walked over to the lift, pressed a button there, and spoke to it.

"Does Esmeralda look any different?"

Danny pressed a button to make the lift go. I hoped he'd ordered some food or something. Like Esmeralda phoning up and then, magically, thirty minutes later—pizza at the front door.

"No, not really."

"So your only evidence for this new kind of magic is Esmeralda healing her fingers?"

Tom started to answer, but I didn't hear what he said. The lift doors had opened and Jason Blake was stepping into Danny's apartment.

"Oh, no," I said, cutting across Tom.

"What? What?"

"My grandfather is here. Jason—" The phone flew out of my hands and halfway across Danny's flat.

24
Strong Magic

"Reason? Reason?" The phone had gone dead. Tom redialled and got a strange beeping sound. He tried Danny's landline. It rang and rang until Danny's smooth movie-star voice announced, "You missed me. If you're feeling it, leave a message. If you're not, well, that's cool. Catch you later." *Wanker,* thought Tom, before putting the phone back in his pocket and running downstairs.

"Esmeralda! Esmeralda!" She wasn't in the kitchen. "Esmeralda!"

Where could she be? What should he do? Jay-Tee was dead to the world upstairs. He fished his phone out and dialled Danny's mobile again. This time it went through to voicemail with an equally annoying message. "Hi," Tom said, "it's me, Tom. Could you call back?" He gave the mobile number just in case. "I'm worried. Are you okay, Ree? Let us know." He tried the landline again with the same result, but this time he left a message.

Esmeralda came out of the bathroom. *Good,* he thought, *she'll have some clue what to do.* Then he remembered he didn't trust her anymore.

"What's wrong, Tom?"

"Jason Blake's got Reason. We were on the phone talking, you know, and then she said that Blake'd shown up, and then the phone clicked off, and I've rung and rung but there's no answer."

Esmeralda said nothing, but the expression on her face was not happy. Tom found that he was biting his bottom lip. He stopped.

"What would he want with her?" Tom asked, though of course he could think of many things Blake'd want from Reason.

Esmeralda raised an eyebrow. "More magic. A longer life."

"We have to do something."

"We do. We will. First, though, we'll need winter clothes."

"We're going through the door?" Tom asked, feeling stupid as soon as the words left his mouth. How else were they going to rescue her?

Esmeralda nodded. "Is Jay-Tee awake?"

"She was, but then she got tired again. Do you want me to check on her?"

"No, I'll do it. Run next door and get clothes, enough for a couple of days, toothbrush, whatever else you'll need. Tell your father you're going, that you're not sure when you'll be back."

Tom returned with a chock-a-block backpack dangling from his left shoulder, carrying a big winter coat with pockets stuffed with other winter gear, and his ears full of his dad's messages to Cathy, which Tom wasn't at all sure he'd have a chance to deliver.

Jay-Tee was sitting at the kitchen table eating porridge, looking terrible. The bruise on her cheekbone was red, purple, and blue. There was a bandage on her hand.

"You're not coming," he said, dumping his stuff at the other end of the table.

Jay-Tee pulled a face. "Can if I want."

"Sure, but you can't if your body won't let you."

Jay-Tee began what looked like a shrug and then stopped, wincing.

Tom raised his eyebrows and said, "See?" because his eyebrows were not renowned for their visibility. Then he remembered Jay-Tee claiming *she* could see them.

"I'm not coming," she admitted, "but I couldn't stay in bed. Not with Reason . . ." She blinked, and Tom realised how upset she was. He felt stupid. Of course she was upset. Jason Blake scared her so much she wouldn't even say his name, and now he had Reason.

"There you are, Tom," Esmeralda said as she entered the kitchen carrying her briefcase and a black leather winter coat lined with sheepskin. Even folded over her arm Tom could see how elegant its lines were.

"Lucky you have a spare coat," he said. "What with the other one getting eaten by the door and . . ."

Jay-Tee grimaced. Tom wondered if it was meant to be a smirk or a smile. "Second spare," she said. "She's lost two now."

"When did that—"

"How are you feeling, Jay-Tee?" Esmeralda asked, ignoring the discussion of her coats.

"Sore, achey. But I'll live. For a while, anyway."

"Has Reason rung?" Tom asked.

"No," Esmeralda said, turning back to Jay-Tee. "Do you think you're going to be up for this?"

"Probably not, but I'd rather be here than lying in bed upstairs *imagining* what was happening."

"Up for what?" Tom asked.

"I'm going to try a spell on my own, to get the door open and to make me strong enough to deal with the old man on the other side."

"Oh," Tom said. "Is that all?"

"Very droll," Esmeralda said, moving closer to the door. Tom noticed there were even more feathers lining the bottom now. Mostly green ones that were longer and curvier than the first lot they'd magicked.

"That sounds like a big spell. Won't it be kind of risky?"

She nodded. "I'll need you and Jay-Tee to keep an eye on me. If it starts to look dangerous or too strange, I'm depending on you both to pull me out of it."

"How, exactly? You're a lot more powerful than we are now. Are we supposed to slap you or something?"

"If you need to," Esmeralda said. "But I don't think it should come to that. A gentle shake should be enough."

She closed her eyes and reached out towards the door. Tom grabbed her hand. "Esmeralda. You don't know anything about the old man's magic. It might not be safe. You haven't used it for a spell this big—"

"I'd say healing broken bones was rather large."

"But how do you know what you're doing?"

"Reason is in danger. I have to rescue her."

"I know that." Tom was close to shouting. "But how's it going to help her if you wind up dead?" He looked at her right hand. Her fingers moved as they always had, as if he'd never lost his temper. Tom thought about all the things Esmeralda could do with a magic that didn't eat up your life. She would never steal from him again. If this magic was everything she thought it was, it would mean he could trust her again.

"That won't happen."

"How do you know? What if this magic lulls you into thinking everything's right as rain and then burns you up? Look at Jay-Tee! Look what the old man's magic has done to her."

"Hey! I don't look that bad."

"Yes, you do," Esmeralda said. "Tom, everything you say is reasonable. But sometimes you have to take risks. Think of the old man. *Old* man, Tom. He's been using this magic for a very, very long time without ill effect—"

"Without *ill effect!* Reason says he's some kind of monster!"

"Without his magic, Tom, I'd be dead already. Every second I live from now on is a bonus. I want to rescue my granddaughter."

"But it nearly killed Jay-Tee. What if it's turning toxic inside you as we're talking?"

"It's not turning toxic, Tom. It feels right inside me. It feels like it belongs."

"Doesn't mean you can trust your feelings."

"Tom, this argument is over. I'm doing this."

Esmeralda closed her eyes and put her hand palm first on the door. The wood began to ripple outwards from her fingers. A metal-against-metal sound started small and grew. Tom and Jay-Tee put their hands over their ears and looked at each other.

25
Jason Blake

Danny's phone landed on the other side of the television with a sharp crack. Pieces of it skidded across the floor, one stopping in front of Jay-Tee's bedroom, another near the far windows.

Danny glanced at his broken phone and then turned to Jason Blake. "You're the jerk who was messing with my sister."

Jason Blake nodded, agreeing that he was.

"Get out," Danny said, stabbing the lift button. The doors opened immediately.

"I don't think so. I need to speak with my granddaughter."

He was looking at me, not Danny, his stare eerily like old man Cansino's. I stared back at him as if I was unafraid.

"She doesn't want to speak to you."

"I think she does."

"Not really," I said, speaking for myself. "I'd like you to leave."

Blake flicked his hand, and something arced through the air at me. I caught it. Grey-brown, almost like putty. A piece of the old man. It even smelled like him, fresh-baked bread. It began to sink into my hands, sharp and biting. "No," I said, concentrating on the golden spiral, letting it uncurl within me, growing wider and wider, expelling the old man's stuff so that it bubbled up into my hand. I shaped it into a perfect ball, tossed it back at him.

Blake caught the ball, held it lightly in his left hand, not bothering to watch as it sank back into him. "Well done. I see you've already met Señor Raul Emilio Jesús Cansino? I thought as much."

"Who?" I said, but then I remembered that name. I'd seen it etched on marble in the cemetery on the other side of the door. The cemetery in Sydney. The one Tom had shown me, where the remains of my family were kept. "Died 1823."

"Except he didn't," Jason Blake said, "did he?" He took a step towards me.

"All right, that's enough," Danny said, moving closer. Blake was tall, but Danny was taller. He loomed over him. "Get back in the elevator."

The smell of baking bread became more intense. One of the kitchen stools flew past me. I called out. Danny turned just in time for it to hit him full in the face and knock him over.

My grandfather dashed across the room. I stepped back, running into the kitchen table. He reached out and grabbed my shoulders. His hands were hot, burning my skin. I screamed. Something inside me began tearing itself loose, racing through my body towards Blake's hands, into his body. He was seizing my magic.

"No!" I yelled. "No!"

"I don't have to ask anymore."

I closed my eyes, reached for my ammonite in a pocket that wasn't there. I tried to clear my mind without it—I thought of the night sky out bush, filled with tens of thousands of stars, too many to count at a glance. I coaxed my Fibonaccis, prodded them to unfurl inside me, radiate out, but they curled tight, into an Archimedean spiral, not golden, the distance between each coil the same, like a roll of paper, not like my ammonite. And then the spiral wasn't even that. It unravelled, raced burning through my veins, through my skin, into Jason Blake.

He was not the Jason Blake he had been, cautiously using only enough to keep from going insane. Taking other people's magic in only the most economic of ways—asking, never taking. Taking used too much magic.

But he was stripping me bare. Through blurred eyes I saw the magic growing in him—the old man's magic floated in every part of my grandfather's body. And something else, too: Jason Blake was related to old man Cansino. He was a Cansino, too.

"Asshole," I heard Danny say from somewhere far away.

Jason Blake grunted; the burning pressure of his hands lifted. The flood of magic stopped. Shockingly sudden. I fell back, landed hard on my arse.

"Get up," Danny said, grabbing my hand. "You have to get dressed. We have to go."

Jason Blake was unconscious on the floor. A broken stool lay beside him.

I stood up and wobbled. Danny steadied me. I looked up at his face. His cheek was bleeding. A trickle of blood ran down his jaw onto his neck.

"We have to go now. Before he wakes up and starts throwing furniture again." Danny hauled me over to Jay-Tee's room. I got dressed as quick as I could, stuffed my ammonite into my pocket. I've had a lot of practise getting dressed on the run, grabbing everything, exiting out the nearest door or window. Even with the awkward winter clothes and in my shaky state I was fast.

Danny dragged me to the lift. As we stepped around Jason Blake he groaned, his eyelids fluttering before closing again. Danny punched the button and the doors sprang open. We lurched inside, stabbing the button for the ground floor.

The door slid shut just as Jason Blake started to stir.

Stepping outside was like walking into a freezer. I shivered, hugged myself. Jumped as a truck's horn blasted loud enough to wake the dead. On the other side of the highway, lights gleamed out across the black of the Hudson River. The river was the only true darkness I could see. The sky glowed orange-brown from the city and its pollution.

Danny grabbed my arm and started walking as fast as he could. I stumbled, struggling to keep up with him.

"Where are we going?" I asked, my words emerging in puffs of condensation.

"Away from your grandfather. What did he do to you?"

"Stole my magic."

"Bastard. All of it?"

"No, but enough. I don't . . . I don't feel very strong."

Danny picked up his pace, dragged me around the corner of the nearest busy street, and turned off the highway.

"Where should we go?"

"Away from your grandfather."

"He'll follow us. You don't understand. He has *so* much magic now." I coughed. The cold burned my lungs. "He'll find me wherever I go."

Danny kept dragging me along the street. "There has to be somewhere he won't find us."

I couldn't think of anywhere, but I could think of someone who might protect us. It was risky. "We could go back to the old man."

"The old man? You figure he can handle your grandfather?"

I nodded. "They might be doing this together, though. . . ."

"Then why didn't the old man try"—Danny lowered his voice—"to steal your magic? He didn't, did he?"

I shook my head.

"If we go anywhere else, what will happen?"

"Blake'll take the rest—"

"Let's get a cab," Danny said, sticking out his arm and moving onto the road. A yellow taxi pulled up straightaway. Danny looked surprised.

"Hurry," I said, opening the door and scooting to the other side. Danny jumped in after me.

"Where to?" the driver asked.

"East," Danny said. "Seventh Street and Avenue B."

Danny sank back next to me. He reached out and squeezed my hand.

Something tugging at me sharply. I twisted around to look out the back window. Jason Blake was running towards us.

"He's coming."

Danny turned. "Damn."

I leaned forward to the driver. "Do you think you can go faster? Please?"

The driver started to tell me no. "I'm going as fast—"

"There's twenty bucks in it for you if you can get us across town in less than ten," Danny said.

The driver looked in the rear mirror, caught Danny's eye. "Make it fifty and I'll see what I can do. And you pay any fines if those policemen bust me."

"Done." Danny fished out a few bills and handed them over.

"Put your seatbelts on!" the driver told us. He pressed heavily on the accelerator.

I turned and saw Jason Blake less than a metre behind.

26
A Different Kind of Magic

Jay-Tee wondered if the old man's magic was chewing Mere up. It didn't look like it. She hadn't moved an inch since she'd put her hand on the door, closed her eyes, and shut Jay-Tee and Tom out. She stood still and steady, her skin glistening with a light coating of sweat, as if she'd slept in Central Park overnight and woken to find herself covered with dew. The door, on the other hand, had gone totally wack, making the most awful high-pitched metallic noises, bucking and kicking like an enraged horse.

"This is foul," Tom said, putting down Mere's phone for what seemed like the hundredth time. Danny and Reason still weren't answering. "She shouldn't be doing this."

"But we have to save Reason," Jay-Tee said, even though she sort of agreed with Tom. Esmeralda *was* messing around with magic—something Jay-Tee's father had told her never to do. Hell, something *Mere* had told them not to do. (And which, naturally, Jay-Tee had done over and over again, with the fabulous result of almost dying at fifteen years of age.) But Mere was forty-five. She'd said she was all about caution, but after one dose of the old man's magic, here she was experimenting like crazy, almost wiping out Jay-Tee and now possibly killing herself. "Anyways, she's doing it, isn't she?" Jay-Tee continued. "Nothing we can do now. Let it go, Tom."

"Easy for you to say."

"Huh?" The door let out a shudder and then an even louder high-pitched metal scream. Neither of them jumped, they were used to it now. Besides, Jay-Tee was drained beyond jumping.

"You go along with whatever Esmeralda says."

She stared at Tom. "Excuse me? Ah, little flashback, you know, to before you knew Esmeralda had drunk from you and you thought she was God's gift to the universe."

Tom's pale skin went even whiter, making the freckles stand out. His lips got really thin. Then he let out a big breath that turned into a sigh. "I just wish there was something we could do. How long has it been now?"

"Four minutes later than when you last asked me."

"So, fifteen minutes?"

Jay-Tee nodded. She reached over and patted Tom's shoulder. "It'll be okay," she told him, though she wasn't at all sure that it would be. "Nobody's perfect. Not Esmeralda or Reason or anyone. You just have to—"

Esmeralda had begun to move, her hand reaching to turn the doorknob. Suddenly her whole body shook. Her head and arm and back snapped back violently, looking like they would break at any moment. But her right hand grasped the doorknob and started to turn it.

Tom stood and moved toward her. Jay-Tee tried to stand

up, wobbled, had to steady herself on the table. "We should do something," she said, even though that was obvious.

Tom took several steps forward and grabbed Mere's shoulders. She shook even more violently, and Tom lost his grip. He tried again, and this time she moved so suddenly she knocked Tom to the ground. The back of his head struck the kitchen floor with a crack, and he lay there, still.

"Tom!" Jay-Tee shouted.

He didn't answer.

27
Chased by The Devil

The driver drove as if the devil were after him, which was, I reckoned, at least half right. If magic existed, who was to say devils didn't? And Jason Blake was as good a candidate as anyone I'd met in my life.

I watched Blake lose ground before the cab turned a corner and I lost sight of him.

Every corner the cab took I was thrown against Danny or he against me. "Sorry," I said the first time it happened, though I wasn't sorry. The feel of him against me turned my fear and the soreness inside me into something wonderful.

"No problem," Danny said as the driver ran a red light and a cacophony of horns erupted. He squeezed my hand and I remembered the feel of his mouth against mine. I wanted to kiss him again. "Here's hoping we don't die!" he said, grinning.

I twisted again to look out the back of the cab. My eyes were dazzled briefly by the headlights of the cars behind us, but I caught a glimpse of Jason Blake behind us, running in easy, loping strides that looked natural and yet moved him along much faster than they should have. I stayed twisted around, staring out the back window, even as the violent cornering of the cab made the seatbelt dig into me painfully.

Two blocks behind, a tall, running figure turned the corner, weaving through the winter-bundled people on the footpath as if they had become so overburdened by the weight of their clothes that they were hardly moving. Blake was fast as light; they were as slow as the earth.

"What?" Danny said, before turning back to the driver. "Yeah, this is it, left side. Thanks, here's great."

The cab came to a stop.

"He's only a block behind, Danny."

"Thanks, man," Danny said to the driver, handing him more money.

I jumped out, momentarily shocked by the cold after the over-heated cab. "Hurry, Danny," I said, running towards Esmeralda's door, glancing over my shoulder at Blake running towards us. Funny how I could see him clearly through the crowds. Not funny, I realised: he was more vivid than anything else, absorbing all the electric lights around him. As he ran, he shone.

I belted up the steps, through the dozens of misty trails, to the door. The old man was nowhere in sight. I glanced back. Jason Blake was getting closer. Danny bounded up the stairs, stood beside me. I heard a popping sound and looked down. At my feet the old man began to bubble up out of the steps.

"Where is he?"

"He'll be here soon," I said, wondering that Danny couldn't see the old man emerging in front of him. "Jason Blake, too." I pointed at my grandfather weaving through the crowd towards us. "You have to stop him from touching me."

Danny dropped down a step. He nodded. "I see him."

I smelt the old man as he came together. The old vomit smell transformed into lime; the burnt rubber, toasting bread. Good smells that made my stomach rumble, reminded me of how hungry I was, and also of Danny and me last night.

The same smell, I realised. Limes and baking bread. Last night . . . Danny and I . . . that smell had filled the room. The old man's smell, but appetising and comforting.

"Damn," Danny said, staring at the old man, no longer a pile of bubbly goo. He was all I could smell, every breath full of limes and baked bread. He placed his hand on my stomach. I gasped, expecting to go blind or be paralysed. Danny moved towards me.

"I'm fine," I told him.

Instead of pain I felt warmth radiating from him, spreading across my stomach. We stood facing each other—the gnarled old man and me. Suddenly I could see inside him without blurring my eyes. I could see his magic, the same shape as the magic in Jason Blake, but bigger, even more pervasive.

The old man drew back his hand, and I was on the steps, back at the surface of things. He was smiling at me, nodding as if I pleased him. I half expected him to say, *Well done.*

"Are you Raul Cansino?" I asked.

He continued to smile; the warmth from his hand grew hot. I gasped.

"Reason?" Danny said, catching my eye, raising an eyebrow as if to say, *Are you okay?* I forced a smile. "His name. It's very Hispanic. Want me to ask him in Spanish? ¿Cómo se llama, señor? ¿Raul?"

The old man clapped his hands, gave what could have been a nod.

"What do you want?" I asked. "Ask him, Danny."

"¿Que quiere, señor?"

Raul cocked his head as if he was trying to understand.

"¿Que quiere, señor?"

The old man's eyes widened. He reached his hand to the door, touched the keyhole, almost pawed at it.

"Well, that we knew," Danny said. "He wants to get into your grandmother's house. But why? ¿Porque, señor?"

The old man smiled more broadly, brushed his knuckles past my stomach again, leaned back against the door. What had he wanted in that cemetery, searching through every grave? Why had he filled me and Esmeralda and Blake with his magic but almost killed Jay-Tee? *Because we're all Cansinos*, I realised, *and Jay-Tee isn't.*

"Danny!" I screamed.

Jason Blake was running up the stairs. Danny turned, met his charge with raised fists. Blake tried to shove him aside, tried to reach past him to me. My knees buckled. The old man picked me up, carrying me as Danny had on the way to the green seaweed restaurant.

My eyes blurred, looking at the old man's face. He was

dense with magic, inhuman, but not animal, either. There was no blood in him, no waste.

"I have to talk to you, Reason," Jason Blake yelled. My eyes cleared, took in Blake, stumbling down the steps. *He* had blood. It was on his face, dripped down his chin.

"We're talking, aren't we?"

"Not really. It's a little difficult with your magic-deficient gorilla in between us."

Danny took a step towards him, and Blake moved closer to the curb.

"Mongrel," I told him. "You shit me worse than anyone I've ever met. I don't care if you *are* my grandfather."

Blake started to do something. I felt the air begin to be displaced, but then it was gone. "Interesting," he said, his eyes unfocused. "Oh," he said in surprise. "You have been naughty."

"What?"

He smiled at me, smug as a cat that hasn't had its throat slit open. "Well, now I know why he chose you." He let out a short laugh. "My being your grandfather does mean something. You have magic flowing into you from more than one source—not only the Cansino women, but from me, too, and now Raul. He's chosen you. It makes you more powerful."

"Or dead faster." *Chosen me?*

"Does Raul look dead to you?"

"He doesn't look like any kind of alive I'd like to be." Raul Cansino didn't feel dead, holding me in his arms. He radiated warmth, comfort, soothing smells that made me want to stay there. Jason Blake couldn't do a thing to me if Raul Cansino didn't want him to.

Jason Blake shrugged dismissively. "That's now, but, remember, he's survived for centuries."

Danny turned to me. "Do you want me to—" He stopped, staring at the door. It had started to open. Before any of us could register it, Raul Emilio Jesús Cansino had slipped through to Sydney faster than thought, me held close to his dry yeast-and-lime chest.

28
Cemetery

Mere had barely opened the door a crack before the strangest creature Jay-Tee had ever seen came sliding through. He was all-over red-brown, the same color as his little golem, with eyes the same size and shape as almonds. He was not much taller than she was. Reason's scary old man was an elf; a pixie; a spry, lean hobbit. He carried Reason as if she weighed no more than the few bedraggled feathers protecting the door.

The elf man pushed past Mere, ran through the house as if he were floating, leaving a strong scent of something sweet and soothing that Jay-Tee couldn't quite identify. A smell that made her smile. How had the smell of him made Reason hurl?

"Hah!" Jay-Tee exclaimed. She jumped up, though it killed her to do so and she really needed to pee. But Tom was still unconscious, and anyway, neither he nor Mere could run as fast as she could. It was up to her to save Reason.

Jay-Tee ran after him, ignoring the commotion behind her, leaping over Tom. The pixie wasn't hard to follow—he left a trail of red-brown dust behind him.

Jay-Tee couldn't help giggling as she sprinted after him, even though this could be life or death. She could feel the hollowness in herself growing bigger with every step, but the elf man looked so ethereal, so unthreatening. She wondered if he was stealing Reason to take her down into his elf kingdom to be his queen. Reason would look funny with a golden crown on her head.

Jay-Tee chased him down the street but couldn't get close to catching him. She was running as fast as she could, sweating, panting, feeling the pain of every bruised muscle working, whereas he skipped past the ground as if it didn't concern him. She half expected him to laugh, *ha, ha, ha,* at his escape from gravity.

Jay-Tee was relieved it wasn't as hot as it had been the last time she'd run like this. When had that been? Yesterday morning. She sprinted past gnarly trees growing up out of the sidewalk, sprouting branches in all directions so that there was barely room for a small child to get past.

Yesterday had been torturously hot; the distances had shimmered like crazy mirrors. Today the air felt almost cool rushing past her. Everything was as bright as ever—gleaming, cut-glass bright. She wished she had sunglasses. She wished she had a hat. She fixed her eyes on the elf—somehow he was soothing to look at, made her eyes sting less.

She sprinted past an old woman struggling to pull her wobbly shopping cart over the uneven, broken-up sidewalk, and wondered what the old lady thought of the elf with the girl in his arms zipping past. Or had she seen something else? Reason clearly didn't see the pixie the way she did. How could she describe him as an old man? He didn't look that much older than Reason.

She ran past a bar with tiled walls and large-screen TVs. The people inside were all watching a strange sport where everyone wore white and stood around on a large green field. Up ahead the elf man had reached the slightly busy road and floated across it to the sloping park Tom had shown her on her first day in Sydney, when Reason had been sleeping and sleeping and sleeping.

Jay-Tee ran to catch him, narrowly avoiding being hit by a kid on a skateboard who had no sense of balance and no clue what you were supposed to do with a board with wheels on it. "Watch it!" the kid yelled. "Bloody drongo!"

Jay-Tee giggled and sprinted across to the park. The elf stuck to the concrete pathway, whereas Jay-Tee ran on the springy grass. He reached the other side of the park and turned right on the narrow street. Jay-Tee accelerated as he disappeared from view. When she reached the corner she couldn't see him, but she could see his browny-red dust floating in the air, catching the sun high above. He'd turned at a churchyard. St. Stephen's, said the sign. It wasn't a Catholic church.

Jay-Tee slowed down because her legs were screaming at her. She leaned briefly on the low, rusting iron gate, caught her breath as best she could, staring at a scary-looking prehistoric tree almost as big as the one in Mere's backyard, though this one's roots came high out of the ground, sinewy and sprawling, like giant lizards dozing in the sun. Not at all how trees were supposed to look. She half expected one of the roots to rip free from the ground and wrap itself around her like an octopus tentacle.

She went through the gate, walking because she could no longer run. Her breaths were hot and sharp and painful. She staggered along the path past the church, her legs and lungs aching, past a slew of broken and worn gravestones. It was a cemetery.

She followed the fairy trail past stone monuments with rusting iron fences around them. There were trees everywhere, even some palm trees, as if this were a beach instead of a graveyard. Everything was green and overgrown, and all the graves were old and broken.

She followed the trail to where the elf and Reason were standing by one of the biggest monuments. On top of it was a grumpy-looking stone angel with huge wings, holding a sword and a book. Jay-Tee just bet the book had instructions on how to behead people who piss off angels.

"Are you okay, Reason?" she asked. She'd been aiming for a shout, but she was out of breath and couldn't raise her voice above a whisper.

Reason appeared not to hear. Jay-Tee dragged herself closer. Reason was still wearing all her New York winter gear. She must be broiling.

"You okay?"

Reason turned, gave Jay-Tee a half smile, and put her fingers to her lips. The elf was running his fingers along all the names on the monument. Jay-Tee read them over his shoulder, keeping her feet, although her legs were still wobbly. They were almost all Cansinos and almost all women. She saw lots of Esmeraldas and Sarafinas, Milagroses, and Marias. The elf man only touched the women's names. She and Reason followed him around all four sides. She became aware that he was humming softly. A tune she'd never heard before.

He stopped in front of a man's name right at the top of the monument: Raul Emilio Jesús Cansino, died 1823. He ran his fingers over it and then brought a finger to his chest.

"That's you," Reason said.

He inclined his head slightly. Jay-Tee figured it was a nod. She had an urge to say, "Hi, Raul. How you doing?" But she was too tired to say anything. Anyways, she didn't think she'd get much of a laugh out of him or Reason.

Then he ran his fingers over the name immediately below his own: Esmeralda Milagros Luz Cansino, 1823–1841. He was humming. He was smiling.

"Your daughter?" Reason asked. *Well, duh,* thought Jay-Tee.

The same slight movement of his head. Then he pointed from the name to Reason, to her stomach. His smile grew.

He pressed harder on Esmeralda Milagros Luz Cansino until his hand started to sink into the stone. He put his other hand on Reason's belly. Reason's eyes grew wide, but she made no move away from him. His fingers sank into her belly.

"No!" Jay-Tee shouted.

29
Golden Spiral

I couldn't move. The old man's hand was in my belly. I could feel his fingers twisting, pulling, tweaking. His magic scorched through every part of me, was centred there, below my bellybutton. His fingers were finer than wire, manipulating my cells, I was sure. I wished I could turn my gaze inward. See inside myself the way I could see inside everyone else.

Jay-Tee started shouting, then threw a punch at the old man. Her fist sailed through him, through air. Cansino's hand inside me felt fainter, as if he wasn't solid anymore. Jay-Tee stumbled, fell to the ground, struggled to get up. Her breath sounded frayed, unravelling like loose thread. Cansino moved his left hand slightly, like a ghost waving. Jay-Tee froze. Cansino pulled himself together, became solid.

I sent my magic at his hands twisting inside my belly. But it didn't send him screaming out of me; it nibbled at his edges, playful as a small dog. He pulled the magic into his hands, made it his.

I was suddenly sure that *this* was what Raul Emilio Jesús Cansino wanted: to become me. Inhabit my body. Be human again.

Even if it meant killing me.

Then the old man pulled his hand from my belly and held it in front of my eyes insistently, as if he was trying to tell me something. I stared at it, even blurred my eyes, though I didn't think I had much magic left, but I had no idea what I was looking at.

What did he want me to see?

Cansino pushed his hand into his own belly, made his fingers into long, thin wires, thinner than hair. I could see better now what he was doing. He reached inside his cells, forcing my vision to narrow, to see the components of each cell, the strings of DNA that were so like my own, even though there was so little humanity left in him. He stared at me as he did it, nodding at me at each stage. As if to say, This *is how you do it.*

Through my blurred vision I saw old man Cansino altering the cells of his body with his wire-thin fingers, performing minute surgery on himself. As he worked, his legs began to turn into bubbling brown stuff. The same stuff that I had seen emerge out of the steps in front of Esmeralda's door. The stuff that had turned into Raul Cansino.

Then he pulled his hand out. His legs rippled, changing from bubbling mass to a kind of flesh. He nodded at me. Gently waved, setting me free.

I stumbled forward, turned to Jay-Tee, opened my mouth to speak. The old man froze me again, shook his head, and took my hand in his, plunged it into his belly.

If my mouth had worked, I would have screamed.

He pushed my hand past his skin, into the muscle below, but there was no sinew, no blood. It didn't feel like flesh; it felt like the piece of him he had thrown inside me. More like plasticine than flesh.

We were so close that I could see his skin had no pores. It was in constant motion, as if tiny worms flowed underneath. I could smell his breath. It was faintly sweet, like homemade lemonade.

Raul let go of my hand. I could move it but nothing else, not even my eyelids.

He nodded, his face centimetres from my own. His eyes stared at mine, unblinking. Like a croc's, only they were the same brown throughout, no variation. His irises were as uniform as his black pupils, as if they were made of glass.

He nodded again, almost impatient with me. What did he want me to do?

Cansino waved his wire fingers almost close enough to cut me. He shifted his body so that my hand moved through his dense but yielding flesh. Fine hair stood up all over my body.

I understood.

He wanted me to tinker with his cells. Just as he had done.

Raul Emilio Jesús Cansino was teaching me to do magic the way he did it.

Jason Blake was right. Raul had chosen me—to be his student, to learn how to be like him. Nausea rose in me, but with a gesture he made it go away. I tried to pull my hand out, but it would not respond to my commands. I wanted to run to the other end of the earth. I did not want to become like him: to have flesh without blood, to no longer speak, to no longer be human.

But my brain already accepted that I had no choice. He was stronger than me. If I didn't learn his lessons, he wouldn't let me go. And if I did learn his lessons, my mind whispered, maybe they would help me save Sarafina and Jay-Tee and Tom.

I did what he had done, but it was impossible with my clumsy, round-tipped fingers. I slid past clusters of cells, crudely breaking his flesh. I had to make my fingers long and less than a micron wide. But how?

I concentrated my magic, drew it through the brooch pinned to my jacket, the ammonite in my pocket, thought about changing my fingers just as Esmeralda had taught me to make light, as Sarafina had taught me to use the golden spiral to detect anything living nearby. I concentrated. Sweat ran down my face, past the backs of my knees.

Nothing happened. My fingers remained fingers.

Raul plunged his hand back into me, moving his fingers. But slowly this time, so I could follow what he was doing. I couldn't see it, but I could *feel* it. The changes made my fingers inside him start to stretch, to elongate, to grow harder, to become fine metal cell-manipulating instruments.

I set about altering his cells. Or rather, shearing them in half. He smiled and drew the cells back together again. I tried again, flailing about, as uncoordinated as a newborn foal. But

Raul was patient, repairing my wreckage, nodding for me to try again. I was a puddle of sweat. It was so hard.

And then I did it—I minutely shifted the sequence of DNA in one of his cells. Feathers sprouted across his forehead.

Raul smiled, and the feathers above his eyes shifted. If I'd been able to move anything other than my hand, I would have giggled. He was pleased with me, I was sure: his strange skin and eyes glowed. He drew his hand out of me and took a step away. Gradually, the feathers disappeared.

He unfroze me. This time I stood where I was and ignored Jay-Tee. He had another lesson for me.

Raul Cansino began to dissolve again, as he had when Jay-Tee attacked him, but he was showing me how to do it. How to shrink the cells into near nothingness and then how to bring them back together again. He did it by concentrating on the size of each cell.

He took a step back, the signal for me to try. There were so many cells inside me, and I couldn't see them the way I saw them inside everyone else. I had to go by feel. I thought about them being smaller, and slowly, they shrank.

It didn't hurt, but it filled my body with dizzy nausea. I felt light and strange and awful—the world shrank to a million kilometres away, as if I were on another planet looking at Earth through a telescope. Raul Cansino brought his palms together, drew them apart, and then put them together again. It took me a moment to realise that he was clapping, applauding my success. He was almost grinning.

I made my cells big again, felt myself pulling together, solidifying, sickeningly fast. It was like being in the back seat of a car going way too fast along winding roads.

But I was whole. Raul nodded again. And thrust both his hands into me. He started dissolving, unravelling the connections between his cells, pulling them apart until all I could see were particles of what had been him in air, particles drifting into the ground to join his dead relatives, particles still inside me.

The lesson was over. He was unravelling. I felt him sigh, almost as if he were happy.

Jay-Tee stumbled forward and into me.

"Sorry, Reason," she panted. "Where'd he go?" Jay-Tee wavered on her feet.

In front of my eyes the old man continued to dissolve into a mass of spirals. They radiated downwards, growing bigger and bigger. Algorithmic spirals, Fibonacci spirals, golden spirals. They consumed our family monument, dispersing into the ground, into the remains of his family underground, into me. All those magic Cansino bones. Spirals sped up through the ground to meet him. Together they faded back into the soil. I wondered what they were. The remnants of my ancestors speeding to meet the remnants of Raul Cansino?

But they were dead. They couldn't come back to life like that.

Raul Cansino was gone, but I felt him even more strongly within me, like a bonfire in my stomach. I couldn't see the cemetery anymore—not Jay-Tee, not the monument, not the gum trees or overgrown grasses. Everything flattened out and stretched forever, became a map dotted with points of light. A map of magic.

I *could* see the monument and Jay-Tee, but now they were faint dots of light. The biggest light was not far off: Esmeralda's house, I was sure: Tom, Esmeralda, the door, all those magical objects. There were others. Further away, Sarafina glowed. I knew it was my mother, not from the shape or size of the light, but because I recognised the feel of her. Some part of me had recognised the magic in her my whole life.

I looked farther out, across Sydney, saw other lights. I wondered if they were people, doors, or magic objects. I pushed further, across Australia. Clusters of brightness—I imagined they were cities, where people were, where magic was, but none of it was as blindingly brilliant as Esmeralda's house.

I couldn't count the lights; there were too many stretched out too far. It was like trying to count all the grains of sand at the beach. There weren't hundreds of magic people, places, objects: there were thousands and thousands of them.

I was seeing what Raul Cansino saw, not people or houses or doors, but patterns of magic. He had replaced my sight with his. Was he going to take me over completely?

I turned my thoughts to Danny, to Sarafina, to Tom and Jay-Tee. My last thoughts weren't going to be of Raul Cansino. I said goodbye. I thought about the munga-munga who had created the valleys and the hills and mountains but not the

people or their cities or their magic. I wished I'd had a chance
to go back to Jilkminggan and stay, tell them my name was
Reason, not Rain, and ask them for more stories. I wished my
mother hadn't gone mad. I wished I'd never killed anyone. I—

"Reason? Reason? Are you okay?" I felt Jay-Tee's hands on
my shoulders, though I couldn't see her, only the fading, tenu-
ous light of her magic. "Reason! Reason! Wake up!" She
slapped me.

I blinked, half fell forward, flashing back and forth between
the old man's vision and my own. A stuttering fall between dots
of light and the cemetery. Glimpses of me falling against Jay-Tee,
pushing her back against the Cansino family monument—
glimpses of an expanse of dark punctuated by light, by magic.
Jay-Tee managed to stop my fall, and we slid to the ground.

"You're okay, Reason," she told me.

"Am I?" I could still feel him inside me. The heat was there.
I saw black ants crawling along a fallen piece of bark; I saw
Jay-Tee looking down at me, tired and worried. I blinked again.
Briefly, the world became points of light, magic stretching out
as far as I wished to follow it. Eyes open, I saw sunlight, grave-
stones, gum trees, overgrown grass.

But when I blinked . . .

"Well, thank God for that." Jay-Tee made her strange gesture across her forehead, chest, and shoulders. Her face was
drawn. I closed my eyes. Her magic was the faintest glow.
"'Cause I don't know how I'm going to be able to walk back to
the house, let alone carry you."

I stood up, dusted myself off. I felt strong. I held out a hand for Jay-Tee, who took it and stood shakily. I put my hand on Raul's name engraved in marble and then on his daughter's below. There were a few specks of grey-brown dust. As I touched them they sank into my skin. The heat in my belly shifted. I blinked, and for an instant I saw his map of magic.

"What is it?" Jay-Tee asked. "That dust?"

"Raul."

"Is he dead?"

I nodded, though it felt like he was still alive inside me. "He was tired. He wanted to come home and die."

"That's what he wanted? Banging at the door?"

"I think so."

"Then what did he need you for? Why did he fill you and Mere with his magic?"

I opened my mouth and then shut it, shrugging instead. What could I say to her? Either my ancestor had invaded my body or he'd turned me into the same kind of monster he was. Or something else I hadn't even thought of. I couldn't begin to talk about it until I understood. And even then . . . What would Esmeralda make of it? Would she want to become like me? Would she try to take it from me if she knew? I blinked again, saw the world transformed into magic light. How could I explain that?

"But you're sure he's dead?"

I wasn't sure of anything. I hadn't been sure of anything for days and days, not since I opened a door that led to another world. Everything since then had led me to this moment, standing here dazed in a cemetery with my ancestor's magic pulsing in me, turning me into something else, something that could see like a dead man. What was I supposed to say?

"The old man is dead, right?" Jay-Tee asked again, staring at me anxiously.

If I told Jay-Tee, she might tell Esmeralda. I couldn't be sure, so I made myself nod. "He's in the ground with the rest of the Cansinos." At least, *some* of him was. "It's where he wanted to be."

Two sulphur-crested cockatoos landed in the tall gum tree. "Wow," Jay-Tee said, pointing. "Check out those birds! They're gorgeous." The birds let out their raucous cry and Jay-Tee jumped. "Jesus! They sound like someone being strangled. That is deeply messed up."

Not compared to how messed up I was. What had Raul's magic lesson turned me into?

What was I now?

30
Triangles and Diamonds

Tom woke up to a loud noise. He opened his eyes as someone jumped over him. He was lying on the kitchen floor, which made no sense. Then he remembered. He sat up, blinked.

Esmeralda was still standing at the door, gripping its handle tightly, but she wasn't shaking anymore. The door was open. Tom was staring at the other side of the world. He was sitting in daylight, looking at night; sitting in warmth, feeling a freezing wind blow across him. He shivered. He was sitting in Sydney watching Jason Blake trying to force his way in from New York City.

Tom stood up—he felt wobbly but not too bad. The back of his head hurt. He wondered where Jay-Tee was. Where Reason was.

Jason Blake's hand reached into the kitchen, into Sydney.

Tom picked up one of the bones from the box on the table, pushed magic into it, and hurled it at Blake's hand. Reason's grandfather flinched, pulled his hand back into New York. Tom reached for another bone, magicked it as well, and stepped closer to the door, ready to hurl it at Blake's face. That's when he saw that Blake's other hand had hold of Esmeralda, was dragging her into winter. She clung to the door. Blake was as powerful as she was, he realised. He must have the old man's magic, too.

Esmeralda wasn't how Tom had thought she was. She didn't know everything about magic, and she wasn't as brave or honest as he'd imagined. She'd kept so many secrets from him. He hadn't known about her daughter, Sarafina, or her granddaughter, Reason. She'd failed to teach him to protect himself from magic-wielders, to protect himself from *her*.

But even so, she'd rescued him from insanity, from turning into his mother. And she was a much, much better person than Jason Blake.

Tom magicked three more bones, flung them at Blake, who screamed and lunged forward at Tom with his right hand. Tom felt something sharp across his face, like a cat's claws. It stung, the cold air from New York digging in, making it filthy painful.

"Bloody mongrel," Tom said, putting his hand on Esmeralda, adding his lesser magic to hers.

Everything dissolved into true shapes, crystal dodecahedrons floating through the air. Jason Blake became sharp diamonds, moving in and out, swiping at Tom, slashing at his eyes. Esmeralda was an ocean of triangles, tinkling up against the cold dodecahedrons, flinging herself amongst Jason Blake's diamonds, trying to break him open.

"Let me through," Blake roared. "This new magic doesn't last. You have to let me through." His words turned into more diamonds that shot across the blurring, rumbling edge between Sydney and New York, the exact spot where night met day, cold met summer. Tom swatted at one, then another, then another, but one diamond buried itself in his cheek, and another hit his chest. He kept swatting at the rest, his hand sliding back and forth through icy cold and balmy warmth.

The diamonds inside him were a wrecking crew, bulldozing their way through blood and gristle. His whole body shuddered in response, screaming from every nerve receptor that this was wrong, wrong, wrong.

"No!" Esmeralda roared back at Blake. The *n* and the *o* splintered, turning into long, thin, acute triangles that flew, knifelike, for Blake's throat.

The diamonds inside Tom cut and dug, heading for his bones. The old man's magic. Tom moaned low, trying to keep his sight focused on the battle, where Mere needed his help. He continued to clutch her with his left hand, using his right to call the remaining bones into his hands. He shot them through with magic and hurled them at Reason's grandfather, cursing him with all the foulest words he could think of.

Then Tom felt hands on his shoulders and back—Jason Blake had somehow gotten behind him. He turned to see Reason, and behind her Jay-Tee, her shapes confused and crumbling as she swayed on her feet. Reason pulled Tom away from Mere. He staggered, slid to the ground still clutching one of the bones, and watched Reason place one hand on Mere's shoulder. Her other reached out to her grandfather.

Reason was shimmering, her true shape a swirl of triangles, triangles that spiralled larger and larger into infinity, and smaller and smaller into nothing. She was anchoring herself to Sydney and to Mere, forcing Jason Blake back into New York City.

Tom felt something cutting behind his eyeballs. He tried to keep his eyes open, to ignore the pain inside him. His body started to slide from his control, to strike against the kitchen floor as Jason Blake's diamonds ate him from the inside.

The door between Sydney and New York City slammed shut. Tom heard the overlapping echoes bouncing back and forth against the walls and ceilings in every room of the house. Through his eyelids he saw dodecahedrons spill into the kitchen.

Then something cool pressed on him, and the knives cut upwards, away from him, out of him, towards the cool thing pressing down. The pain stopped.

He opened his eyes. Reason was leaning over him. She smiled. Sunlight from the windows lit up her face, made her eyes brighter, her skin a soft golden brown. Each hair of her right eyebrow seemed to glow. He imagined touching that eyebrow, kissing her cheek.

"Good," Mere said, pulling off her winter hat. Her hair spilled out, lit gold by the sun. "Your grandfather's gone, Reason." She peeled off the rest of her winter gear—gloves, scarf, coat.

"I used up all the bones," Tom said, sitting up and discovering that he didn't feel as bad as he feared. He touched the back of his head and winced. He had quite a lump there. "How are we going to add more protections and keep Jason Blake away? Those feathers must be pretty buggered."

Mere touched his cheek. "You're bleeding. Let me clean that." She saw to his face with a clean wet cloth and stinging antiseptic and a large Band-Aid. Mere had to lean so close he could feel her breath. He wished it were Reason touching him.

"But what about the protections?" Tom asked.

"We'll add more. Alexander won't get through."

"Who's Alexander?" Tom and Reason asked at the same time.

"Jason Blake," Esmeralda said. "That's what he told me his name was when I first met him."

"Did you meet him back there?" Reason asked, nodding at the door, looking at her grandmother curiously.

"Yes."

"Did you like him back then?" Reason asked. "Was he different?"

"He was very handsome."

Jay-Tee snorted.

Esmeralda laughed. "He was! Funny, too. Yes, Reason, I liked him back then. I liked him *a lot*. And his magic gave him glimpses of the future. He told me we'd have a daughter together. Then he kissed me. My first kiss." She smiled. "I'd just turned fifteen."

Tom tried to imagine such a vast chunk of time. Thirty years ago: flared jeans and maxiskirts, cork-heeled shoes. It seemed an impossibly long time.

"What happened to the old man?" Esmeralda asked.

"Raul Emilio Jesús Cansino is dead."

Tom recognised the name but couldn't place it.

"What?" Mere said. "Well, of course he is. He's been dead since 1823."

"Raul Cansino?" Tom asked. "The only male Cansino in the cemetery?"

"That's right," Reason said.

"He didn't die back then," Jay-Tee said. "The old man was Raul Cansino."

"How could he not have died?" Mere asked, her voice full of disbelief.

"He just didn't," Jay-Tee said.

"Somehow his magic changed and he became something else," Reason said. "Not human and not an animal, either—something that could keep on living, no matter how much magic he used."

"But didn't you say he was dead?" Tom asked, feeling deeply confused.

"He is *now*," Jay-Tee said, as if it were obvious. "That's what he came back for—to die and be in the cemetery with all the other Cansinos. Pretty cool cemetery, by the way."

"Isn't it?" Tom said, wondering why the old man had to scare them all with his assault on the door if he was only trying to off himself.

"That's all he wanted?" Mere asked. "Why couldn't he have *asked?*"

"He wanted to be with his family," Jay-Tee said. "With his daughter."

"Then why did he try to infect us with his magic?"

"I don't know," Reason said. "Maybe it was his present to us before he left."

"Not much of a present for Jay-Tee. And anyway, Jason Blake said the magic doesn't last," Tom said.

"He said that?" Reason asked.

Esmeralda nodded. Tom noticed her hands clench in her lap. "There's no reason to believe him. Why would he tell us the truth?"

"I guess," Reason said, but she looked worried. "Raul's magic only worked for his relatives, for us Cansinos. That's why he sent that bit of himself through the door—to find us."

"But it worked for Alexander."

"He's family."

"He's *your* family," Esmeralda said. "But he's not Raul Cansino's family."

"Jason Blake's a Cansino, too."

"What?"

"I saw it in him. You and he are related. Not closely, but it's there. He has Cansino ancestry, too. Tom and Jay-Tee don't. His magic works for us, not for them."

Tom sighed. He felt deflated knowing that he wasn't going to become a superwitch like Esmeralda and Reason (and Jason

Blake). Nor would his mother. When he finally got the chance to talk to Cathy, he wasn't going to have very good news for her.

"Ewww, so you and *him* are cousins?" Jay-Tee asked, looking at Mere and screwing up her nose. "*Kissing* cousins? That's gross."

"More distant than first cousins," Reason said. "More like fifth or sixth."

"Whatever. It's still gross."

"But he hasn't just given us magic, has he?" Mere said. "He's changed us." Tom watched as she blurred her eyes, looking into Reason. He wondered what she saw in place of true shapes.

Her eyes widened with shock. "You're pregnant!" she said.

Reason was up the duff? No way. How? Reason's face had gone tight. Then Tom remembered Danny and had a sudden vivid image of Danny kissing Reason. He felt sick. Reason and Danny. So he, Tom, was too daggy for her; she'd gone for a poxy wanker with the try-hardest voicemail messages Tom'd ever heard.

Jay-Tee sat up. "Holy crap! *That's* what he was doing? The elf man—I mean, Raul Cansino—made you pregnant? He put his hand in your belly and . . . Oh, my. Oh, Reason. Oh, no! You poor thing."

"Really?" Reason looked at Mere. "You're sure?"

She nodded. "I'm sorry. I didn't mean to blurt it out like that. I was surprised."

Reason shrugged. "You and me both."

Not Danny then. Tom's heart began to beat again. Not Danny. Then he thought about what it would be like being up the duff to a freaky old nonhuman magic guy who just happened to be your ancestor. Deeply weird and wrong. "The old Cansino bloke made you pregnant with magic?"

Reason looked too shocked to say anything. She and Esmeralda were staring at each other. Tom imagined Mere would have a lot to say to her. She knew what being pregnant at fifteen was like. He wondered if there was anything he could do.

"I'm starving," Reason said at last. "I swear, I've hardly eaten since Raul hauled me through to New York City."

31
The Family Way

Between us we polished off four-and-a-half family-sized pizzas. There was some talk of dessert and watching a movie, but Jay-Tee almost fell asleep halfway through the fourth pizza.

We all went to bed—Tom to his house; me, Jay-Tee, and Esmeralda to our separate rooms.

I showered, brushed my teeth, put on clean PJs, climbed into bed, checked under the pillow for any feathers or bones, even though I knew I was strong enough to undo their magic, even though I almost believed Esmeralda that she'd put them there to protect me. But the habits of a lifetime, even a short lifetime, are hard to shake. I put my ammonite there. I needed it close to me.

I lay my head down, closed my eyes, and saw darkness dotted with light. Where there wasn't magic, there was nothing. Raul Cansino, I realised, had been able to see magic.

I opened my eyes, to colours and shapes and textures, to the world as I'd always seen it. I couldn't turn the old man's vision off. How was I going to sleep if every time I shut my eyes, I saw what Raul saw? My eyes burned with the effort of not blinking.

Why was Blake determined to get through the door? What did he want in Sydney? He *had* the old man's magic. If Esmeralda was right and it was infinite, then he didn't need anything else, did he? He'd finally gotten his wish: lots of magic that it didn't kill him to use.

Why take mine? Because he wasn't lying: Raul's magic didn't last.

I closed my eyes again and was plunged into the world as Raul Cansino saw it. The old man hadn't done this to Esmeralda or Blake. Raul Cansino had done more to me, given me more. Why had he chosen me and not them?

Because I was *pregnant*? What would Danny say about that? What would Sarafina say? Could I give my mother some of the old man's magic, make her sane again? She was a Cansino.

But I didn't trust Raul's magic. It might make me stronger, and live for a long, long time, but it would also turn me into something like Raul: not human, not animal, either. I didn't want that any more than I wanted to die young.

There was a knock on the door.

"Come in," I called.

Esmeralda opened the door, leaned against the frame. There were two letters in her hand. The ones she had written and slipped under my door and then taken away before I'd finally decided to read them.

"Are you too tired to talk?"

"No," I told her. I wanted to talk to her. I *needed* to talk to her. What would she do if she was certain her new magic didn't

last? Would she try to steal it from me like my grandfather
had?

Esmeralda placed the letters on the bed, then sat down
beside me.

"How do I know those are the same ones?"

"They are. You can ask Jay-Tee to verify that I'm not lying."
Esmeralda looked tired. Older, too. The skin under her eyes
slacker than it had been.

"I will," I said, though I was fairly sure on my own she was
telling the truth.

"You only really need to read the second one. That's the
one I decided I didn't want you to read."

"Why?"

"I told you the truth in it. I told you I was dying."

"And now that you're not, you're going to square with me?
What makes you certain that you're not dying?"

Esmeralda looked at me for a long time. Her eyes were so
much like Sarafina's, big and brown and intense, seeing
through me. I could never fib to Sarafina.

"You don't know," I said. "Not for certain."

"I feel different," Esmeralda said, speaking slowly, as if she
had to grope for each word. "Before the old man's magic . . . I
was fading. Getting fainter. I was running down. That feeling's
gone now. I feel stronger. The magic crackles in me. There's so
much of it, and there's even more in you." She leaned forward
a little. I leaned away.

"We have no idea what it's doing to us," I said. "I don't

want to end up like Raul Cansino. I like being human. What do you see when you close your eyes?"

"What?" she asked. The question didn't make sense to her. She didn't have Raul Cansino's vision. If she knew about it, would she want it?

"Nothing. I don't trust the old man's magic."

"It just—"

"Magic brings out the worst in people. Why should I trust *you*, Esmeralda? Will you tell me the truth from now on?"

"Yes. No." She smiled tiredly. "I don't know, Reason. I want to be straight with you. I want to be someone you can trust."

"Then give me the keys to the house next door. Let me use the library whenever I want."

Esmeralda blanched. "I can't."

"Then why should I trust you?"

"Reason, there are things in the library you wouldn't understand."

"Explain them to me."

She sighed. "I have made rather a mess of things."

"A right dog's breakfast."

"Is there any way I can fix it?"

"Sure. Don't lie to me, don't hide things from me, let me into the library."

"All right. I'll start by telling you that I know Raul Cansino didn't make you pregnant. It was Danny, wasn't it?"

I nodded, relieved that someone knew, even if it was Esmeralda. "He didn't . . . I kissed him first. I wanted to."

Mere—I stopped myself from thinking of her by that name—*Esmeralda* put her hand on mine. "I know," she said.

I didn't pull my hand away. "I have a lot of questions. Will you answer them?"

Esmeralda nodded.

"What did you do to Sarafina's cat? Why did you cut Le Roi's throat and bury him in the cellar? Why did you keep Sarafina locked up? Why did you keep searching for me and Sarafina even when you knew we didn't want to be found? Why couldn't you let us be? You were the witch who haunted all my dreams when I was little. I never ever felt safe. You were around every dark corner, waiting."

She squeezed my hand. "I'm so sorry. I was trying to find you, to help you. To teach you who you really were . . ."

I let go of her hand, pulled myself to sit up properly. "Were you teaching Le Roi who he really was when you cut his throat?"

Esmeralda blanched. "Le Roi died."

"Because you killed him."

"Le Roi died of natural causes. Sarafina loved that cat. She couldn't stand that he was dead. She put her hands on him, made him live again. But he wasn't really alive."

"But . . ." I trailed off. "How could she do that to a cat?"

"Le Roi had magic. Most animals do. Cats in particular have a lot of magic. Le Roi had more than most."

"And Sarafina really made him live again?"

"Yes. And I had to teach your mother a lesson about what

you can and can't do with magic. I had to teach her that she had overstepped. That she had done something awful. I slit Le Roi's throat in front of her. I made her take her magic back from his blood."

"You tied her to a chair?"

"Yes."

"That's brutal."

"Magic is brutal. It's what my mother would've done."

"That doesn't make it the right thing to do."

"No. That's when Sarafina started to hate it. That's when she started to convince herself it didn't exist. I didn't handle any of it right. I taught her the way my mother taught me. But it didn't work. And I lost her."

"You were a terrible mother."

"Reason, I was a *young* mother. I was fifteen years old when she was born. My own mother died before Sarafina's third birthday. I had my mother's money, but I didn't have my mother. I had Rita—"

"The cleaning lady?"

"She worked for my mother and for my grandmother before that. But she's afraid of us. Always has been. In awe of us Cansino women and afraid of our magic. She wasn't much of a substitute for my dead mother. But she helped me with Sarafina. A lot. I could finish high school, go to university—"

"Drive your daughter insane. Sarafina was fifteen when I was born."

"And look what she did to you! Lied to you about what you

are. Left you completely unprepared for all that could happen to you. I had to find you, teach you—"

"Tie me to chairs and kill my pets? *That'd* be grouse."

"I wasn't going to make the same mistakes with you that I did with Sarafina. I wasn't going to—"

I held up my hand. "I'm tired. I need to sleep. I need to think about what you've said."

Esmeralda stood up, walked to the door, then turned back to me. "Most of what Sarafina told you about me was true, but she didn't ever put it in context."

"You ate babies? What's the context that makes *that* okay?"

"No, Reason, I never ate babies. I said *most* of what your mother told you was true. And she never explained why I did things that look so bad on their surface. She didn't explain, because she *couldn't*. Because she lied to you about the most important thing." Esmeralda opened the door. "Good night, Reason."

"Good night," I said, but only after she'd closed it and couldn't hear me.

There wasn't any sleep for me after that. Any tiredness I'd felt evaporated. I opened the glass doors onto the balcony, leaned against the railing, felt the cool breeze against my skin. A flying fox glided by, its leather wings making a whooshing sound against the air. The bat landed in one of the bottlebrush trees growing out of the footpath. It squeaked and rustled before taking off again.

I put a hand on my belly. There was a baby growing inside me. I couldn't quite believe it was there. But the old man had seen it, and Esmeralda, and, I realised now, Jason Blake. I couldn't see it, though, or feel it. Would my baby be like the old man and see only magic? Was that what he had done to the baby? Could I *un*do it?

Would I be able to use what he had taught me? Manipulate my own cells? I blinked, saw a nanosecond of magic lights, stretching into infinity, beyond my ability to count. I wondered if I would ever be able to close my eyes again and see nothing.

I thought about Danny, about making the baby. I wanted to live, to have my baby and be with Danny again.

"Reason?" asked a voice out of nowhere.

I jumped. "Bloody hell!"

Jay-Tee stepped onto the balcony from her room. "Sorry. Thought I heard you out here. Can't sleep?"

I shook my head.

"Me either." Jay-Tee stood beside me, leaning forward to rest her forearms on the wrought iron railing. "So much has happened." She waved her fingers in the air, making circles. "Too much. Makes my head spin."

"Me, too." I blinked, saw magic.

"I'm not going to use my magic ever again." She glanced at me, waiting for me to say something. I didn't. "Even if I go nuts. I think you can fix it, Reason. I think you can save us from going crazy or dying young. Jason Blake saw it."

"He what?" I stared at her. Maybe she'd gone mad already. She certainly wasn't talking like the Jay-Tee I was used to.

"In one of his dreams, but he didn't understand it." Jay-Tee grinned. "In his dream you change everything. He thought that was a bad thing, but it's not—it's a good thing."

"Why didn't you tell me about this before?"

Jay-Tee shrugged. "Have you been telling me everything?"

I looked down.

"You might not know right now how you're going to save us. But you will."

"But I don't—"

"I'll wait till you do know, even if I'm pulling my dress up over my head, dancing on tables, and trying to eat cock-roaches."

"Yuck." I half-smiled, but it was hard not to think of my mother, blank and staring at the walls.

"You'll save us," Jay-Tee repeated.

"I hope so." I thought of her and of Sarafina and Tom. Maybe I could save them all.

Glossary

amari: grandfather. A word used by Aboriginal people in the Roper area of the Northern Territory.

bickie: short for *biscuit*, the Australian word for *cookie*

bitumen: can mean either a paved (sealed) road or the black substance (usually asphalt) used to pave (seal) the road

boong: racist term for an Australian Aboriginal person

bottlebrush: an Australian tree or shrub with spikes of brightly coloured flowers

bugger: damn. The thing you say when you stub your toe and don't want to be *too* rude.

bunyip: legendary creature of Aboriginal legend, haunts swamps and billabongs (waterholes that only exist during the rainy season)

chunder: vomit

countryman: an Aboriginal person. A word used by some Aboriginal people in the Northern Territory.

croc: short for *crocodile*

crook: bad, dodgy

daggy: a dag is someone lacking in social graces, someone who is eccentric and doesn't fit in. The closest U.S. approximation is *nerd*, but a dag doesn't necessarily know a thing about computers or mathematics or science. *Daggy* is the adjectival form.

demountable: a school building that can be removed from its foundations and moved somewhere else. However, this never actually happens. The "temporary" demountable classrooms end up staying forever.

dodgy: sketchy

dog's breakfast: a mess, a disaster. To make a dog's breakfast out of something is to really mess it up.

drongo: someone who's not very bright

dunny: toilet

footie: in New South Wales and Queensland means Rugby League (Rugby Union is known as rugby); in the rest of the country usually means AFL (Australian Football League, popularly known as Aussie rules)

grouse: excellent, wonderful, although it can also be a verb meaning *to complain*, as in, "I wish you'd stop grousing about everything"

jack of: to be jack of something means that you're sick of it

jumper: sweater

knackered: very tired, exhausted

lift: elevator

li-lo: a blowup rubber mattress

loo: toilet

mad: in Australia it means *crazy*; in the United States, *angry*

munanga: white person. A word used by Aboriginal people in the Roper area of the Northern Territory.

porkies: lies

poxy: unpleasant, crappy, or annoying

pram: stroller

recce: from the military term *reconnaissance,* meaning *to look around, check out thoroughly*

ropeable: angry, as in "fit to be tied"

Shire, the: Sutherland Shire, a district of Sydney that's a long way from the city

skerrick: a very small amount

skink: a small, insectivorous lizard with a long body

spag bol: spaghetti bolognese

spinifex: spiky grass that grows in the desert

stickybeak: a person who always sticks their nose into other people's business

stoush: fight, brawl, rumble

thongs: flip-flops

tracky-dacks: track pants

tucker: food

unco: short for *uncoordinated.* Someone who's unco isn't much chop at sports or juggling. For some unco types, even standing can be a challenge. Your humble author has been known to be unco, though only since infancy.

wanker: poseur

Winnies: short for Winfield's, a brand of cigarette

white man place: city

widdershins: counterclockwise

Acknowledgments

I'm very lucky to have such smart, incisive, hardworking editors as Liesa Abrams and Eloise Flood. Thank you. Thanks also to Andy Ball, Chris Grassi, Annie McDonnell, Polly Watson, and Margaret Wright.

My first readers are eagle-eyed and amazing. Thank you, John Bern, Gwenda Bond, Pamela Freeman, Carrie Frye, Margo Lanagan, Jan Larbalestier, Karen Meisner, Sally O'Brien, Ron Serdiuk, Micole Sudberg, and Lili Wilkinson. Thanks also to John Bern, Jan Larbalestier and Kate Senior for research help.

My gratitude to the people of Ngukurr and Jilkminggan for looking after me and teaching me all sorts of cool stuff when I was little. Special thanks to Sheila Conway, and Betty and Jessie Roberts.

Janet Irving answered all my questions about fashion and fabrics. (If I still managed to get it wrong, blame me.)

Allen Haroothunian let me use his home in Camperdown (Sydney) to finish the first draft and the first round of rewrites. Much appreciated. Large chunks of the first draft were also written at Drink Me café (New York).

Lastly, to John Bern, Niki Bern, Jan Larbalestier, and Scott Westerfeld: you four make everything easier and more fun. Here's to more good food and wine together.